STARFISH MOON

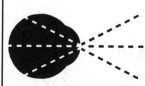

This Large Print Book carries the
Seal of Approval of N.A.V.H.

STARFISH MOON

DONNA KAUFFMAN

KENNEBEC LARGE PRINT
A part of Gale, Cengage Learning

Farmington Hills, Mich • San Francisco • New York • Waterville, Maine
Meriden, Conn • Mason, Ohio • Chicago

GALE
CENGAGE Learning·

ALL RIGHTS RESERVED
Kennebec Large Print® Superior Collection.
The text of this Large Print edition is unabridged.
Other aspects of the book may vary from the original edition.
Set in 16 pt. Plantin.

LIBRARY OF CONGRESS CATALOGING-IN-PUBLICATION DATA

Names: Kauffman, Donna, author.
Title: Starfish moon / Donna Kauffman.
Description: Large print edition. | Waterville, Maine : Kennebec Large Print, 2016.
| © 2016 | Series: The brides of Blueberry Cove | Series: Kennebec Large Print
superior collection
Identifiers: LCCN 2016008394| ISBN 9781410489173 (paperback) | ISBN 1410489175
(softcover)
Subjects: LCSH: Large type books. | BISAC: FICTION / General. | GSAFD: Love
stories.
Classification: LCC PS3561.A816 S73 2016 | DDC 813/.54—dc23
LC record available at http://lccn.loc.gov/2016008394

Published in 2016 by arrangement with Zebra Books, an imprint of
Kensington Publishing Corp.

Printed in the United States of America
1 2 3 4 5 6 7 20 19 18 17 16

For Marty & Brik

Marty, for your big, loving heart
and for including me in it.
And Brik, because I know you would have
gotten the biggest kick out of it.
I miss you.

ACKNOWLEDGMENTS

Special thanks to my Aussie connection, Lorraine Fletcher, who helped me find Cooper's voice. Please forgive any inadvertent lingo transgressions. I'm American. You know how we are.

And a shout-out to a very special young lady, the real Madison Diba. Thank you, Maddy, for being so generous and allowing me to play a bit with your namesake character. I hope you (and Dart!) love her as much as I do.

CHAPTER ONE

She didn't mind being known as the single sibling, the last remaining unmarried Mc-Crae. She didn't. Kerry McCrae's life was too big, too bold, to settle herself down in one place, with one person.

Let 'em eat wedding cake!

"Refills in the back!" The shout came from the pool table area in the rear of the Rusty Puffin, the lone pub in the tiny harbor town of Blueberry Cove, Maine. The same town where she'd been born and raised.

The same pub she'd been helping her Uncle Gus — who owned the place — run for a little over a year now, her big and bold life on hold. She'd come back for her older brother Logan's wedding the previous summer, then stayed on for her oldest sister Hannah's Christmas wedding. And now the middle McCrae sister, Fiona, was driving them all bonkers as she reached the final planning stages of her impending wedding in just a few weeks' time to Snowflake Bay Christmas tree farmer Ben Campbell. None of those were excuses for Kerry not heading out on her next grand adventure.

If she was looking for an excuse — and she wasn't — it was the stroke that Fergus had suffered a mere few weeks prior to Hannah's holiday wedding. Technically, he was her late grandfather's cousin, but he was Uncle Gus to her and to her siblings. He was her port in a storm, the one Mc-Crae who truly understood her, who recognized that glint in her eye, because it matched the one in his own.

He'd been in his fifties when he'd up and moved from County Clare, Ireland, to America, offering to help his distant cousin raise his orphaned grandchildren when her grandpa's own health began to fail. Kerry had just turned ten and thought her new-found great-uncle was the most exotic thing she'd ever seen, with his short, stout frame, wild fringe of white hair ringing his bald pate, and vivid blue eyes. But it was that rich, lyrical brogue of his, as he told her bold tales of exploration and adventure, that truly entranced her. The fact that Fergus had stuck it out in the Cove going on twenty years now didn't mean he wasn't a wayfarer at heart.

Gus knew she couldn't contain her spirit in a small seaside town, no matter how dear the Cove was to her. And her hometown was dear, as were each and every one of her family members. It was their strength, stability, and support, after all, that had given her the confidence, the assurance, the daring, to leave home at the tender age of nineteen and go forth to conquer the world as she pleased. And she'd pleased herself a great deal, gypsying around the globe for more than a decade, hitting every continent except Antarctica. And that was only because the floating science lab she was going to crew on, from Tierra del Fuego all the way down to the penguins and back, had been docked for funding reasons a week before she'd been set to leave.

Gypsying until last year, anyway, she thought, when she'd come home again. For the weddings. And to help Uncle Gus. If staying, helping, and playing bridesmaid time and again also kept her from thinking about the last adventure she'd been on before she'd returned home to the States, then all the better, really.

"Are the brews coming anytime soon? We're thirsty men back here!"

"Keep your pants on, Hardy," Kerry called out, without even looking up from

11

the bottles she was upcapping and sliding down the bar to two of the other thirsty bar patrons crowding the small establishment. Her musings continued as she pulled four more drafts and set them on a tray. Gus's stroke had absolutely been the reason she'd stayed past Hannah's wedding. He'd always been there for her, so, of course, she'd be there for him. In fact, the thought of leaving, then his having another stroke and her not being there with him — well, she didn't even like to contemplate that.

She carried the tray to the back, weaving her way through the throng, trying to ignore her little voice as it whispered, *He's fine now, no more strokes, or fine enough at any rate. He doesn't need you to stay . . . as he's mentioned a time or a hundred. So how long are you going to cling to that lame excuse before you find yourself yet another? Fiona's wedding? Sure, okay. Then what?*

Kerry gritted her teeth a little, ignoring her incessantly pestering little voice — she'd gotten good at that — and set the tray on the round café table closest to the pool table Hardy and his three fellow lobster fishermen coworkers were using. "Who's losing?" she asked, then grinned as all four men paused in chalking or lining up their cues to look her way. "I only ask so I know whose tab to put this round on."

"Might as well add it to Perry's," Hardy replied as the other two men who weren't Perry chuckled in agreement. "He couldn't sink a shot tonight if he nudged it all the way to the pocket with his nose," Hardy added with a laugh.

Hardy was a tall, well-muscled, good-looking guy, a few years older than Kerry's thirty-one. He wasn't a native of the Cove but had moved up from Boston about four years back, after marrying Caroline Welsh, the third-grade teacher at the local elementary school. So Kerry didn't know him well, or at all, really. What she did know was that he was a natural flirt and cocky enough to think it was perfectly fine to exhibit that character trait wherever and whenever he saw fit. She also knew it had surprised no one except him, apparently, when, after three years of marriage, Caroline had filed for and gotten a divorce almost before he'd known what had hit him. That had happened right after Kerry's return to Blueberry.

He'd stayed on in the Cove, continued working for Blue's, the local fishing company in Half Moon Harbor, the central docking spot for everything seafaring in the Cove. The local gossip was that he'd hung

13

around to woo his ex-wife back, but given that he'd been trying to coax Kerry out on a date since she'd begun helping Gus full time after his stroke, almost seven months ago now, her personal opinion was that divorce had taught him nothing about women. He'd been good-natured enough about accepting Kerry's continued rejections, but she knew, given the twinkle in his dark brown eyes, that he'd try again. She wasn't worried about that. She'd handled men far more aggressive than Hardy on her globe-trotting travels, with a lot less leverage than having her family's pub, currently occupied by a goodly percentage of her entire hometown population, to back her up.

Perry was a half dozen years older than Hardy, also a Blue's employee, and had been since he was sixteen, helping to keep his family's farm going by dropping out of school and working full time as soon as he was able. His face was weathered and he sported a perennial tan, along with a few more crinkles at the corners of his eyes and mouth than he otherwise would at his age. He was as good-natured as he was hardworking, married to Bonnie, the town's one and only EMT, and proud of his wife's accomplishments. They had two little ones and another on the way.

He looked up at her with a sheepish grin, then straightened so he could take a sip of the beer she'd carried to him. "I wish I could say different, but he's right. I'm blaming it on lack of sleep. Bonnie's pulling night-shift work as long as she can — pays better — so I've been pulling double duty with the kids. Her ma's got them tonight so I can get out for a bit."

Kerry just nodded as he handed the mug back to her and bent back over the table to line up his shot.

Across the table, Hardy took a sip of his beer, folding his arms around his pool cue as he leaned back against the wall, watching Perry try to line up a shot that would sink both the seven and the three if it worked. The other two men followed Hardy's example, which was privately why Kerry thought Hardy had really stayed in the Cove. Big-man-in-a-small-pond complex, at least in his immediate circle anyway. The three men took turns sipping and taking side bets on how many rounds Perry was going to owe for by the end of the night.

Kerry had set Perry's mug on the table and picked up the now empty tray but set it back down again and walked around to where Perry was still lining up his shot. She leaned down next to him. "Tap the side of the table," she told him, her voice low.

He paused, shifting slightly to look at her. "Beg pardon?"

"Tap the table," she said again, enunciating the words this time. She'd just delivered their second round of ale so she knew he wasn't buzzed.

Perry straightened, then caught her wink, and tapped the edge of the pool table with the flat of his palm.

Kerry followed suit and tapped hers twice, then took his cue and nudged him out of the way.

"Hold on, hold on," Hardy said, his smile fading, beer suddenly forgotten. "Wait — you can't just —"

"He tapped out. I tapped in," Kerry said. "I'm taking his turn for him."

"This isn't a wrestling match," Hardy protested. "You can't just tap out and tap in."

Kerry lined up her shot, going after the same two balls but taking a slightly different approach. "My bar, my rules." She hit the cue ball, then stood, grinning, as first the three went in, then the seven. She moved around the table. "Excuse me," she said as she slipped between Hardy and the pool table to get to her next shot. "Still Perry's turn, I believe." She then proceeded to run the rest of the table. She'd been playing pool since she could see over the edge of these very tables, a skill that had stood her in very good stead on her worldly adventures. She'd been surprised by just how many countries there were with bars and pubs containing a pool table or two. And how men in every last one of them would underestimate a woman with a pool cue.

A goodly number of folks were watching now as she sank the final ball, and a cheer went up as the black number eight fell in the side pocket. Perry was flushing but laughing, as were both of the other fishermen playing his table. Hardy looked like he was going to complain, but Kerry just held her hand out, palm up, in front of him. "Man's got two toddlers and another on the way. He needs that money for diapers and college funds." She rubbed her fingers, her smile and stare never wavering. "Now, be a nice single guy with no kids and pay up."

"I have a dog," Hardy grumbled as he reached for his wallet to the hoots of the other two men and the assembled crowd. He got a cheerful thanks from a smiling Perry. "A big dog," Hardy added as he slapped the bills on her palm while Perry

17

collected from the rest of the bettors.

Kerry took one of the fives and handed it back to him. "I've seen your big dog, Hardy. Ten pounds of terror, that one. Get little Fritzie some kibble. On me."

"He's my ex's dog," Hardy replied and, to his credit, ignored her offer and picked up his beer again. He grinned as he lifted the mug to his lips. "At least he doesn't steal the covers."

Everybody laughed, including Kerry. It was just past suppertime, a nice breeze coming in off the water as the sun began to set on the first Friday in June, and the Puffin was full up with the hardworking folks of the Cove looking to burn off a little work-week steam and a few dollars from their freshly cashed paychecks while they were at it. They worked hard and played hard and, but for a few exceptions, mostly kept themselves in check.

Despite Gus's stroke leaving him a bit less blustery than his usual ornery Irish self, the folks of the town respected him and knew he ran a tight ship. The Rusty Puffin was the only pub in town, and as he was often fond of saying, "I want it to stay standin', so keep yer balls on the table and your hands to yourself, or I'll cuff one to the other and let you sort out how to get yerself

18

free." That his great-nephew — Kerry's older brother, Logan — was the Cove's chief of police didn't hurt matters any either.

She handed the cue back to Perry, but not before tapping the end of it on his shoulder. "Seeing as Bonnie's also pulling double duty, working and growing you an adorable new baby at the same time, maybe you should spend some of your grandma capital taking her out for dinner and a movie while she can still sit long enough to enjoy them."

Perry didn't flush or look embarrassed. He grinned and leaned closer over the laughs and guffaws. "Our tenth anniversary is coming up, can you believe it? She thinks she's got shift duty and I'll be out running traps, but her ma and I have set up a little surprise. Getting away for a whole weekend, just the two of us."

Pleased, Kerry gave him a fist bump to the shoulder. "Well, then. Good on ya, mate, good on ya." Then she leaned in and bussed him on the cheek for good measure. "The world needs more men like you," she added, plenty loud enough for those close by to hear over the sounds of a pub in full swing.

Grinning at the hoots and hollers that got, she scooped up the tray and skirted the table, taking an order from the three men at the next table as she ducked by. Hardy eased forward just enough to crowd her pathway back to the bar. "Sounds like someone from your little Down Under adventure left a bad impression of men on you. Mate," he added pointedly, copying the bit of Aussie accent that crept into her voice now and again, usually when she was cheering or swearing. So, fairly often. "You should let me fix that for you."

Kerry smiled sweetly up into his handsome, preternaturally tanned and weathered face. "I'm thinking I'll wait until your track record improves."

Hardy clutched his chest and stumbled back a step in mock pain as one of the other players called out, "She shoots, she scores!" causing another ripple of laughter among the slowly dispersing crowd. Hardy grinned and laughed with them, but not before Kerry saw a bit of a hard glint come into his eyes. If she lived anywhere else, she'd have wondered how he knew where she'd been prior to her return to the Cove, given she'd never once spoken of that particular adventure other than to Fergus. But in a town the size of Blueberry, the fact that everybody knew everyone else's business was a given.

Within moments, she was once again swallowed up in the rush of running a small pub on a crowded Friday night. She dismissed any concerns about Hardy. He might be an inveterate flirt who hadn't had the good sense to expend at least some of that natural charm on his own wife, but he wasn't an overly aggressive guy. He'd keep up the pressure, to be sure, but she'd handle it, handle him.

She ducked under the bar in time to bump hips with Fergus as he came in from the tiny kitchen in the back. "Natives are restless," he said. "And hungry. Eatin' us out of house and home, they are. We're down to pretzels and nuts. Need to order more of those cracked corn nuts you put on the menu, too."

He was balancing a tray filled with little wooden bowls in his good hand. She smoothly shifted the tray from his hand to hers, leaning in to kiss his ruddy cheek as she did. "Will do," she said, and carried it to the waiting bar patrons without giving him a chance to protest. He was touchy about the limitations his stroke had left him to grapple with, and she'd learned the best way to deal with that was to do what needed doing while charming her way through his moods.

The stroke had left parts of the left side of his body less than fully functional. He had a very slight droop to the corner of his left eye and the corner of his mouth on that side, but his speech patterns had mostly returned to normal with only minimal slurring. He still had random gaps in his memory, both of current events and ones from his past, and at times he would lose his train of thought or struggle a moment to form a word, but otherwise, for a man in his mid-seventies, he was still sharp as ever.

More troublesome was that the stroke had weakened his left shoulder, arm, and hand, which made him less capable of taking on the normal lifting and carrying duties required of running a pub, though fortunately he was right-handed and still had all his fine motor skills there. According to his doctors and physical therapist, he should be using a walker, as his left hip and knee weren't at full mobility, but Fergus wasn't having any of that. He'd found a way to get his short, stout-framed self around well enough using a thick, hand-carved oak cane that Eula, the local antique store owner, had given him, complete with a large, knotty knob handle that was easy to grip even with his less functional hand.

Still, Kerry worried about him and was

glad she could stick nearby to keep an eye on him. She filled two more drink orders, handed out more pretzels and nuts, and listened to Fergus regale the bar patrons with boyhood tall tales of his life in Ireland. She smiled as she pulled another tray full of drafts, thinking it was likely they'd heard the stories a dozen times or more, but, if they were like her, they never tired of listening to them. The town had rallied around Fergus after his stroke, and the love everyone had for him was made obvious each and every night, right here in the pub.

As comforting as it was to see firsthand that he was doing well enough, maybe her little voice had a point; maybe he didn't need her to stick around. He'd be the first to say so, and had. Often. Pressing her to start planning her next adventure, offering up his opinion on the subject of where she might go, despite never once being asked. She smiled at that. Ornery Irishman he was, but it was hard to ignore the pang she got in her chest every time she really gave leaving a thought. Leaving Fergus, leaving her family, the Cove. It had never been difficult for her before, but now . . .

A roar of laughter from the other end of the bar had her glancing again at her uncle, who was deep into his role as entertainer, truly in his element. He might not be a wayfarer in truth, but he would always be one in spirit. This place gave him purpose, gave him joy; it was a place to share the wonders of his world, as he'd seen them, still saw them in his mind's eye, with people who mattered to him. A blessing, she realized now. It was both his life and his lifeline and she was thrilled and not a little relieved that he'd recovered enough to be able to maintain the place.

So, what gives you purpose, Miss Kerry Mc-Crae, her little voice nagged on, perhaps with a wee bit of a brogue thrown in, just to be truly annoying. *What gives you joy?*

Kerry shook her head and allowed herself another private, if dry smile. Since when had she needed a purpose? Life gave her joy. Her big and bold life. There didn't need to be more, didn't need to be a specific thing that gave her life meaning. Not when she could do so many things, experience so many kinds of joy. She didn't believe that one place, one thing, would hold her interest for long, much less forever. Her thoughts immediately flashed to one place, one person, who'd held her interest far longer than any other. A place and person she'd done her damnedest not to think about. Not since she'd packed her duffels and headed

24

out, headed home. That's what she did. She came, she stayed, she enjoyed . . . then she moved on.

But in that moment, watching Fergus, her heart clutched inside her chest as she felt the love of family, the security of home, and, along with it, a deep sense of fear. Which was ridiculous. She, of all people, didn't do fear. She was the opposite of that; she was fearless.

She went back to work, and maybe her smile was a bit too bright, her laughter a bit too loud, the pokes and prods she enjoyed exchanging with the locals — her locals — a bit too forced. She — Kerry McCrae — wasn't afraid of anything. Certainly not of losing anything. Or anyone. She'd lost more before her second birthday than most folks did in a lifetime. She'd been cured of fear before she was old enough for grade school.

She was in the back of the pub, delivering another round to the guys playing pool at the table Hardy and Perry had left behind for a rousing game of darts, when a hush fell over the folks crowded around the bar and the front door to the place.

A man's deep, accented voice boomed through the sudden hush. "I was told I might find her here, mate," the man was saying to someone. "Kerry? Kerry McCrae.

Her uncle owns the place, yeah?"

If Kerry's heart had clutched in her chest before, it stopped functioning altogether the moment that voice reached her ears. *This is why you don't let yourself think about him, because then you won't stop thinking about him. And now you're hearing things.* Even as she thought the words, knowing rationally that there was no way she'd heard his voice, not for real, some small part of her understood that the impossible had actually just happened.

She looked up, a fierce expression on her face, one meant to forestall even the remotest possibility that he was indeed right there. In the pub. Her pub. Looking for her. It didn't work, of course. Because he was there. And she thought her heart might beat right through her chest wall. *So much for being fearless.*

Someone — she didn't even notice who — took the badly wobbling tray of drinks from her hand as she went toward him, seemingly without even moving her feet. It was like a dream. Maybe it was a dream. Maybe this whole night had been a dream and she was in bed, right now, and would wake up any second and laugh at herself, then swear at herself, for letting him into her dreams. Again.

But it sure didn't feel like she was dreaming.

He was tall, a good half foot taller than her five-foot-seven frame. He was muscular, with thick shoulders and arms above narrow hips, and strong thighs earned over a lifetime of hard physical labor. His thick thatch of curly blond hair was shorter now, bleached almost white from the sun, setting off eyes so blue they blazed from his deeply tanned face like twin lasers. He wore beat-up work Daks, heavy leather work boots, and a forest green polo shirt with a sun-bleached collar and the words *Cameroo Downs Station* stitched in yellow over the front pocket, the threading frayed and faded almost white, too, from hundreds of washings, and the day-to-day abuse it endured while its owner ran a cattle station that was twenty-thousand-head strong and more than fifteen-hundred square miles big.

He could afford better; his family ran one of the biggest stations in the northwestern part of the Northern Territory, but it was just like Cooper not to care about that sort of thing. Damn it all, that was one of the things that had first attracted her to him. He worked just as hard if not harder than the men and women he employed, and did so right alongside them.

Someone pointed and his gaze swiveled to her, pinpointing her on the spot as neatly and securely as if he'd lassoed and roped her to it. And he could have if he'd wanted to, of that she had no doubt. Some dizzying part of her rapidly spinning brain figured he probably couldn't get his bullwhip through airport security. Another part acknowledged that the past year she'd spent convincing herself he was just a man, like any other man, not some larger-than-life action hero she'd foolishly romanticized into someone bigger, bolder, and even more brash than she'd recalled him to be, had been a complete waste of time. Because he was all of that, more than that.

And he was here. Right here. In Blueberry Cove, Maine.

"Cooper," she said. "Cooper Jax." As if saying his name would somehow break the spell, vanquish the mirage she was still faintly hoping she was seeing. It didn't. Instead it brought the mirage a few strides farther into the pub as folks moved to clear a path. "What are you doing here?" she asked as she moved forward until the two were standing no more than five yards apart, encircled by the completely hushed crowd. She wished she sounded strong, strident even. They were on her turf now, in her

28

world. He was the interloper, the traveler. But her voice was hoarse even to her own ears, a mere rasp; her throat was too tight, too dry, too . . . everything, to manage anything more than that.

His smile was brief, a slash of white teeth framed by a hard jaw, but his gaze never wavered. "It's been a year, Kerry. More than. And I've come to realize there's a question I didn't ask you before you left. One I should have. And I can't seem to get on with life until I know the answer."

She had no idea what on earth he was talking about. She'd worked his cattle station for a year, the longest she'd ever stayed in one place. She'd left to come home for Logan's wedding. And, if she were honest, to save herself from having to decide when to leave. Because she'd come close to admitting that maybe she didn't want to. And she never let herself want. At least not something that wasn't in her power to get. *Fear. Of losing.*

If there was nothing to lose, there was nothing to fear.

"What might that be?" she asked, having to force the bravado that was normally second nature to her. From the corner of her eye, she caught Fergus, his gaze swiveling between the two of them . . . a broad grin on his face. *Auld codger.* To think she'd stayed for him. He was the only one who knew. The only one she'd confided in. Of course he was loving this.

Cooper walked closer and a murmur of unease swelled, but Fergus waved his good hand, like a silent benediction, approving of what was about to unfold, and they fell silent again.

Cooper's gaze was locked exclusively on hers, and suddenly it was as if they were the only two people in the room. Everything else fell away, and she felt herself getting pulled in, swallowed up. That was always how he'd made her feel, as if she was this close to drowning . . . and that maybe she should stop trying so hard to keep her head above water.

He stopped a foot in front of her and she lifted her gaze — and her chin — to stay even with his.

"Before, when you were there, working, living alongside us, I thought if I gave you room, gave you space, you'd figure out that Cameroo Downs was where you belonged," he said.

His words, the rumble of his deep voice, that accent of his, held her as surely as if he'd put his hands on her. *But then, that's why you left, wasn't it? So you wouldn't risk*

30

finding out what would happen if he ever did put his hands on you.

"When you left," he continued, "I told myself once you were gone, then you'd realize it — you'd have to — and you'd come back."

She struggled to listen to his words, to take in their meaning, but they were so completely at odds with what she'd thought, back when she was working for him and every single day since. Thinking he'd been business only, that her thoughts, her fantasies, about him, about them, were hers alone — that was the only way she'd kept her sanity intact, kept her yearning from consuming her.

"But a full year has gone by. And you haven't come back. Not so much as a word from you."

"Cooper," she said, the two syllables not much more than a broken whisper. She cleared her throat. "I never said — you knew I wasn't coming back. You knew when I started that I wasn't staying."

"When you started, yeah," he said, then moved another inch closer, and what little air she seemed to have pulled in deserted her just as swiftly. "But by the time you left . . . I thought . . ."

She let herself sink deeper and looked into

his eyes. "You thought what?"

"It's been a year," he repeated, and for the first time, she saw something behind that bold, fierce, confident gaze of his, something she'd never seen before, though she couldn't quite say what it was. "And I realize now that I should have asked then."

"Asked me to stay?" she said, hating the tremulous waver in her voice, hating more that she wasn't quite sure how she'd answer him if he asked now. "You could have just called."

A titter went up in the crowd and was just as swiftly snuffed out by shushing sounds. It all barely registered with her.

"No, not that. I mean, yes, I wanted you to stay. But not as a jillaroo. Or not only as one."

And then she realized what it was she saw. She would have recognized it right off if she'd let herself acknowledge that it was the same thing she'd seen in her own eyes. *Fear.* What could Cooper Jax possibly be afraid of? *Fear of wanting what he can't have? Of losing what he wanted most?* But that couldn't be, because that would mean —

"I wanted you to stay, Kerry. As my wife."

The crowd gasped as one, and she might have gasped with them.

"I've come all this way, Starfish, because I

need to know. If I'd asked you then, if I'd pursued it, pursued you, would you ever have considered marrying me?"

CHAPTER TWO

The world around her consolidated into a loud buzz, reverberating in her ears. Which made no sense, because in that single moment there was a complete absence of sound.

The drumming of her heartbeat should have been deafening. Only that wasn't a noise, it was a feeling.

Feeling.

Kerry had spent the better part of the past year trying not to do exactly that. There were very few things she'd failed at as spectacularly as she had that single-minded mission. And that had been when the man responsible for her uncharacteristic failure was half a world away.

Now he was standing directly in front of her. Saying the most shocking and, frankly, terrifying things to her. One part of her understood where she was, accepted that the unthinkable had just happened, knew that there were people crowded all around her — around the two of them — gaping, holding their collective breath, waiting for her response. Her response to his completely insane and utterly ridiculous question. Who did that?

Who waited a freaking year, then traveled a bazillion miles, spending untold numbers of hours on a plane, a train, an automobile, and, very likely, a horse and sheep cart or two, to publicly lay his heart bare? When in all the time they'd spent together, he couldn't be bothered to so much as hint at the possibility, that he was maybe, kind of, sort of interested in her as anything other than a station hand? While she tossed and turned and suffered through the most unthinkable, untenable — for her — feelings and emotions she'd ever had. So much so that when the invitation to her brother's wedding arrived, she didn't so much leave Australia and Cameroo Downs . . . she fled them.

WHO DID THAT?

The words screamed inside her head. Inside her chest. Begging — no, demanding — to be let out, just like that, in full caps and with a string of exclamation points, and possibly a longer string of expletives after them. It was only the fair certainty that

35

she'd fly apart, in equally overly exclamatory fashion, only to end up in teeny, tiny, never-to-be-reassembled pieces at his big, booted feet, that had her, mercifully and quite severely, biting her tongue almost in half at the very last second before self-implosion occurred.

"Kerry —" he began, shattering the silence and any chance she had of wishing herself into invisibility. Or onto another planet.

She instantly, instinctively, swung her palm up to halt him. To halt him and that voice. That deep, rich, oh-so-mellifluous voice, with that accent that seemed to curl around the vowels and loop between the consonants of her name, making her feel like he'd stroked some part of her every time he said it. A part of her she could never keep from shivering and shuddering in an instant and uncontrollable response.

Stupid, really. How many accents had she heard in her life? How many of them uttered by men who were charming, good-looking, and all but oozing sex appeal in her general direction? More than she could count. More than most women would in a lifetime. Two lifetimes.

How many of those accents had worked on her, gotten to her, made her want to wriggle out of her beaten-up chaps, worn-out jeans, and faded chambray shirt and beg to add physical touch to the verbal stroking? How many men, born with the kind of accent that made commenting on something as innocuous as the weather sound like pornography, had made her nipples achingly, painfully hard, like he'd murmured the words with his lips wrapped around them? Made her as wet as if he'd slid his hand inside those chaps, toying with her while he talked of cumulous clouds and threatening thunder bursts? Torturing her into finding new and exceedingly more challenging mental hoops to jump through so she could keep her mind on what he was actually saying, on her work, and dear, merciful God, off what her body wanted him to be saying and what kind of work she wished he was proposing they get busy on.

Yeah. Exactly none.

Other than the one standing right in front of her.

Her focus shifted from his face, from those eyes, pulling back to focus on her hand, still held up in front of her. Her fingers shook; only slightly, but any sign of weakness was unacceptable. She jerked her hand back, then folded her arms to hide the evidence of her reaction, trying hard to make it look like a defiant, squared-off stance. And not like she was wrapping her arms around herself the way a vulnerable child would a hastily erected, makeshift shield.

"Cooper," she managed, hating the hoarse, grating sound. It was a name she'd quite purposefully never spoken, not once, to anyone, even herself, since driving through the north gate and away from Cameroo Downs. "I don't know what possessed you to come all this way," she began.

"I believe I've explained that," he said, the tension in his face starting to relax a little, though his big, rangy body still radiated coiled energy.

He'd always been like that. Which had made that whole sexual energy thing between them like being one breath away from touching a live wire. At all times.

His mouth kicked up a little at the corner as he added, "Of course, I might've made a bit of a blue, choosing this place to do it in."

"You think?" she shot back, hands involuntarily flying up to punctuate the outburst.

And just like that, the freeze frame clicked off and the world around them snapped back to life. The crowd laughed at her snapped response, sounding almost collectively relieved to hear Kerry sounding like . . . well, like Kerry.

38

"Haven't you mentioned me to your mates here?" He took a brief moment to acknowledge the still-assembled crowd with a short nod and a brief smile. "My apologies for intruding on your Friday night."

Just then Hardy emerged from the bodies crowding in behind her to bump at her left elbow. "Kerry, you want me to escort your . . . *mate* here outside?"

She might have jumped, just a little, at the contact. Any contact at the moment would have done it. She quickly corralled her thoughts, or tried to. "No," she told him. "That won't be necessary. I — thank you. But I've got it."

Hardy started to move around Kerry, intent, she figured, on placing himself between her and their uninvited guest. Hardy was a big man, and while his musculature was a bit thicker than Cooper's, Kerry would give Cooper the edge in a matchup between the two. She knew Hardy's occupation was a very physically demanding one, but Kerry had seen Cooper in action with several thousand head of recalcitrant livestock during mustering season. He was more long limbed, rangy in build than Hardy, but he had a few inches in height on the other man, and in addition to being powerfully strong, Cooper was also quick and agile. In body and in mind.

She put a hand on Hardy's arm, stopping his forward progress, glancing up at him as he shifted his gaze from Cooper to her. "Thanks, but it's all good. Go back to your game. I've got this."

He looked as if he was going to argue the point, but when she met his retractable gaze with her own, knowing it was every bit as steely, he finally relented. Not, of course, without tossing a look Cooper's way that made it clear he was keeping an eye on the newcomer.

Kerry shifted her attention from Hardy to the rest of the still-milling crowd and tried to ignore the murmurs that included Cooper's nickname for her and speculations on there being yet another McCrae family wedding. She needed to put an end to that before it even started. She clapped her hands, drawing everyone's attention to her, then strode to the bar and hoisted herself right up on it, straight to her feet. She was no weakling herself. "Okay, listen up, everyone." The noise abruptly wound down again, though not to the complete silence of before. "I'd like you to meet Cooper Jax, from Cameroo Downs cattle station, Northern Territory, Australia."

Heads swiveled and Cooper smiled, nodded several times, shifting his gaze around the room as he did, easily meeting everyone's avidly curious gaze. But when that gaze went back to Kerry, despite the smile creasing his handsome face, the look in his eyes was anything but casual.

Kerry ignored that. Or tried to. She shifted her attention back to the crowd. "I worked the Jax family's station for close to a year, just before coming home for Logan's wedding." Blueberry Cove was small enough that everyone knew who Logan McCrae was. Not only due to his police chief status but, as it happened, the McCraes were also a founding family of the Cove. There wasn't much the general populace didn't know about the entire history of her family, past and present.

"Long time for you," came a voice from somewhere in the crowd. Kerry recognized the scratchy voice: Stokey Parker. A Rusty Puffin regular and one of Fergus's cronies. "Heard tell you don't stick in one place too long. Guess we know now what the draw was Down Under."

A chuckle went up in the crowd, and Kerry knew this wasn't going as she'd planned. Not that she'd had much of a plan. "Thanks, Stokey. Australia is a beautiful country. I loved it there." That much was sincere. All the same, she carefully kept from looking anywhere near Cooper's direction. "But I'm home in the Cove now." She expanded her gaze to encompass the full crowd again. "I appreciate that you're all entertained by this . . . little surprise." She swallowed hard and looked at Cooper as she added, "But there's not going to be another McCrae wedding."

There was a collective groan from the audience, and someone shouted, "Come on, don't break the guy's heart." Someone else added, "That's cold, Kerry. Even for you."

She might have blanched a little at that. Cold. She wasn't cold. She just wasn't . . . overly friendly. At least not in the way some of the men in the place — and not only the single ones — hoped she'd be. "Come on now," she said. "I'm not breaking anything here. You get what you see with me. No subterfuge, no leading anyone to believe anything that isn't true. You all know that." She didn't bother looking at Hardy, though it couldn't hurt to get him the message again, too. She did look at Cooper again, though, as she added, "Anyone who knows me, knows that."

His laser-beam gaze didn't falter for even a blink. She drew in a steadying breath and pasted a big smile on her face. "So then," she said, clapping her hands together and keeping her fingers woven tightly in front of her, her damp palms belying her I'm-so-in-control-here attitude. "The entertainment portion of the evening is over. Nothing to see here. Let's shoot some pool, throw some darts, and a round for everyone, on the house."

That got the rousing cheer she knew it would and she quickly hopped down behind the bar and immediately began setting up glasses. She knew her grand — and not inexpensive — gesture would quiet them for a bit, but she also knew life in the Cove was going to be rife with all sorts of gossip for the next day or two, until something else came along to replace it on their juicy little grapevine. She had no idea where Fergus had suddenly gotten to and was surprised he hadn't tried to orchestrate something, anything, between Kerry and Cooper. Hopefully with her little demonstration just now, he'd never have the chance.

No sooner had the thought passed through her mind than Fergus was there at her elbow. "I've got this," he said, uncharacteristically low key as he edged her out of the way.

"Gus —"

He nudged her again with a bit more force

than was necessary, then wedged his cane in between them to emphasize the point. "I'll pour and pass. You go talk to your young man."

"He's not my —"

Fergus turned his bright blue eyes on her. "I know who he is." His voice might brook no argument, but there was a world more feeling in his gaze than in his quietly spoken words. "So get on out while the getting's good. We're not too far from closing. I'll get Sandy to help shut the place down. You're officially off duty until tomorrow."

"But —"

Now his gaze did turn steely, reminding her where she got the look from. "I believe I still own and run this place. So when I say you're off until tomorrow, you're off until tomorrow."

Kerry swallowed hard and was as shocked as anyone to feel the tiniest prickles behind her eyes. No matter what her latest exploit, he'd never, not once, looked at her with even a hint of disappointment. Until now. "Yes, sir."

His gaze softened, even if the set of his face did not. He leaned in and bussed her on the cheek, then whispered in her ear, "And I'm taking this round out of your pay, Sprite. Giving away my ale," he added in a grumble.

The grumble made her smile, and she gave him a quick, one-armed squeeze around his shoulders and a kiss on the side of his forehead, taking care not to put him off balance on his bad side. "I had to do something to throw them off the scent."

"I believe the something that is still on your scent is waiting for you by the door," he said, then turned back to help Sandy, who manned the griddle in the kitchen on busy nights, fill and slide mugs down the bar.

Kerry glanced up and over the heads of the folks crowding the bar to the tall man who, indeed, was standing by the door, his old Akubra in hand. Her gaze shifted from the ever-present drover's hat he always wore for work to the penetrating and unwavering look in his beautiful eyes.

"Get on, lassie," Fergus said, his brogue thickening, "before the wolves slake their collective thirst. I'll nae be serving more free lager this evening."

Kerry went to the other end of the bar, toward the front and away from the pool tables and dartboards in the back, where she was fairly certain, if she looked, she'd find Hardy tracking her every move. She appreciated his willingness to step in, but

45

she doubted it was an entirely altruistic gesture on his part. She shoved thoughts of Hardy aside, knowing she'd deal with whatever he thought he had in mind when the time came, and turned her attention to getting herself out of her apron and out the door while she could.

She gave Cooper a quick nod, indicating she was going out the back, and didn't wait around to see if he understood her meaning. She pushed through the swinging doors to the small kitchen in the back, snagged the keys to her truck from the hook, and replaced them with her apron. She gave a quick glance to the grill, making sure Sandy hadn't left anything to burn on it when he'd been pulled out front, but everything looked in order. *Stop stalling.*

She sighed, shook her head, but the rueful smile that accompanied the movement was fleeting. For what might be the first time in her life, she had absolutely no idea how she was going to handle what came next.

"Only one way to find out," she murmured. Tightening her grip on her keys, if not her emotions, she let herself out the back door of the pub and found herself staring straight up into the crystalline blue eyes of Cooper Jax.

CHAPTER THREE

She was every bit of everything he remembered about her, all at once and all at the same time. That was Kerry McCrae in a nutshell, he thought. All at once, full on, 100 percent real. No bullshit.

She froze on seeing him, and while the wariness in her beautiful green eyes wasn't a surprise, the vulnerability sure was. "Starfish —"

"Don't call me that," she said, then immediately, and less stridently, added, "Not here." She ducked around him before he could react and was down the set of wooden steps leading off the narrow cement loading dock that ran along the back of the pub, heading across the gravel lot.

He started after her. He might not have handled any of this even close to how he'd planned, but he wasn't flying all the way back home without at least a conversation. A private conversation. *You might have*

47

wanted to lead with that, you yobbo. "Kerry, wait."

"Not here," she repeated, then opened the driver's side door to a beat-up old navy blue truck that looked like it was more rust than actual metal. "Get in."

"I've got a rental. I'll be happy to —"

She swung her laser green gaze to his. "Get in." She slammed the door without waiting for a reply, then slammed it a second time to get the handle to catch.

He climbed in the passenger side, not all that surprised to find the inside of the cab surprisingly clean and as well maintained as possible, given the thing had one tire, if not two, in the grave. Kerry McCrae had never fussed about how she looked or what she wore, but when it came to property or equipment, whether it be her own or simply entrusted to her care, no matter how old or worn out, she had a dab hand at keeping it clean and neat, all systems go. Her concern was never about appearance, just functionality and getting the job done.

It was sexy as hell then, and it was sexy as hell now.

"You just spent a whole lot of money and wasted even more of your time so I could turn you down in front of an entire town's worth of people," she said, giving him a

48

sideways glance as she pulled out of the rear lot and swung the truck down the narrow back road toward the harbor down below. "So, what have you got to smile about?"

He settled back in his seat and put the old felt hat he'd taken off when he'd entered the bar back on his head, and let his smile slide into the grin he realized he'd been holding back. "It's good to see you again, Starfish."

She scowled at that, as he'd known she would, but she didn't call him on it. No point in it, really. As well as he knew her, she knew him equally so.

"I can't believe you did this," she said a moment later, and he noted that along with her irritation, she was gripping the steering wheel as if her life depended on it.

That shouldn't have reassured him, but it did. "Which part?" he asked with a chuckle.

She gaped at him, then turned her attention back to the road. "All of the parts." She drove on for another few seconds, making the turn onto the road that led down to the harbor, then suddenly stomped on the brake, causing him to brace a quick hand on the dash. She jerked the truck to the side of the road and came to a full stop before turning to him, her expression urgent. "Did something happen? To your family? Cooper, don't even think about not —"

"What?" he asked, honestly surprised by the sudden barrage, and more so by the clear concern in her eyes.

"Your family," she repeated, as if he was a bit slow. And maybe he was. About a lot of things. "I was just thinking I can't imagine them being thrilled with you taking off like this, halfway around the world no less, leaving them shorthanded and — then I thought, oh no, something must have happened, because why else would you —" She broke off, shook her head, and seemed to look sightlessly at her hands, still gripping the steering wheel.

"Because why else would I what?"

She finally looked at him, and along with that goodly dose of agitation and not a little honest confusion, he saw that sliver of vulnerability again. "Because what else would cause a man I knew to be perfectly sane and fully committed to running one of the biggest cattle stations in the Northern Territory alongside his big, loud, boisterous, and very close-knit and beloved family — to up and run halfway around the world chasing after a . . . after —"

"You?"

She blinked, closed her mouth, opened it again, then simply shook her head and looked away. A beat passed, then another. "So, they're all okay?" she asked him anyway, back to staring at her hands. "Big Jack? Ian? Sadie?" She glanced at him. "Little Mac?"

He lifted his hand, palm out. "All safe and sound, I swear. Last I checked anyway." His grin settled back to a quiet smile. "The only one who's lost anything is me."

She ducked her chin; then he saw her pull herself together. And when she raised her eyes to his once more, she was all Kerry McCrae. Bold, confident, smart, and more than a little smart-assed. Potent combination, that. Or so he'd learned.

When she'd first come to their station, hired on by his father, Big Jack, as a jackaroo — or jillaroo, as the female ranch trainees were called — Cooper had told his dad and his two siblings that the American wouldn't last a fortnight. A wanderer who'd gone a bit troppo more than likely, traipsing around the world for kicks, thinking station life was some romantic outback romp, was about to find out she'd bitten off more than she could chew.

He bit back a grin at the memory of how she'd taken on Cameroo and every single member of the Jax family, wrapping them around her like they were a comfortable,

51

well-worn coat. And the only chewing that had been done was by him, eating his words.

"You know, a more prudent man might have wanted to use that newfangled thing called a phone, or to shoot off an e-mail on that fancy laptop Sadie was so excited about finally getting for her schoolwork," Kerry said, more quietly now. "Find out if the other party even remembered his name, much less if she was interested in doing anything more with him than trying to herd ten thousand head of cattle all over the godforsaken outback."

"Twenty thousand. And you just told your entire town you loved Australia and its godforsaken outback."

She nodded but said nothing; there was not even a hint of that earthy, easygoing smile that was usually never more than a breath away.

He let the silence continue as they drove along the harbor road. She pulled into a sandy lot on the far side of the endless rows of jutting piers. Just ahead the road disappeared behind a thick stand of pine trees before winding its way back out of the harbor and on to destinations unknown.

"Tide's out," she said, then got out of the truck, closed the door, and banged it shut again to make it stick, before making her way down the rocky ledge to the seaweed-strewn ocean floor below. She hadn't asked for company, nor did she look back to see if he was going to follow.

Cooper wasn't a particularly well-traveled man. His idea of a big holiday was to go with the family to one of the beaches in Darwin after they'd sold off the annual lot of cattle at the ports there. He'd flown as far away as Auckland, New Zealand, to visit extended family, but he'd never been to any part of the Americas, and had never seen anything that rivaled the coastline of Maine. He'd heard Kerry's stories about her childhood here, so many of them, but despite how vividly and lovingly they'd been recalled and relayed, they hadn't done the place justice. He'd read up on the country, and specifically the state, before making his flight, had read about the big tidal swings, some of the biggest and most rapid depth changes in the world. Seeing it with his own eyes, however, was far more impressive . . . and yet his gaze remained fixed on one particularly fiery and unsurprisingly recalcitrant redhead.

She claimed not to want him, not to want what he offered. She'd even made it seem as if his interest in her, his belief that there was something far deeper between them than simply a working relationship, or even a strong friendship, was coming as a surprise. But he knew what he knew, knew the air had fair sizzled between them, all but crackling with the kind of sexual tension that took a sort of superhuman control to resist. He knew, firsthand, because he'd had to find that control.

He'd been her boss, her employer. She'd been temporary, had made that clear from the start. But then her summer stint had turned into a six-month stay, then nine, and then her first full year anniversary was on the horizon . . . and he'd been forced to admit any ability he had to resist his feelings for her had long since begun to seriously falter. He'd finally stopped denying that there was something there, something special. He just hadn't known how to take things a step forward. He had been considering the ways, contemplating that first move, what felt like every waking minute of every day. Then she'd gotten the note from her brother. And before Cooper had found the words to ask her to stay, or, at the very least, to come back, she'd been gone.

But he knew what he knew. There had been something there. Something real, and solid, something that because of his superhuman control — and he had to believe hers, too — had allowed a true and deep friendship to form between them. Not all at once either, but slowly and surely, over time. The kind of time that, by its very nature, brought with it a long string of events that forged lasting bonds. Everything from grand and momentous holiday occasions to the mundane, everyday, mettle-testing drama that was the reality of running a station the size of Cameroo Downs.

So it wasn't lust, though she still delivered a fair wallop of that to various parts of his body, and it wasn't some shallow, love-struck notion of what a relationship with her might be. He knew what it would be. He'd lived it. In all the ways except the most important one. He'd seen with his own eyes, and heard with his own ears, the feeling, the emotion in her voice when she said she loved Australia.

He knew what he knew.

It was because he knew what he knew that he got out of the truck. And followed her.

CHAPTER FOUR

She could feel him, sense him, more than hear him. Of course he'd followed her. Kerry knew him. Even if he hadn't flown halfway around the world to make a preposterous proposition, she knew he wasn't one to give up when he'd made up his mind about something. It was a Jax family trait. And a large part of why the Cameroo Downs station was, and always had been, a Jax family–owned and run operation.

She shut thoughts of Cooper's father, Big Jack, his younger brother, Ian, his thirteen-year-old sister, Sadie, even his damn cattle dog, Little Mac, from her mind. She'd missed them all like a physical ache even before she'd driven off the pastoral property, and had learned early on that the only way to keep that deep sense of loss from consuming her altogether was to simply not allow herself to think of them, of the people who had become, despite her very best and concerted efforts, a second family to her.

And that yawning chasm of emotion had been complicated by crushing guilt. Guilt for not being able to rise above the pain of leaving to do as she'd promised, to keep in touch. Not for Cooper, or even Big Jack, though she'd told him she'd write. But for Sadie. The only female in a family of boisterous, rowdy, hardworking men, and one of only a few on the entire station, she'd bonded with Kerry like a pearl cleaved to a clam. Kerry had done her damnedest to be friendly and professional while remaining firmly off limits to the wise beyond-her-years youngster, but Sadie was a Jax after all. She'd been determined to weasel her way over, under, and through every protective layer Kerry could construct between them until she wore down her very last defense. And damn if she hadn't, too.

The fact that Sadie was cute as a bug, small, but gangly for her age, with her freckled pip of a nose, pointy little chin, eyes as blue as her big brothers', wild, red-gold ringlets that always looked like they were wrestling their way out of the single thick braid she wore every day, not to mention being smart as the proverbial whip and twice as sharp in the observation department, hadn't hurt her chances either.

57

Kerry ducked her chin and kicked ineffectually at a clump of kelp, then bobbled and almost went down on her ass when her other foot slipped in the muck. She should have grabbed her Wellies from the bed of the truck. *But why start being smart now?* Her rash decision to take a beach walk had stemmed mostly from needing to be out of that cab, needing to put more space between her and Cooper. Before she did something even more phenomenally stupid. Like lunge at him. So she shrugged off the fact that she'd just trashed another pair of work shoes less than five steps through this ocean muck and steadied herself. Lose the shoes to save some face. "If not my ass," she murmured, continuing onward.

Cooper caught up to her less than twenty yards down the shoreline but said nothing. He simply fell into step beside her, seemingly also uncaring about the muck that was accumulating on his leather work boots, taking the occasional slip and slide in stride, quickly finding his balance on this new-to-him terrain.

Of course he did.

"I know you don't owe me a damn thing," she said at length, "but I'm going to ask a favor anyway."

"Ask," he replied, simply.

She didn't glance at him, keeping her eyes on the rocks as they began to crowd out most of the seafloor and the kelp beds, which were strewn over and in between them. "Please tell Sadie that my being a total shite of a friend was not in any way about her."

"What was it about, then?" he asked, the barest hint of amusement in his tone, when she'd expected — and earned — censure. Or worse.

She sent him a quick, sideways glance, but his gaze was fixed downward, as hers had been, as he navigated the exposed seafloor under their feet.

"I meant to," she said. "Write her," she added. "I know she was upset that I left."

"She's a tough little sheila," he said.

Kerry glanced at him again, not missing the barest hint of an edge in his voice this time. *More like it,* she thought. More like what she deserved. "I know. She has to be, living with the likes of the rest of her family."

That got a quick look from Cooper, and maybe the first bare hint of a smile from her. He caught that, looked back, and this time their glances caught and held. Her smile faded, but the honest affection came through in her tone when she said, "She shouldn't have had to be where I was concerned."

Kerry was surprised at the bark of laughter that comment earned her. She merely lifted her eyebrows in response.

"Says the woman who made it as hard as humanly possible for Sadie to connect in the first place. That girl could make friends with the meanest croc alive with little more than a smile and a laugh. You, on the other hand, made her work for it."

"Did you just compare me to a mean old croc?" Kerry asked, the thread of amusement back in her tone.

"If the tough hide fits," he said, but not unkindly.

Kerry nodded, gave him a considering look. "True that," she said. She picked her way over a tricky stretch of kelp-covered rock, then added, "Maybe I was trying to save her from her own friendly nature." She looked back as Cooper hopped his way over the last pile, his heavy-booted feet sinking into a narrow stretch of sand before starting over the next rock bed. "I knew I was going to leave. You all did. No point in breaking hearts." She held his gaze more directly now, turning back slightly to look at him full on. "I might be a tough old croc, but I'm not heartless."

"I didn't say —"

"You didn't have to." She opened her mouth, closed it again, then took in a slow, steadying breath, letting the deep salt tang tickle the back of her throat and the tart brine of the sea fill her senses. Anything to keep his scent from doing that instead. "As a rule, I don't do good-byes well. I know that about myself. I also know that I have the attention span of a sand fly. A well-intentioned sand fly," she added, trying to inject a bit of humor, mostly failing judging by the unwavering look in his eyes. "So, given my wanderlusting, gypsy life, I learned early on to keep things friendly and light. Easy, breezy. I've made friends all over the world, but none so close that —"

"That missing them causes a pang," he added. "Here maybe," he said, pointing at his own head. "But not here." He pointed at her chest, more specifically at her heart.

This was how they were, how they'd been from the start. Finishing each other's sentences, following each other's train of thought, even when the exchange of words was a bare minimum. She glanced up into his steady gaze and thought, *or when there'd been no words at all.* That was why they'd worked so well together. And also why she'd had a tough time keeping her feelings for

61

him strictly professional. . . . She'd forgotten how threatening it felt, to have someone read her so easily. Most folks never look past the surface. Cooper — hell, the entire Jax family — hadn't even blinked at surface Kerry before barreling right on past all of her well-honed, automatically erected barriers.

"Like I said," she went on, "I don't do good-byes well." She continued walking down the beach then, knowing she was avoiding continued eye contact, but it was unnerving enough that he was here, in her personal orbit, in her world. Her home world. Wasn't that invasive enough?

"Would a postcard or two have killed you?" he finally asked her retreating back. "Not for me; I never expected one."

She didn't glance back at that, but just as he knew her too well, she knew him the same way. She'd heard that little hint of disappointment, of long-held hope. Of course the very fact that he was there, on her beach, was proof enough that he'd had hopes where she was concerned. And in that moment, she thought, *the hell with this,* and stopped. Running halfway around the world apparently hadn't been far enough to leave him and all of what had transpired between her and the entire Jax family behind. So why did she think she could escape it along the span of one low-tide beach?

She stopped so abruptly that he banged into the back of her, then immediately grabbed both of her arms when she pitched forward and lost her balance on the slippery rocks. He pulled her back against him, and the shock of the feel of that hard body lined up so perfectly with hers, so much better than she'd ever imagined it would feel — and oh, she'd imagined it — was far greater than almost pitching face-first against the rocks.

The instant she had her balance she said, "I'm good" and moved out of his grasp. She wasn't sure what it said that she was disappointed he didn't take advantage of the moment to press his cause . . . or anything else he might be interested in pressing against her. But he let her go, and even stepped back for good measure.

"Sorry," she said, turning to face him. "I just — this isn't solving anything."

"What is it that needs solving? To your way of thinking," he added.

She gaped at him, then shook her head and laughed. "Oh, I don't know. Your coming thousands of miles to declare yourself to me, a year after I left and, as far as you knew, never looked back?"

"You've already solved that one, haven't you?" he said. "Back there in the pub. I believe you shut me down pretty effectively and quite definitively."

"So why are you here?" She gestured to their immediate surroundings, perhaps a bit more wildly than was technically necessary. "Why aren't you trotting back to the airport and back home again? I'm sure your family can't be thrilled with you up and taking off like that. It's the middle of dry season."

"It's always the middle of something," he said. "And if you want to know the truth, it was Big Jack who presented me with the plane ticket."

Her mouth dropped open. Cooper was a pragmatic man, had to be to keep a place as big and complex as Cameroo running smoothly and successfully. But Big Jack took pragmatic to a whole new level. Where Cooper was sensible but reasonable about how things should be done to minimize risk and maximize potential, it was well known that Big Jack went well beyond frugal. *Stingy* was a term she'd heard used more than once. Not that he didn't have a big heart; he did. He was all for providing opportunities and encouraging others to reach for more, but there was usually a price tag attached.

"I believe his exact words were, 'Go sort this out, and don't come back until you're certain you can keep your mind on what matters.' " He smiled at Kerry, then. That big, broad grin that crinkled the deeply tanned skin at the corners of his eyes, the one that made all that bright blue twinkle and added a shadow to that hint of a cleft in his chin.

"That sounds more like Big Jack," she said. He'd just been making it clear he wanted Cooper's head back in the game. She wondered if Big Jack was shocked when his oldest son had taken him up on the offer. *Probably,* she thought, a smile hovering again as she imagined the look on his broad, still handsome, craggy face.

"He also said, 'And, if what matters happens to be about yay high' " — Cooper lifted the palm of his hand level with the top of Kerry's head — " 'with firecracker hair and a temperament to match, well, you'd best be bringing her back along with you.' "

"He did not say that," Kerry declared, even as she knew damn well he probably had. She could hear him, see his own crinkled-at-the-corners, twinkle-eyed gaze.

Now it was Cooper's turn to shrug. "He'll be deeply disappointed when I come back

65

empty-handed." He lifted his palms. "But what's a bloke to do?"

She swatted his shoulder, only it might have been a little more like a punch. "Don't you dare try to emotionally blackmail me or make me feel bad about this. I didn't ask you to fly halfway around the globe and could have saved you the trouble if you'd given me so much as a hint what you were thinking. Besides, you don't want me — or anyone else — on the station who doesn't want to be there. Who doesn't feel the same as you."

His smile stayed, but the look in his eyes was nothing short of the fierce gaze of a man who pushed himself to the limits of his ability every single day and wasn't the least bit afraid of a challenge. "My mistake, then."

Kerry tried to hold his gaze but ended up ducking her chin. "You never so much as hinted —"

"Starfish —"

Her head shot up, but the automatic rejection of the nickname died on her lips at the look on his face, in his eyes. "Nothing ever happened." *Only because you didn't let it happen,* her little voice supplied. She tried desperately to ignore that part.

"As you said, you weren't staying. We all knew that."

She felt the catch in her heart but worked to ignore that, too. What difference did it make now who should have said or done what? They hadn't, and that was her point. "My family needs me," she told him. As close to an admission as she was willing to make. "Your family needs you. Two different continents. Two different lives."

"You stayed. Here, I mean." His tone made it clear he'd been surprised by that.

"There ended up being another wedding. Hannah got married at Christmas. And there's another one still. Fiona's. Dropping like flies around here," she added, trying for humor.

Failing, apparently, when he said, "Good news for them. Congratulations. But . . . was it just the weddings? You sound as if —"

"Fergus had a stroke. Right before Hannah's wedding." From all her stories, Cooper knew how close she was to her great-uncle.

"I'm so sorry. That was him, behind the bar there when I came in, right? I recognized him straight off from your stories."

She nodded. "He likes to think he's capable of running the place on his own again. He's doing well, better than predicted, but between his age and some of the permanent

67

limitations left from the stroke, he really isn't up to that. Not on his own."

"Sounds like a long-term gig for you, then. From what you've told me about him, I can't imagine he's happy with that arrangement. You staying on just for his sake, not getting back to your wanderlusting life."

She almost smiled at that. Almost. Cooper worked hard, worked his employees hard, but somehow always remained an easy man to be around, an easy man to like. *To lust after, too.* "He's family," she said, veering away from that thought. "That's what you do. My sisters are both staying in the Cove, too. Well, Hannah is up in Calais most of the time, but she's home. So is Fiona. She'll be living up in Snowflake Bay, but her new design business is in the Cove." She was rambling. Stalling.

"You're good with sticking in one place, then? With your family all here now?"

She searched his eyes but didn't see anything more in the question than what he'd asked. "I don't know," she said, more honest with him than she'd been with any member of her family who had asked. And they all had. Repeatedly. Fergus most especially. "I am for now. He needs me."

"That's not going to change, based on what you said. You taking over the place as your own, then?"

"I don't know that either. I can't believe he'd ever sell the place and retire, and I don't know that I fancy myself a pub owner anyway." She let a small smile curve her lips. "Any more than I saw myself working one of the larger cattle stations in the Northern Territory. Or any of the other things I've done since I went walkabout back when I turned eighteen."

"Could be that's changing. A year spent at Cameroo. Your longest. Now here, longer still."

"How did you know that? About my stint at Cameroo being my longest," she clarified when he looked confused by the question. She'd made sure they'd known she was hiring on for the remainder of the dry season, nothing more; then she'd stayed on when the wet season started that fall and on into the next dry season, late the next spring. But while that unplanned extension had allowed her the time to form solid friendships with pretty much every member of the Jax family, sharing many a family tale with them along the way, she'd never once mentioned that the duration of time she'd spent there was an anomaly of any kind.

"I thought I'd have to work a lot harder than I did, tracking down your whereabouts," he said in response.

Her eyes widened briefly. "Right. I hadn't thought about — how did you know I was here? I could have been anywhere, like looking for a needle in a global haystack."

"As I thought the task would be when I started tracking you down. The only base you had that I knew of was Blueberry Cove, so I started there, hoping I could get someone to tell me where you were. Turns out, that's as far as I had to look."

She cocked her head, doing a quick mental tabulation, trying to figure out who'd been so chatty with her former employer, then neglected to tell her about the inquiry. Only one person in the Cove even knew about Cooper, about the Jax family, about anything having to do with her time in Australia other than the fact that she'd been working in the Land Down Under before she'd come home again.

But surely, if Fergus had actually spoken to Cooper, he wouldn't have have kept mum on that little detail. *Who are you kidding?* The man thrived on meddling, especially where his beloved McCrae girls were concerned. That would also explain why he'd so conveniently disappeared once Cooper had taken the floor. And why he hadn't come back out carrying the shotgun they kept handy in the back. "Uncle Gus" was all she said.

He smiled briefly. "I thought that was a better bet than your chief-of-police brother. I've already guessed Fergus didn't tell you about our little conversation."

She shook her head. "How long ago?"

"A week. Not so long as all that."

Long enough, she thought, already mentally rehearsing the conversation she'd be having with her uncle the minute she got back to the pub.

"We only had the one chat."

"One was apparently all that was needed. What else did he share with you?" She immediately held up her hand. "On second thought, don't tell me. I'll have that little chat with him directly."

"He wants you to be happy," Cooper said.

"And he thought encouraging a man I haven't seen in over a year, a man who was my former employer and nothing more, to hop on a plane and bop on up this side of the equator to see me was what would make me happy?"

Cooper's smile deepened, and that twinkle sparked to life in his eyes again, making them so fiercely blue it caught at her breath. "He might have mentioned that you'd be less than welcoming of a surprise visit. He also said if I had a prayer of your still being here when I arrived, a surprise visit was pretty much my only shot. And how the frosty reception I was sure to receive was simply your automatic defense system, and how I should just ignore all that and 'press my suit' anyway, as I believed he called it."

Kerry closed her eyes, willed her short fuse to wink out before it had the chance to get dangerously lit up. *Yep, too late.* She turned abruptly and moved to go around Cooper, aiming herself back toward the lot where the truck was parked. Cooper's hand shot out and took hold of her arm, releasing it the moment she stopped and turned to look at him, her balance intact.

"His heart was in the right place, Starfish. He warned me. It was my choice to come here and risk it anyway. Don't go unloading all the frustration you're feeling about my unexpected arrival, not to mention the unfortunate public spectacle I made of this whole thing, on your poor uncle."

Cooper was right of course, which just fired her up more, but it was all too much to sustain really. The shock, the anger, the pure ache that seeing him again brought to her heart . . . the unrelenting lust that brought other things to other parts of her body. Dammit. Still, the anger winked out as fast as it had blown up, before she even opened her mouth.

She debated what to say to him, then decided she didn't owe him a thoughtfully prepared anything. She hadn't asked him to come here, to put her personal life on the gossip vine, number one with a bullet. Emphasis on bullet. "I need to get back to the Puffin. Sandy is great in the kitchen, but let's just say being a people person is not his strong suit. Fergus sounds like his old Irish rascal self, but he still wears out fast."

Cooper simply lifted his hand, gesturing back the way they'd come.

Kerry didn't stomp off, which would have been impossible anyway, given the terrain, but she wasn't mentally stomping off either. One thing this past year had taught her that the previous thirty had not was patience. Well, a modicum of it at any rate. Dealing with Gus's stroke, and even more so with his slow recovery, had forced her to become, well . . . still. Or more still than she'd ever been. Kerry moved. It wasn't only how she lived her life, it was how she lived all the moments inside of it as well. She didn't sit; she definitely didn't ponder. She took the leap, made the jump, dove in. Reflecting was for folks who could no longer get out and go, see, and, most importantly, do. She was a doer.

Being back in the Cove had definitely altered those standard operating procedures. Not all at once, but gradually, over time, so she'd had no choice but to conform. *Time,* she thought. Time was always the enemy. Giving any one part of her life too much time was the surefire way to ruin everything. Whenever she found herself settling in, settling down, the ennui would almost certainly come in close behind it. That itch, that urge to find a new place to explore, give herself a new chance to challenge herself, doing something completely different than she'd ever done before.

And if change coincided with preventing her from making any more than surface-level friendships along the way . . . well, that was fine, too. She had a long list of happy contacts she remembered fondly and felt fairly certain that feeling was reciprocated. Folks who could be called on for a place to sleep or a job so she could earn some extra cash, maybe even a little help out of the occasional jam she got herself into. Contacts. That's how she thought of them. Points along the journey, associated with people whose lives had intersected with hers for a short time. Not so much friends, really. And certainly not family of any kind.

She'd never seen any point in diving in too deeply. It would just set everyone up for sadness when she left, as she most assuredly would, and who wanted to be maudlin about things? Not her. Nor anyone else either, as far as she knew. She was doing herself and all of them a favor by keeping things light. At least that had been how she'd always looked at it, and believed it to be.

Until Australia. And Cooper. And Sadie Jax. Then all the rest of the Jaxes.

The Cove, however, wasn't another point on the journey. It was home. Filled with people who had known her since birth. Nothing here was like life out there, and the adjustments she'd had to make, to basically fit back into what others would call a "normal life" hadn't been so simple or achieved so smoothly as all that, though she'd done her best to make it seem that way.

She wasn't blind, though; she knew those who loved her most, knew her best — her family — were all essentially waiting with bated breath for her to up and leave at any random moment. She let a rueful smile curve her lips as she maneuvered over a tricky rock and kelp tumble. Knowing her family, there were money bets in place, odds being given.

She felt Cooper just behind her as she scrambled up the rocks at the end of the wash and on to the gravel lot just above. She climbed in behind the wheel of her truck and he was in his seat and buckled in before she got the motor running. She put the truck in reverse, then put it right back in park and looked over at him. "I'm sorry you came all this way," she said quietly, sincerely. "I am. Sorrier to be disappointing you." She paused a moment, then added, "It is good to see you again." Also true. He was from a part of her life that, if she allowed reflection, she'd be forced to admit she cherished. "That said, I know I'm still not in the position to be asking favors, but if you'd tell your family hello from me, especially Sadie —"

"It's all over your face, Starfish. You know that, don't you?"

She blinked. "What is?"

He sighed, and she caught the edge underlining the exhalation. "Let me ask you this, and be honest. At this point, there's no reason not to be, right?"

She nodded warily. "Sure. I mean, yes, I'll be honest."

"For about the last month or so, before

you left, I'd been trying to find a way, the right way, to let you know my interest in you was more than business, more than the friendship we'd developed. I was fairly certain I wasn't alone in feeling that way, but as your employer, or part of the family who employed you, I didn't want to risk ruining what we did have. I knew you were on borrowed time and had convinced myself that once you'd seen both seasons, maybe that would be enough for you. But then you stayed into the next dry season, and . . . well, in my heart, I . . . I'd begun to think that maybe you'd admit to what we could all see. That you were born for the place."

"Cooper —"

"Let me finish. I've waited too long, and if I'm to go home without what I came looking for, I'd at least like the chance to say all the things I should have when I could have."

"I thought you did that back at the Rusty Puffin," she said, forcing a hint of dry amusement into her tone. It was that or clutch at her chest to keep her heart from going crazy again. She'd found the courage to turn him down once. She wasn't sure she could do it again, especially if she let him spill his beautiful heart all over her.

His determination didn't waver. "I see now that your situation here has changed, you have obligations to family. I respect that, as I do your refusal of my awkwardly staged proposal back at the bar. But I'm — please indulge me in answering one more question." He didn't wait for her to accept or refuse the request. "Had I found that way, found the right words, before you'd gotten your invite back to the States for your brother's wedding, had you known what I thought of you, of . . . of us, or the possibility of there being an us, would you have been interested in exploring what we had? Am I completely wrong about that?"

Kerry knew what she should say. She should tell him the thought never crossed her mind and now it was a moot point and, again, how sorry she was he'd come all this way. But what she saw on his face, in his eyes, wasn't so much a request for her response so much as a man left questioning his own instincts, his own intuition. And while she didn't want to give him — a man so naturally driven to achieve whatever challenge or goal he set for himself — so much as a hint of hope, they had been friends, the real kind, the good kind. And she owed her friend, Cooper Jax, the honest truth, as she'd hope he would do for her were the situation reversed.

She held his gaze, which was almost as

hard as telling him something she'd never thought she'd have to say. "I would have," she said carefully, then hurried on when the resulting flare in his eyes, the way she saw his throat work, did what everything else about him did to her. "Considered it," she added, emphasis on the *considered.* "But even without what's going on here with my family, it would have been a lot more complicated than simple attraction. We both knew that, and I think that's why we remained the good friends we'd become." She looked at that handsome face and shoved all those maybes and might haves away for the last time. "And nothing more. It was the right thing to do."

She settled back in her seat and finally broke their gaze, staring straight ahead, unseeing anything except the myriad of memories of her time on Cameroo, her time with him, with his family. The long days that didn't end at sundown, working her body until she swore it wouldn't be able to give any more, and still wanting him with an ache that no amount of rest would ease when she finally crawled into her bunk. The joys, the sweat, the frustration, the triumphs. The laughter, even the occasional tears.

"If that wasn't true," she finally said quietly, not wanting to admit she was aching for more than just him in that moment, "you'd have just up and done something about it the moment you wanted to, and not spent so much time trying to figure out how."

She pulled out then, forced her thoughts back to the here and now, back to the Rusty Puffin, to Fergus, who needed her, to her family, all home again and happy about it. So what if her siblings had found a way to meld their lives and their loves into one big melting pot of happiness, while she couldn't even figure out what she wanted to be now that she'd finally been forced to grow up. She was where she was supposed to be. That much she knew.

Cooper said nothing on the drive back, and she couldn't feel his gaze on her so he must have turned it forward as well. She hoped he was turning his thoughts forward, too. Back to Cameroo Downs and his home, his family.

She pulled in behind the pub and put the truck into park, paused for a moment, then quickly shut the engine off, yanked out the key, and slid out of the cab without looking over at him again. She had her memories of him, of them. Now she had a few more. That was all there was to it.

She heard the passenger door close and

made herself turn around when what she wanted to do was run inside, slam the door behind her, and begin the long, sure to be agonizing process of putting him behind her all over again. "Like I said," she began, only to have the *"it was good seeing you again"* stall behind her lips. Lips that were now only a hair's breadth away from his.

He'd been right behind her, head bowed, and had taken her by the arms when she turned, her face uptilted so their noses were almost touching, mouths almost brushing, before catching themselves at the last possible second.

He took his hat off and put it on top of the truck cab, his eyes never leaving hers. "Can I satisfy my curiosity about one last thing?" he asked, his voice gruff in a way she'd never heard it before. Then she noticed his attention, his focus, was on her mouth now.

Heat flared through her so fast she couldn't control it. Like a wildfire fueled by a raging wind, it consumed her, ravaging any hope she had of containing it. "What would that be?" she said on a choked whisper, though she had absolutely no doubt she knew the answer. She blamed a year of not having to manage her defenses around him for not being able to rally them now. Truth was, though, she wasn't sure she would have, even if she could.

"This." He closed the whisper of a distance between his mouth and hers, only he didn't go for the alpha-male, take-all, conquering kiss. That might have swept her off her feet, quite literally, for at least the time it took for it to begin and end. No, what he did decimated any chance she had of being simply swept away, able to write off the moment later as nothing more than a mindless, primal response.

No, what he did was make love to her mouth. She hadn't even known it was possible to do such a thing. His kiss wasn't demanding, it wasn't desperate, or, worse, a sad good-bye. It was a slow, deliberate, and confident wooing. That last part being the most heady, and the most dangerous. It was a kiss that didn't ask for her complete and utter participation; it simply, by its most intimate nature, demanded it.

He didn't lay claim. He made love to her mouth with his, like he'd known this, all along, and just hadn't had the chance to show her yet.

He drew her in, sharing with her the experience of utter communion that was the two of them, together. He kissed her slowly, intently, and so utterly sensuously, that she was kissing him back, fully partnering him in this communion of so much more than mere lips, tongues, and breaths, without it even being a conscious decision on her part. His tongue slid in along hers as if it had found its mate and was simply happy to be home, curled up again, sated and content. But that beautiful sweetness was all mixed up with the pulse of something darkly sensual, making her crave the discovery of what every part of him communing in this way with every part of her would be like. So deeply satisfying and urgently primal.

She was in trouble here. Real trouble. Because somewhere along the way she'd forgotten he wasn't a man who called anything quits, and he surely hadn't come all this way to turn around and head home without making damn sure she knew exactly what she was turning away from.

CHAPTER FIVE

While he would likely regret many parts of this ill-forsaken journey for the rest of his days, he'd never, not ever, regret this one kiss.

She sank into him as if she'd finally found that part of him that was meant to fit her, and only her. He'd known she'd be that for him, his perfect fit, instinctively known it, but nothing could have prepared him for the wallop that was the God's honest truth and reality of it.

He could have kissed her forever, until he drew his last breath. They didn't fumble, didn't grope. Her arms had found their way over his shoulders, and she'd wound them around his neck. His had slid around the small of her back, pulling her in and up so their mouths could mesh even more fully, that much more deeply. That's as far as the rest of their bodies got in this moment, which remained purely a union of mouths, lips, tongues. Of deep breaths and racing heartbeats. *Of souls parted,* his mind whispered, *and finally reunited.*

He had no idea how much time had passed when she slowly loosened her hold, let her mouth trail softly from his, as they caught their breath. Her cheek slid to his chest, her head tucked just under his chin, as they stood, hearts still racing, wrapped up in each other in ways that went much farther than tightly clamped arms and damp lips.

She said nothing, but she didn't make a move to extricate herself. He would have stood there until their legs gave out and the earth stopped spinning, but he wasn't sure how much longer he could expect them to have privacy, even in this small back lot, just up from the shore, in this small coastal town. And he wanted one more moment of privacy before the world intruded again.

He pressed a kiss to her hair, smiling at the smell of some spicy scented shampoo, rather than the lingering beer and pool hall he'd expected. She was so much more than he'd expected. Always had been. *Some things never changed. Thank God.*

He nudged until she looked up at him. He felt her begin to draw herself inward, arming herself, as she did whenever he, or anyone, got too close. He didn't try to stop her; it was ingrained in her, for reasons he'd yet to determine, but whatever the cause, he knew it would take time and patience and who knew what else to penetrate. All he wanted was a chance to do just that.

When her gaze finally met his, he wasn't sure what to expect and got another little wallop, right in the chest, when he saw that even though her natural defenses had slowly straightened her shoulders, the detachment hadn't made its way to those lovely green eyes of hers. Those were still dark and vulnerable and more open than he'd ever seen them. So much so, for a moment, he almost faltered in saying what he wanted to say, because he felt he would be taking advantage, when what he should be doing was protecting what was his. Or what he wanted to be his, proving his worthiness of being hers as well.

But it was the only moment he would have. Ever.

"I've arranged to be here a month," he told her, his throat as parched as the banks of the Wollamaroo River in dry season, the words even rougher. "My grand entrance notwithstanding, I didn't expect to come and sweep you off. I just wanted time to find out what's what."

"A month," she repeated, and that open gaze shuttered.

He silently cursed, but it wasn't entirely a surprise.

"But how can you be gone so long?" she asked, still looking a bit stunned. "It's —"

"Important," he finished for her. "Possibly the most important thing I've ever done. Whatever way it goes, I need to know."

"But the station —"

"Has been around far longer than I've been alive and will survive a few weeks of my absence. Besides," he said, convinced that kiss had closed a distance between them that had nothing to do with the number of miles she'd put between her mouth and his, "I've stayed back the past several holiday jaunts Dad took with Ian and Sadie, so I've earned a bit of a walk-about of my own."

"But in the end, won't it be that much harder for you to —"

"Anything is possible," he said, thankful he'd seen that unguarded look in her eyes, before she'd pulled back again. It was a look he'd never forget, and one he might need to call upon from time to time, to see him through the upcoming weeks.

"Cooper —"

"Ultimately, our lives are our own to lead.

We love our families, each of us, and they love us back. Obligations aside, not a single member of my family, and not one of yours either, from what you've told me of them, would want either of us to sacrifice our lives, our happiness, in service of theirs. In fact, at least with mine, that would be the worst thing I could do to them. Else I wouldn't be here. And they wouldn't have seen me off with smiles and good wishes."

She smiled briefly, and he saw the sincere and honest affection in her eyes every time he mentioned his father and siblings. Why hadn't she stayed in contact? At least with Sadie? Despite her best efforts to keep her heart fully her own, and her acquaintances — even the ones with whom she'd become quite fond — at a bit of a distance, he knew her to be warm, generous, and kind, with a heart — guarded or not — as big as the summer moon. He'd seen it in the way she worked with the animals, with her work mates on the station, with his own family. Or he wouldn't be standing where he was at that moment.

The Kerry he knew wasn't cold of heart. Couldn't be if she tried. So why hadn't she looked back? Even if just to say hello and how are you doing?

"I have pretty much been selfishly servicing my own desires and needs for my entire adult life," she told him. "And my family's supported me all the way. Now they need me, and I think it's their turn. You know?"

"I do know, yes," he said, taking a moment for her words to truly sink in. When put that way, he could understand how she saw it. And she had a point. A good one. Yet that didn't answer his other questions. "So, then, when I go back home to Cameroo and leave you to do what must be done . . . when it's your turn again to do as you please, would you come down, give me — us — the time to find out what we could be to each other? Would you be willing?"

He'd obviously surprised her with that request. It took her a moment to regroup. "You'd leave now, just go back and wait for me to come?"

"No, I'll take my time here with you. It will be more time for us to learn, the way I see it. Life goes on," he said. "Nothing is ever on hold. So we'll see what we see, and if there's more to see when my time here is up, I'd want and hope you'd come back to Cameroo when you were able, and we'll keep on seeing what we see. And during all that, we'll get along with the living of life as it comes, both of us. Who knows what that might lead to, and if whatever happens

89

might change the choices we may want to make now. But in this moment, I'm asking, would you come?"

"I — don't know." There was the slightest hint of a tremble in the words. And that wall she'd so hastily put back up wavered just a tic.

He traced a finger along the side of her cheek, then over her bottom lip, and felt her body shudder against his. "Would you come back to Cameroo and give this a chance?"

He held her gaze for the longest time and thought he'd never tire of the scenery.

"I'd consider it," she finally said, searching his gaze as well. She sighed, then melted against him when he dipped his head, kissed her quietly. "Yes," she whispered against his lips before he lifted them away. "I would."

"Good," he said, lips spreading, grin deepening.

A car rumbled down the alley, startling them both, and their intimate bubble burst as the outside world intruded once again.

Kerry pulled back and then moved fully out of his arms. She made no show of smoothing her shirt or tidying her hair, which made his grin deepen. She might be tangled up when it came to family and future and her real needs and wants, but she was, at core, still the same guileless woman he'd fallen in love with a world away from here. He snagged his hat off the roof of her cab and walked toward his rental.

"So you're staying then," she said to his back, not making it a question. "You don't think — maybe it would be better if you went back, until I had time to — we could stay in touch somehow, still be in contact — because I don't know if it's a good idea for you to —"

"It's not good-bye," he said, turning back as he reached the car, liking that he'd unsettled her enough to make her stammer. "Not just yet."

"But —"

"I respect that you've got demands on your life. I do. I don't expect you to drop everything to spend every moment with me. But I'd like to have what moments you can spare." When she might have argued further, he said, "It's my turn. The only one I'm likely to get. I've got a month, Starfish."

Her eyebrows narrowed a bit at his use of her nickname, and he relaxed further as they eased into a far more familiar back and forth. Lord, but he'd missed her.

"Like I said, let's take the time we have now and find out what we find out. Then, when it's your turn, we'll already be that much closer to knowing what we know."

91

Her eyes remained narrowed, his feisty Kerry fully back at the fore. "Why is it that I feel like I just got played?"

His grin got bigger. "Oh, we haven't begun to play, love. There was nothing playful about that kiss. But next time?" He let that statement linger with no immediate follow-up. Instead, he dug the keys to his rental from the pocket of his Daks and unlocked the door to the sleek black roadster. At least he'd walked to the correct side this time. Took some getting used to, the whole wrong side of the road thing. Still, the little two-door BMW was a beauty. And about as far away from anything he'd ever driven on the station as it was possible to get. Which was exactly why he'd rented it.

He looked back over to where she stood, arms folded now, defenses fully back up and battle ready. *Good,* he thought. *Do what you need to do. Be sure of yourself, of me. Of us. Just remember, I know how to get you to lower those defenses.* And he was looking forward to finding out how she'd come apart for him when he melted them completely.

"Thirty days," he said, opening the door. He tugged at the sunglasses that had been hanging down his back on a pair of Croakies and slid them around, putting them on before popping his hat back on his head.

He rested folded forearms on the top of the open door, his grin still in place. "And I don't know about you, but I'm really liking how Day One has worked out." He tucked his long, rangy frame into the low-slung car and lowered the window as the sport engine purred to life. "Can't wait to see what Day Two holds in store. G'day, Starfish."

CHAPTER SIX

Kerry groped her nightstand and smacked at the clock until she silenced the buzzing alarm, then rolled to her back and stared at the gabled ceiling of her loft bedroom, perched up in the eaves above the second story of the pub where Fergus had his little man cave of an apartment.

After returning from her impromptu outing with Cooper, she'd defied Fergus's take-the-night-off orders and spent the next three hours on her feet, and a few more after that on her hands and knees. The former had been spent pulling, pouring, and hustling drinks out to the tables, all while working twice as hard ducking comments, whistles, and inquiries about her possible engagement that she doubted would end anytime soon. But that was precisely why she'd gone directly back into the fray. Tackling it head on and letting them all get it out of their system was the best way to squash the whole debacle sooner rather than later.

That, and the knowledge that being run ragged by the Friday night crowd — which included a healthy influx of tourists who'd discovered the Cove now that they had Brodie's historic schooner replica running summertime cruises out in Pelican Bay — was possibly the only thing that would take her mind off what had happened in the parking lot behind this very pub.

When that hadn't worked, she'd stayed on after closing and nearly scrubbed the shellac off the teak bar and the polish from the wide, age-old cypress plank floors with her own two hands in an effort to blank her mind to the events of the day. *Fat chance of that.* It had been close to three in the morning by the time Kerry had headed up the back stairs of the pub, and even as exhausted as she was, she'd still found it impossible to wipe that image of Cooper from her mind. The sun setting over his back, highlighting the breadth of his shoulders, sending shadows under those cheekbones, made more chiseled by the ridiculously gorgeous, shit-eating grin that had been on his face when he made it clear he was in town to stay.

"For another twenty-nine days anyway." Kerry pulled her pillow over her face and groaned. Part of her was still in utter shock that he was actually there, in her town. Hell, in her orbit at all. Other parts of her — most of them hormonally activated — were still all aquiver from that kiss. She groaned again and ground clenched fists into the mattress on either side of her hips. *Damn, but that kiss . . .*

How many times had she lain in bed, just like this, only in a bunkhouse at Cameroo Downs, and wondered what it would be like to be kissed by Cooper Jax? Okay, okay, a whole lot more than kissed. But *damn . . .* that kiss alone had been worlds better than the best sex she'd ever had. So much so, he'd probably ruined her for having sex with mere mortals.

So I guess you'll just have to have sex with him, then.

"Not helpful," she grunted at her little voice, jerking the pillow off her face and thumping it on the bed beside her. Besides, even if she was willing to have some kind of fling with Cooper, fulfill even a sliver of the many, oh, so very many fantasies she'd had about the man, he'd made it clear from pretty much the moment he'd set foot back into her world that he wasn't looking for a fling. He'd strolled right in and made it clear he was looking for a — no.

She squeezed her eyes shut and tightened her lips, willing her mind to go blank.

It didn't work. She couldn't shut it out. Cooper Jax had, basically, proposed to her. Then he'd walked all up and down a kelp-covered, low-tide seashore and listened to her enumerate the reasons why they couldn't even contemplate such a union. Right before kissing her in a way that defied science and made her wonder if she might need a pregnancy test, before pretty much declaring he was going to spend the next four weeks making it as impossible for her to say no to his doing that again, and maybe more, as he could.

Which, when she looked at it that way, well . . . it would almost excuse her for having a fling. Wouldn't it? He was going after what he wanted, so why shouldn't she? He'd learn that no really meant no, and she'd get her uncharacteristic and now even greater hunger for him out of her system, then send him packing back to Australia. If he pushed and they got naked, well . . . if he was ultimately disappointed in the outcome, then that was on him. She'd warned him after all.

She swore under her breath and kicked the sheets and quilt off her bare legs. "Yeah. That's who you want to be. That girl." She might have been wandering the globe for pretty much her entire adult life, but while she'd been decidedly footloose, she wasn't in any other way loose. She'd had sex, yes. On several continents even. But her partners had been far fewer and far more carefully chosen than most would assume, given her bohemian approach to living.

Not that there hadn't been times when she hadn't wished it were otherwise. She liked to blame her conservative, New England upbringing, but the truth was, for all she wasn't a put-down-roots kind of person, she had always been a one-woman-one-man kind of gal. She didn't want to be dallying with more than one person at a time and didn't want her partner dallying either. But it was sort of hard to demand exclusivity from a person you were likely never to see again after, at best, a few months' time. The most she could hope for was temporary exclusivity. Which wasn't so easy to come by.

Hence the "few" part, and the "far between." But, even for her, it had been really, *really* far between lately.

She thought about Hardy and his pursuit. There had been a few others as well, since her return, though none of them had been locals. She couldn't lie and say she hadn't thought about saying yes — not to Hardy — but there had been a pro fisherman here and a thru-hiker there who had made her look twice. Unfortunately, while her body had been interested, the rest of her . . . not so much.

And yet every part of her, every last microbial speck, had had no problem whatsoever waving the giant green flag for Cooper. And that had been before *the kiss.*

She glanced at her clock and groaned. She didn't hear any signs of Fergus being up and about yet, which meant she'd better get up and get about herself. The apartment was small, even with the loft space, and consisted of a bedroom, a bath, and an open living room and kitchen arrangement below, and her loft space and shower above. She and her siblings had long since given up trying to get Fergus to move into a small cottage with a bit more room and a place to grow the garden he was always going on about. After his stroke those arguments had briefly resurfaced, with Logan even discussing moving him to their family's ancestral home out on Pelican Point, where he lived with his wife of nearly one year, Alex. But Fergus had proven that a little stroke wasn't going to whittle his ability to stand his ground when it came to his living quarters.

99

Every time he went down the steep, narrow, indoor set of stairs that led to the kitchen, Kerry held her breath. She'd forbidden him to use the outside set of back stairs completely, and on that argument she'd won. Privately, she felt she'd just allowed him to save face; he'd known he couldn't really risk using his cane on the open board planking that comprised the outdoor steps. At least indoors, the stairs had a hand railing.

Kerry had taken over the loft bedroom long before the stroke, though. It had been her room as a teenager, before she'd left the Cove, so it had seemed the most natural place to return to when she'd come back for the wedding. It was as much home to her as their big old house out on the Point. She'd initially come to stay with Fergus at the age of fourteen so her grandfather could have her old room on the main floor of the Point house when it became too hard for him to get up and down the stairs to the master suite.

When she'd opted to stay on in the Cove after Hannah got engaged, she'd briefly thought about looking for a short-term lease somewhere in town, but in all her travels, she'd never once leased a whole house of any size, usually making do with a room rental or whatever doubled as one, depending on what country she was in at the time. She'd never stayed in one place long enough to need bigger digs than that, and Fergus had made it clear she was welcome to stay, so . . . she'd never really looked all that hard. Then the stroke had happened and, well . . . here she still was.

She looked around the small room, tucked under the gabled eaves over the front of the pub. All her worldly possessions fit just fine in the tiny loft bedroom. *Just as they had in that bunkhouse in Cameroo.* She'd slept in that bunk every night that she wasn't out at one of the station campsites, but the truth was, before she left, she'd been spending more and more of her downtime with the family at the homestead, which was both the central building and offices for the entire station as well as their family home.

Initially, she'd come by to help Sadie with her schoolwork. There was no school on the station, so the station kids went to School of the Air, which had been around since the days of radio signals but was largely done via computers now. Then, more often than not, she'd get invited to stay on for dinner, followed by a rousing game of checkers with Big Jack, before heading outside with a mug of hot tea or hot chocolate, depending on how successful their cook, Marta, had been in convincing Big Jack he could stand something a little sweet to go with his tart tongue.

They'd sit around the stone fire pit as the moon rose and the temperatures fell, telling tales, sharing a few laughs. Cooper usually kept to himself, having already given his report on the station goings-on to his father in the office before the workday had ended, thereby letting Ian have the floor, to fill them in on everything happening on the business side of the station and, invariably, his ideas on how to improve this bit or that, each idea being met with varying degrees of open-mindedness by his father. Big Jack was set in his ways, but Kerry had admired him for at least trying to look forward, despite how uncomfortable he was with the prospect, knowing it was vital to the continued success of the station. Much as he likely had pushed his own father, or so Cooper was wont to point out, on the few occasions he'd joined the fray.

Big Jack, who'd married twice, made a widower by his first wife and divorced by his second, was close to Fergus in age, but while his mind was sharp as ever, his body had begun showing the effects of a life hard lived. At thirty-two, Cooper had long since taken on the day-to-day running of the station, but now the twenty-six-year-old Ian, who'd gone off to university in Melbourne and come back as the only Jax with a master's degree, was slowly taking on the business side. Everyone seemed happy about that arrangement. Kerry had privately wondered if they saw the spark in Sadie's eyes when she'd demand another story about Kerry's life of adventure, and how they'd take it when she up and left the station herself someday, as Kerry was fairly certain she would. Like recognized like after all.

So many memories of Cameroo, she thought, feeling awash in them, and all the emotions they roused in her. It was a lot to take in, a lot to feel, to process, after so deliberately closing herself off from them for so long.

She looked around her small loft room once more, with different eyes this time. So many memories here, too. And she realized then that the memories felt much the same. Some happy, some not, but all grounded in the same undeniable sense of family.

She didn't try to shut any of them out now, but let them all come in and swim together inside her mind. And her heart. The walls, the furniture, all of it was exactly the same as she'd left it at the age of eighteen. It had been her childhood bedroom, really. Not that anyone would guess by looking at it. Even as a child, she hadn't been a nester. Whatever she needed, she'd just crammed into her pockets and taken with her. She'd liked it that way then, and the habit had continued. Compact, secure, always ready for the next adventure.

So why aren't you out there, adventuring? Or, barring that, Miss Happy Memories, why aren't you leaping on Cooper's invitation to go back to the land of good times and even better hot chocolate? Better yet, why aren't you leaping on Cooper?

The buzz of her cell phone mercifully saved her from further self-examination. It was one thing to allow a ramble through her memories and wallow a bit in the realization of how happy she'd been while making them. Quite another to analyze what those feelings meant, much less what she should do about them. She grabbed her phone like a drowning person would a lifeline and punched the Accept button without even looking at the screen to see who the caller was. "Yes?"

"Well, good morning to you, too, sunshine," her middle sister, Fiona, chirped.

Kerry rolled to her back, rolling her eyes

at the same time. "You were insufferably perky before you were engaged. Now you're simply intolerable."

"I do it to balance the cosmic scales against your unrelenting grouchiness. Consider it a karmic service. You can thank me later. Right now your presence is requested down at the Harbor, at Delia's new place."

Kerry groaned, and not silently. She supposed she should have been prepared for this, but she'd barely had time to process her new reality herself. Last night had been spent fending off a town full of way-too-nosy-for-their-own-good gossips and rumormongers, then scrubbing up the remains of their sloshed beers and crushed pretzels.

Of course those were the same gossips and rumormongers who kept the Rusty Puffin and every other business in the Cove alive with their patronage, and who she'd pretty much known since birth, but still . . . "I hate to disappoint, but I don't have time to be interrogated about my personal life. I have orders to enter, food to prep, and —"

"I'm sorry," Fiona said sweetly. "Did I say *requested*? I meant commanded. As in command performance. We have a table in the back."

Kerry's eyes narrowed. "We?"

"Hannah, Alex, and Delia are here, too.

The wedding powwow?"

Kerry groaned again. With everything else, she'd completely forgotten about the bridal breakfast Fiona had set up for this morning. Or the bridezilla brunch, as she'd privately named it. "Start without me. I'll be late."

"Don't pretty up on our account. We don't have that kind of time."

"Har-har," Kerry groused, swinging her legs over the side of the bed. She caught sight of herself in the old vanity mirror she'd propped up on top of her grandfather's steamer trunk in the corner and shuddered. *You give new meaning to bed head. And bed face. And . . . yeah.* "I'm taking thirty to shower and give myself a full body lift. You'll thank me later," she parroted back to her sister.

"Says the sister who was born looking like an Olympian. Wah-wah."

Kerry stood and stretched, stifling a groan as every muscle in her body protested. So much for the restorative powers of sleep. She grabbed her last fresh pair of khaki shorts, decided which of her already worn T-shirts was the least questionable, made a mental note to take her laundry basket with her when she left, then sighed as she caught sight of her restless night, wild-child hair once again in the mirror. *If only Cooper could see your oh-so-sexy self now,* she thought, *he'd book the next flight out.*

"Kerry?"

"Well," she said, making a face at herself in the mirror, "if there was an Olympic event for bed head, I'd take the gold right now, no question. Even the Russian judge would have to cave and give me a ten."

"I'd say give me a break, but come to think of it, I have seen you in the morning."

"Bite me."

"Oh, and because you brought it up," Fiona added, her voice dripping with sugar once again, "make sure you book some extra time to tell us every last detail about your dead-sexy Aussie fiancé."

"He's not my —"

"Hurry!" Fiona interrupted as group laughter echoed through the phone from somewhere behind her; then she hung up.

Kerry looked at the dead phone, then tossed it on the bed, mumbling swear words in several languages under her breath.

Thirty-five minutes later — the extra five was her just being her typical rebellious self — she was finally heading down the back stairs. Her body was freshly scrubbed and her hair washed and conditioned, her old faded green shamrock T-shirt not so much, but beggars couldn't be choosers. They wanted her on demand, they got what they got. A fresh mug of Delia's coffee along with a plate of her awesome biscuits and sausage gravy and Kerry was pretty sure she'd feel mostly human again.

She propped the laundry basket on her hip and was negotiating the narrow space between her truck and the old, metallic blue Chrysler behemoth Fergus was no longer allowed to drive, when the one person she'd been studiously avoiding thinking about since climbing under the blistering hot spray of her shower banged over the curb and into the back lot, neatly blocking off her exit by parking behind both her pickup truck and Fergus's boat of a car.

She shielded her eyes from the sun, her truck keys dangling down the back of her free hand, as Cooper lowered the passenger window and leaned forward so he could see her. "G'day, Starfish. Need a lift?"

She needed a lot of things. Hot coffee, sisters who weren't nosy, a clear vision about what should be next on her life agenda. Being inside a small, sporty vehicle, trapped mere inches from Cooper Jax, even for the short ride down to Half Moon Harbor? That she definitely did not need. "I'm good, thanks. And can we retire the nickname? Please?"

He'd begun calling her that after she'd regaled him with a steady string of childhood stories of life lived by the sea, and he'd commented that she seemed too big a fish for such a small pond. A starfish, as it were. She'd rolled her eyes at the very bad pun, but the nickname had stuck. Aussies were big on nicknames. And the honest truth of it was, she hadn't minded hearing him call her that, even though it had been a joke, delivered as a ribbing, not an endearment.

Now? Now she wasn't sure how he meant it, or what it made her feel when he said it. *Better to just bury it right, Ker? Like you do everything that makes you uncomfortable.* She really needed to find a way to strangle her little voice. "I've got a meeting," she went on, not giving him a chance to respond.

He nodded to the basket in her arms. "Yes, I can see that. Demanding lot, laundry."

She glanced down, then back at him. "No, with my sisters. About Fiona's wedding."

"Yes, I heard about it."

She didn't ask how he could possibly know that, or who he'd been talking to this time, because any person in town could have brought him up to speed on the goings-on about pretty much any person he wanted to know about. The downside to being home. One of the great things about being a wanderer was that folks only knew whatever parts of her story she opted to share with them. Cooper, she realized now, had already known more than pretty much anyone she'd met in her travels up to that point. God only knows what he'd learned in the twenty-four hours he'd been in the Cove. She didn't want to examine how that made her feel either.

"Three McCrae weddings in less than a year," he commented, as if casually discussing the weather. Then he grinned. "Is it catching?"

He could be so damn cute. And sexy as hell. His charisma and charm had been hard enough to resist before. Now that he'd unleashed it in full force, with every bit of his desire for her out there in the open for the world to see — and for her to feel — it was like being caught up in a kind of constant foreplay. It was one thing when she could just observe him in all his alpha-male glory, her thoughts about his sexy self and her desire to get all naked and personal with him safely hidden away inside her head for her own private enjoyment.

But now he'd kissed her. And she'd kissed

him back. And it had been so incredibly intimate, so ridiculously hot, so every other thing that usually requires full frontal nudity to experience, that she couldn't even look at him without getting squirmy and tingly and far too turned on for her own — "I hate to disappoint you," she blurted out, needing to get out of there, away from him. "But I really need to —" She lowered her hand and motioned to her truck and its trajectory as she backed out, right into where he was parked.

"Lunch, then? Fergus said you're off this shift."

"Oh, he did, did he?" No wonder she hadn't heard him rummaging about in the apartment. He must have woken early and gone downstairs to his office. To hide. *Old meddler.* She'd have a little chat with him after the bridezilla brunch.

"He also said he's taken care of the orders, so no need to hurry back."

Kerry dipped her chin for a brief moment, then busied herself with wrangling the driver door open and all but shoving her basket in and across the bench seat of the ancient rig. She closed the door halfway, her sandaled foot still propped on the running board, and looked back at Cooper. "You've made yourself quite at home, I see."

111

"You've a nice one here, Kerry," he said quite sincerely, his smile still sparkling with equal sincerity. "Good people, nice little town. I find I'm liking it a great deal. Your ocean is everything you described and more. I'd like to see more of it, through your eyes. When you have the time."

She debated the wisdom of trying to put him off as long as possible, but hell, he'd talked to half the town already and even had Fergus playing wingman for him. "Apparently I have time today," she said dryly. "I don't know how long this meeting will go, and I have errands to run. I still have to buy tonight's special — unless you're about to tell me that's already been handled, too."

"Not that I'm aware of," he replied easily. "But then, I just got into town late yesterday, so I'm not fully up to speed yet."

Oh, he was speedy all right. "It scares me to think what you'll know after a full twenty-four hours. If you want to go with me to Blue's to look at the early morning catch, I can meet you down in Half Moon around two."

He grinned. "We have a date, then."

"We have a meeting. Blue's is —"

"I'll find it."

"I'm sure you will." She went to climb in the cab of her truck, then paused. "I don't

112

guess it will do me any good to ask you to stop talking to people about me, will it?"

"I don't guess it would, no."

His accent, the way it wrapped around the os, making them sound like two delicious syllables in one, shouldn't affect her like it always had. Like it still did. To be fair, given her protracted stay Down Under, she'd grown accustomed to the accent in general. It was the deep, smooth timbre of his voice, speaking in that vowel-curling way of his, that rolled right through her like ocean waves relentlessly lapping at the shore. Lapping at her.

"Well, be warned," she told him, trying to ignore the delicious little shiver that was snaking its way down her spine, and all she was doing was looking at him. "Folks here can tell you everything you ever wanted to know about me, my family, and the entire history of Blueberry Cove, but just know that they'll also be telling everyone in the Cove every last detail they learn about you, too."

"Not much different from life in the Downs, then."

No, she supposed, in that way, it wasn't. In truth, his family's cattle station was far bigger in square miles than the Cove. And though its population was comprised of far

113

more cattle than people, the folks who lived and worked there had long since formed their own village of sorts, complete with a small company general store, a tiny restaurant bar, a gas station, and a post office. A lot like life in the Cove. Only with a sea of grazing land stretching out as far as the eye could see rather than the ocean. Funny she'd never thought about or noticed the similarities before. Maybe that's what had drawn her to the Downs, made it feel so familiar.

"Two o'clock then," he said, shifting back into his seat and putting the sports car in gear. He ducked his head so he could look through the window at her. "See you then, Kerry."

She lifted a hand in a short wave, smiled briefly, and watched him drive off. Now that there were no witnesses, she closed her eyes and let herself enjoy the last tingling tendrils of that delicious little shiver. Then she hoisted herself into the cab of her truck, revved the engine . . . and tried really, really hard not to mind that he hadn't called her Starfish.

CHAPTER SEVEN

Cooper climbed out of the shower, wrapped a thick, white-and-navy-blue–striped towel around his hips, then grabbed another one just like it to rub the wet from his thick hair. He shook his head when he was done, shaking the curls loose again, sending a water spray onto the mirror. "Like a wet dog you are, mate." He'd taken to wearing his hair a bit shorter, then groused about having to get it cut all the damn time. Still, he should have made the time before leaving. Despite his many daydreams about reuniting with Kerry — and more than a few night dreams as well — he hadn't actually put a lot of planning into the trip.

His father and siblings had gone from nudging to practically begging him to go after her, but the longer the time spun out without a word from her, not even to Sadie, the more the rational side of his brain told him he really was dreaming if he thought he'd ever see her again. He'd missed his chance. He'd said as much to his dad about the hundredth time Big Jack had told his oldest son he'd made the biggest mistake of his life. His father's reply to Cooper's insistence that he'd missed his chance with her? "Son, those who wait on chance never recognize it, even when it's staring them right in the face. Success comes to those who make their chances, then take them."

It was nothing his father hadn't expressed in a myriad different ways already. But something about that particular day, and those particular words, had stuck in Cooper's mind, niggling at him, digging at him. The truth was, his father was right. He supposed he could make another chance. He could track her down, tell her what was on his mind. Or, better yet, go find her. It wasn't the sort of thing a man did over the mobile or a computer screen.

Of course that was also when he'd had to admit to himself the real reason he hadn't jumped the first flight out after she'd taken off. As long as it was a chance not taken, it was also a failure not risked. He could continue what-ifing forever, enabling himself to keep that slender thread of hope alive. "Which would have gotten you where, mate?" he asked himself in the mirror as he finished shaving. "Old and alone, that's where."

So perhaps he'd been a bit of a slow starter. But he was with her now. And he'd do whatever it took to make back some of the time they'd lost, wherever and however he could.

He heard the sounds of laughter — female laughter — echoing up over his balcony railing from the indoor courtyard below and wandered out onto the inlaid stone and teakwood ledge that jutted out over the central gathering place, two stories below. Unsure of his welcome, he'd originally planned on staying at a small B & B just outside the Cove. Then he'd discovered this spectacularly original little seaside inn on walkabout the afternoon before and immediately changed his mind.

It wasn't like him to treat himself to anything quite so lavish, or at least so unique at any rate. He'd have done fine on a bedroll in the open bed of Kerry's old pickup, with a cooler for supplies and a small camp stove to feed himself. It was how he lived when riding out on the station to check the herds, repair fences, and such. In fact, the bed of Kerry's rusted-out hulk of a truck would have been an improvement on the way he spent many a night each year.

117

Not that he couldn't afford better, but it was a matter of priorities with him, as it was with every Jax for as far back as history had recorded them. He supposed the Jax family would be considered wealthy by any standard, but to their collective minds, assets were only as good as the sweat and labor that went into maintaining them. Cameroo Downs had been owned and run by a Jax since its inception. In the century and a half since then, there had been lean times — many of them — even times when the station came close to closing down or being sold off. But for the past seventy or so of those years, it had found its balance, and even with the fluctuation normal to the cattle business, it could only be described as doing well. Quite well, if the truth were told.

So he didn't feel guilty over the occasional splashy car rental or boutique inn stay. Besides, it could hardly become habit. How likely was he to do anything like this again?

Cooper stepped to the gleaming, restored teak railing, resting his hand on the brass-capped piling that separated the angled sections of the uniquely designed decking so he could glance down to the courtyard below. The inn was unlike anything he'd ever seen or could have envisioned. Designed by Langston DeVry, an award-winning, world-class architect who also happened to be a close friend of the owner, it was one of a kind. Apparently the man was known for his unique design vision and keen eye for finding ways to blend modern conveniences with the historic. At least Cooper knew that now, after reading the small, glossy pamphlet that had been on the restored antique captain's desk tucked in the corner of his room.

The inn itself was a converted eighteenth-century boathouse, originally used in the days of the oceangoing schooners and tall clipper ships built by the Monaghan family, a founding family of the Cove, right there on that very land. So it was soaring in height as well as taking up a decent-size footprint among the row of other boathouses that filled up the heart of the Half Moon Harbor shoreline. The harbor, itself central to the Cove, was apparently experiencing a renaissance of sorts in both productivity and jobs, only part of which were derived from the unique new inn. That part he'd learned over breakfast that morning from his waitress at the small café situated just off to the side of the lower inn entrance.

He let his gaze roam up and over the interior of the transformed building. The guest rooms had been built out from the walls of the boathouse in a cantilevered fashion, circling up in a staggered pattern, each ultramodern in design, like something Frank Lloyd Wright might have envisioned, only styled as historic ship staterooms, with balconies that looked like something you'd spy on a boat deck, complete with the teak and brass-capped rails. Each balcony faced the open center of the building, which remained open all the way to the roof, now inset with sunroof panels to let in the light. The rooms each had clever screens built in to the walls to make them transparent when open, allowing in all the natural light, then opaque when closed for privacy.

Cooper was fascinated by the whole enterprise and hoped he'd have the chance to spend more time talking to the innkeeper, Grace Monaghan, before checking out. There were a few clever ideas he thought might actually be of some use in the bunkhouses on the station.

Cooper was also fascinated by Grace's husband, Brodie Monaghan's boatbuilding business. Cameroo was well inland, and though the Wollamaroo River ran through the property, it wasn't anything you could put more than a flat boat on. Cooper had been to the shores in Darwin on holiday, but the bulk of his life had been spent landlocked by thousands of acres of grazing property. So he was curious and interested in learning more about this seafaring town and its shipbuilding ancestors.

Brodie Monaghan was a direct descendant of the original founding family of the same name, making him a sixth-generation boatbuilder. A recent transplant from Ireland, he'd come to America a few years back to reestablish his family's shipbuilding empire. The Irishman was a celebrated sailboat designer and builder by trade, but Cooper had seen photos and framed news and magazine articles on the walls inside the entrance to the inn. The man's recent construction of a seventeenth century schooner, replicated fully to scale and fully functional, boggled the mind.

That very morning Cooper had caught sight of the tall ship, moored at anchor out on the edge of the deep harbor, right where it emptied into the much larger Pelican Bay, which led out into the Atlantic Ocean. He smiled again, thinking how he'd marveled at the stories Kerry had told of her seafaring town, of the historic lighthouse out on Pelican Point that had been in her family's care for generations, and their own rich history as a founding family of the Cove.

121

Turned out there was far more to the place than the colorful history of that one family. He hadn't known what to expect, but Blueberry Cove far exceeded anything he could have dreamed up.

The rich scents of freshly brewed coffee mingled with the enticing smell of crisp bacon, homemade bread, and something fruity, all wafting up from the café below. He'd learned that Grace's sister-in-law, Delia Maddox, was chief cook and bottle-washer of that enterprise, and had been cooking for the folks in Half Moon Harbor and the Cove her entire life, as her mother had done before her. Cooper hadn't met the woman herself as yet, but he'd told Grace after the dinner he'd eaten there the evening before that if Delia weren't happily married to Grace's brother, Ford, as well as a dedicated, lifelong resident of the Cove, Cooper would have been tempted to bribe her, using whatever means necessary, to get her to agree to come back and set up shop in Cameroo Downs instead.

Marta was wonderful, she was family, but she wasn't getting any younger. And no offense to the older woman's outback style of range cooking — which was stick-to-your-ribs filling and tasty enough — but Cooper already knew that the delicious aroma filling the air right then was making a promise it would deliver on tenfold. Despite having sampled a whole plate full of what he now thought of as "Delia's delectables" earlier that morning before heading over to the pub, he was tempted to go back down for seconds. But he had a lunch to plan.

Speaking of which . . . he shifted his gaze downward, over toward the archway leading into the café, looking for the source of the continuing peals of feminine laughter. One laugh in particular. He had to crane a bit over the edge of the balcony, but given the angle, he could only see a few pairs of feet tucked under a table. None of them was wearing the Tevas he'd seen on Kerry's feet that morning. Still, though he didn't know who the other women were, or how many there were, he knew Kerry was one of them. There was no mistaking that full-throated, rich laugh of hers. No delicate musical lilt for his starfish. No, sir. Her laugh was just like the rest of her; bold, brash, every bit of it straight from the heart, and completely unconcerned about keeping it down to a polite roar.

Though they weren't scheduled to meet for a few hours yet, he was tempted to go down, say hello, see who else was part of the bridal planning powwow — more potential sources of information for him, possibly allies. He planned to be utterly shameless in making all possible use of what time he had here. Then he reconsidered, thinking he'd already made more than his share of uninvited arrivals in front of Kerry's friends and family.

Instead, he pulled on a pair of fresh work Daks and a blue chambray shirt over a white T-shirt, thinking it was as good a time as any to take a stroll over to the Irishman's boat shed to see if he could wrangle an upclose look at that tall ship of his. That led to ideas of maybe combining the two, having a picnic aboard some kind of rental, but because he'd never been on a sailboat, much less operated one, that likely wasn't his best bet. His grin broadened as he thought it probably also wasn't wise to put himself somewhere she could simply dump him overboard and sail off.

He pocketed his wallet, the keys to the car, hung his sunglasses around his neck, then slapped his well-worn Akubra on his still-damp mop out of habit. The summer sun in Maine didn't hold a candle to the searing heat he was used to back home, but he was so used to having it on, it simply didn't occur to him to leave it behind.

Exiting the guest rooms was also a unique

adventure and, he had to admit, the part he liked best. The upper rooms had a pier-style angled ramp system that led out of the room and then switchbacked down to a landing near one of the entrances to Delia's café. Some of the lower rooms also had a circular set of wrought-iron stairs leading down from the balcony to the courtyard. The other lower rooms, like his, had a nautical-style knotted rope ladder that could be dropped down through a trapdoor in the floor, allowing the guest to descend tree-house style. It was all a special kind of genius, really, and made him feel like a kid again, trying to climb the bulbous trunks of the boab trees back home.

Another burst of laughter from the ladies below had him opting for the rope ladder exit, thinking the angle might give him a peek into the adjacent café as he descended. They were a jovial lot. Sounded like the meeting was going well at least, perhaps putting Kerry in a more open-minded mood for their lunch later. He imagined his arrival had been at least part of their conversation, then frowned briefly, thinking maybe he didn't want to know what was at the root of all that laughter after all. Maybe he would drop by, at least long enough to be judged on his own merits. Who knew what Kerry was telling them?

His attention was so laser focused on that possibility, he didn't see the man standing just to the side of the bottom of the rope ladder until Cooper dropped off before reaching the final rungs, then turned and bumped smack into him.

He immediately sidestepped, lifting his hands in apology, grinning as he said, "Sorry there, mate. Didn't see you." When the tall, dark-haired man simply sized him up and down, ending with an enigmatic, somewhat penetrating look, Cooper's grin spread even further. The family resemblance wasn't strong. But then, Kerry was the only McCrae with red hair and green eyes. Her uncle Fergus had called her a woodland sprite in their conversation earlier, and spritely she certainly was.

Her brother, however, from the photos he'd seen in Fergus's small back office, was tall, built as broad as a lumberjack, and wore a police uniform to work every day. Much like, Cooper surmised, the uniform the man in front of him was wearing. Which would explain the dubious once-over.

Not at all perturbed by the surprise arrival and very official-looking demeanor, and yet respectful of it all the same — he'd have done as much or more if some bloke was sniffing after his sister — he doffed his hat and stuck out his hand. "You must be Logan. Or should I call you Chief Mc-Crae?"

Logan McCrae hesitated a short moment, then took Cooper's hand in a quick, firm shake. Cooper was also glad to see McCrae didn't feel the need to resort to some kind of macho game of whose handshake is the firmest to prove who would control their little meeting. But then, he did have a gun strapped to his hip, Cooper noted, so possibly that was simply unnecessary.

"Cooper Jax," McCrae said, sidestepping his name query for now anyway. "I thought maybe we could take a quick walk if you have a few moments?"

"Off a short pier?" Cooper replied, smile unwavering as he gestured for McCrae to lead the way through the courtyard.

The bigger man's dark gaze remained zeroed in, but the tight line of his square jaw relaxed, as did his shoulders. "That depends. We do have one or two."

Cooper knew a lot more about the oldest McCrae sib than he assumed McCrae knew about him, but from all that Kerry had said about her only brother, Cooper was predisposed to like the bloke. The hint of humor underlying McCrae's words told him to trust that instinct. "I'll do my best to keep both feet on the ground then."

"Good start," McCrae replied, then headed through the courtyard.

Cooper followed, wondering if Kerry knew her brother was in the building, but didn't glance over his shoulder to find out. For all he knew, the moment he'd left the pub's rear lot that morning, Kerry had asked her brother to come to the inn to politely — or not so politely — warn her would-be suitor off.

They stepped outside into the crisp morning air; a cool breeze was coming off the water, which lay less than ten yards away. He could only wish summers in Cameroo were as temperate. "I was on my way over to Monaghan's boat shed to see what he's about," Cooper said. "Maybe find a way to take a closer look at that ship of his. Brilliant bit of workmanship, that."

"It is, yes," McCrae said, turning toward the rather large chunk of harbor property that comprised Monaghan's Shipbuilders. Grace's inn sat on the edge of the property and shared the parking lot that ran along behind it with her husband's business. The heavy, wide-planked pier that extended into the harbor, directly across from the entrance to the inn, was dedicated for use by the inn guests but was also interconnected to a much broader network of piers belonging to the shipbuilding side of things.

Some of the boathouses and other buildings had clearly been renovated and were in good repair, while others, including a few that were built out on the piers themselves — he supposed for boat housing, or to work on boats without hauling them up on dry land — looked like they hadn't been used in quite some time. Being part owner of a rather large family spread himself, he marveled that, according to what he'd read in those articles, Monaghan had renovated as much as he had.

"Founding family, I hear," Cooper said, gesturing to the largest boathouse on the property, which had *Monaghan's Shipbuilders* freshly painted on the restored roof. "Impressive to still have it operating toward its original purpose all these years later. Mc-Craes were founders, too, I understand. Lighthouse keepers, your people were, right?"

McCrae nodded as they walked along the harbor's edge toward a smaller boathouse with a sign designating it as Brodie's workshop hanging from a boat's mast that had been sunk into ground out front. "It appears you know a great deal more about us than we know about you." He glanced over at Cooper. "I wonder why that is."

Cooper shrugged. "I can't speak for Kerry. She was a favorite of my family and was a good friend to every one of us. She spoke about you and your two other sisters often. Fergus as well. About many of the folks here, and her life growing up. All with great love."

McCrae nodded, seeming to take his words as truth, making Cooper wonder if he'd spoken to Kerry directly about this latest turn of events yet. Maybe he was just seeing if their stories matched.

"We're a close bunch," Logan replied. "Closer now that we're all back home again."

It was Cooper's turn to nod, and he wondered if he was supposed to read something into that casual statement. "I'm fortunate to come from the same," he said. "We all work together. Family business."

"Funny that she didn't regale us with stories about that. About you and your family. Being as she'd grown so close to you all and everything."

Okay, so either he hadn't spoken to Kerry or she hadn't told him much. He wanted not to be affected by that, but standing there looking at her brother's implacable expression, he began to wonder if maybe he'd misjudged everything. Well, except for that kiss. He hadn't misjudged that.

"Again, I can't speak for her. Is she normally chatty about her adventures? She's been off on walkabout pretty much her entire adult life from what I know of it."

McCrae paused for a moment and rather than respond, he said, "This is the longest she's been home since she first took off."

He could mention that her stint with his family, just prior to that, had also won a longest-stay record, then thought better of offering that up for dissection. "You sound surprised."

McCrae slowed his steps. "I am. We all thought she'd leave after my wedding, but she didn't. She stayed for our sister's wedding, then for Fergus."

Cooper nodded. "Yes, she's said as much. And now there's another wedding in the offing." At McCrae's nod, Cooper added, "But you're thinking it's something else keeping her here? Me, or her time with me and my family, perhaps?"

If Logan was surprised by his directness, he didn't show it. "Honestly, I don't know." He paused another moment, then said, "She's not the best letter writer, and no, to answer your other question, she's not overly chatty, as you put it. But she was good about calling home, regaling us with at least a story or two from each of her various adventures." He looked at Cooper. "And yet not a word about her time in Australia, other than to say it was a good experience. She was there longer than she's ever been anywhere, but that's the sum total of what she had to report about her time spent there."

Cooper held the man's gaze easily, comfortably even. As a big brother himself, he simply put himself in Logan's shoes, while silently praying for the sake of any bloke on Cameroo Downs who might come sniffing around Sadie that he'd never have to. He wasn't sure he could be so calm and contained as the police chief here.

"I know, despite her extended travels," Cooper said, "she considers herself very close to her family. Coming from a close-knit family myself, I recognize deep love when I see it, and she has that for each and every one of you, as I'm sure you're well aware. I'll be honest and say I don't know why she hasn't told you about us, about her time with my family or on the station. I'm as surprised as you are. I believe it meant something to her. I know she mattered to all of us. Or I wouldn't be here."

"More than a year has passed," Logan said, looking less judgmental now, and more like a man simply trying to get to the heart of the matter. "She's talked to Fergus, it seems, which isn't all that unusual, I guess."

"I know they have a special bond, yes," Cooper replied.

"But we didn't know about that until now. And only because you've suddenly shown up talking marriage. A proposal she turned down flat, as witnessed by almost everyone in the Cove. And yet here you are. Still."

Okay, so maybe he was still feeling a little judgmental.

Cooper honestly didn't know what to say to that. All of it was true, and he could understand Logan's concern and his confusion. He was confused himself. He hadn't been aware of Kerry's silence with her family about her time spent in Oz. Talking with Fergus, both when he'd made initial contact and the two times they'd spoken in person since his arrival, Cooper had simply assumed if her uncle knew who he was, then so did the rest of her family. The shock on every last face in the pub when he'd made his grand entrance had been his first clue. But then, she'd remained silent with his family, too, since departing Cameroo. And he knew that wasn't characteristic of her

133

nature either. "I'm guessing you've asked her directly about this. What did she say?"

"I'm more interested in hearing what you have to say."

Cooper spent a moment wondering if he should deflect the question, thinking that Kerry's decision to pretty much treat her entire stay in Australia as if it had never happened, with her family and his own — and maybe even herself — was something he needed to talk to her about. Not her brother. And yet playing his cards close to the vest was what had him traveling halfway around the globe in the first place. Maybe it was time for everybody to start talking to everybody and let the chips fall where they may.

To that end, he held Logan's gaze directly when he responded. "Your sister worked for our family's cattle station for a little over a year. We all got to know her, as she did us, and over time we all grew close. I should say here that while we have a number of folks who have worked for our family a very long time — in some cases for generations — and we consider them to be like extended family, we don't normally adopt every jack or jillaroo and invite them into our home. Hell, we don't always even meet them if they're out on other station sites and camps, working for our station managers. Kerry hired on as seasonal, and it was purely happenstance that she ended up working in our family stables instead of out on the station proper. She has a way with the horses. A natural, really. She worked the station proper, too, prepping horses for work, taking care of that end of things, and did her fair amount of hard work out on the land. Good work ethic, that one. We were all impressed."

"So how did that lead her to —"

"My sister, Sadie. She's thirteen going on thirty, and one of just a few women on the property. My mother passed on when I was in my teens. My father remarried too soon, and Sadie is the result of that short-lived union. Long story short, station life didn't suit her mum, nor did being a mum, so she took off for parts unknown, leaving Sadie to us. For which we're all grateful. She's a ray of pure sunshine, that one is. She took a shine to your sister immediately. I'd like to say it was mutual, but Kerry kept her distance. Polite, kind but professional." Cooper chuckled. "Sadie wasn't so easily deterred. She hung out around the stables every chance she got, then somehow wangled Kerry into helping her with some schoolwork. That landed her in our kitchens, where our cook, Marta, took a shine to

135

Kerry as well. And, well . . . one thing and another and all that." He put his hat back on his head as the sun shifted out from behind the clouds, so he could keep his gaze direct on Logan's. "She wasn't an easy one to win over, to get close to, and I understand why. She made it clear she was temporary. But then she stayed. And stayed again. And, I suppose . . . well, it didn't take a genius to see how much she loved the place, loved the work, too. She was born for it, and the place loved her right back."

"And you?"

This was the easiest question he'd been asked thus far, and he answered it honestly, with his whole heart. "And me. She's a special woman, your sister. I knew that from the start. But I was her boss, and she was temporary. So I respected the distance she put between us, despite wanting things to be different."

"And now? What's different now?"

"Now it's been a year and I can't forget her. I should have told her. Should have asked. And I didn't. A part of me — a big part — thought she'd come back. But that didn't happen. And, as my father says, a man can't wait for a chance; he has to make his own, then take it. So here I am. Making my own chance."

"And her rejection?"

Now Cooper straightened, and though his smile was still at the fore, honest and sincere, he wanted to make sure Logan heard and respected this next part. "We've discussed her reasons for that. I've taken a month's leave from the station and we've decided to see what will come of spending that time together. Maybe nothing; maybe this brief reunion will be all I'll have, and I'll have to be good with that. Whatever the outcome, I will respect her choice and I won't regret trying. It's the only way I'd have known. The only way I can look forward, move forward. I hope you can understand that. And I hope you'll understand also that the rest is between Kerry and myself. If you want her side, you'll have to talk to her."

Logan was silent for a moment, then nodded, though his expression remained somewhat implacable. "You understand my position on this. You have a sister." He made them statements, not questions, but Cooper responded anyway.

Cooper nodded, then grinned. "I've been putting myself in your shoes since I bumped into you back there by the ladder. Let's just say when the day comes, I hope I can live up to your example."

Logan's mouth might have hitched a bit at that; it was a moment of connection, and Cooper wasn't going to be choosy about how he got them. What happened between him and Kerry was personal and private, but her family was part of her, too, as was his family with him, so he had no intention of cutting them out of the picture. Quite the opposite, he hoped. She had gotten to know his family and he was hoping for the chance to do the same with hers.

"Seriously, Logan?"

At the sound of a woman's voice, both men turned to find Kerry, along with five other women — only one of whom Cooper knew, inn owner, Grace Monaghan — all standing not ten feet behind them.

Kerry was front and center, wearing the same Tevas, long, slim khaki shorts, and the well-worn shamrock T-shirt she'd had on when they'd crossed paths earlier. The lean musculature of her biceps showed against the soft cotton in her arms-folded stance, her look of exasperation making the angles of her face stand out more starkly. She wasn't a traditional milk-skinned redhead. Quite the opposite. Her skin was a rich, golden tan so smooth and surprisingly freckle free it looked almost airbrushed. It made her green eyes sparkle even more brightly and her bright white teeth seem a bit feral. At least in their presently bared state. With her taller-than-average frame and the lean and muscular body of an athlete, she seemed far more Amazon warrior queen than the woodland faerie sprite her uncle had nicknamed her as a child of ten. No wonder Sadie looked up to Kerry as her own personal superhero. Cooper thought he might, too.

Even annoyed, as she was now, she vibrated the kind of barely restrained energy that made every part of him spark to life. Some parts more enthusiastically than others. He shifted his weight and sidestepped slightly in an effort to keep that reality as unnoticeable as possible. He'd become a master of that particular skill during the last few months she'd been on the station.

He needn't have worried. She didn't so much as glance at him. Her irritation was focused solely on her big brother. "Did you really just perp walk Cooper down the harbor?"

Logan's eyebrows lifted along with his hands, which he held up at his sides, palms out. "Hold up, I didn't —"

"Save it," Kerry said. She turned to Cooper. "I apologize. He forgets I'm an adult woman who can handle her own affairs." She glared at her brother during that last part.

"She's right, you know." This came from a little spitfire brunette who, given Kerry's descriptions of her family, must be the middle McCrae sister, Fiona. Fists planted on her hips, managing to somehow look down her cute little nose at her much taller and much bigger brother, she added, "We're trying to plan my wedding and grill her about Mr. Hot and Aussie here. I'd think by now you'd know that we've got this covered." She made a brief gesture to the other women standing alongside her. "If we thought he was a danger to society, we would have called."

Cooper watched the ricocheting dialogue like a spectator at a cricket match, unable to squelch a grin. It was like watching his own sister, all grown up and in triplicate. As Kerry and Fiona closed in on a somehow now hapless-looking lumberjack of a police chief, Cooper stepped forward and stuck out his hand toward the taller, willowy young woman who stood just behind Fiona. Where Kerry was Amazonian and Fiona a little firebrand, their oldest sister was the epitome of cool, calm, and collected. "Hannah Blue, I presume? I'm Cooper Jax. Sorry for the disruption of your sister's wedding plans. I didn't know."

This had Fiona turning his way. "And how could you, given Kerry couldn't be bothered to so much as send you a postcard?"

"Hey," Kerry said, looking at her sister now. "Whose side are you on?"

Fiona looked back at her. "The side that keeps this guy here and you looking all pent up and googly-eyed."

"Googly-eyed?" Kerry shot back.

Cooper, grinning unrepentantly now, turned his attention back to Hannah and continued, as if her sisters weren't getting all up in each other's personal space. "I understand congratulations are in order on your recent nuptials as well."

Hannah gave him a swift, all-encompassing once-over as only a former defense attorney could. Then, in the face of his unrelenting goodwill, she took his hand, her mouth curving up in the barest hint of a smile as she gave it a firm, quick shake. "You're a charmer, Mr. Jax, I'll give you that."

"Go with your strength," he replied; then, while Logan waded into the fray behind him, Cooper turned to the inn's owner, a woman of average height and build with a gorgeous waterfall of dark hair and sharp, lively hazel eyes. "I hope this won't mean

141

you're kicking me out of the inn, Mrs. Monaghan."

"Oh, I'm on Fiona's side. Your side," she said with a grin. "And please, I've told you, it's Grace." Then she blushed. "Though I have to admit, I kind of like hearing the other one. It's still pretty new."

"It looks good on you," he said, chuckling as her blush deepened. In addition to the schooner photos, there were photos of Grace and Brodie's wedding posted on another wall in the reception area of the inn, along with a framed clipping of the announcement that had run in the local paper. Inn owner Grace Maddox and shipbuilder Brodie Monaghan had tied the knot just that spring in an intimate double ceremony out on Sandpiper Island, a wildlife preserve out in Pelican Bay. The other couple had been Grace's older brother, Ford, and his ladylove, Delia O'Reilly, creator of the delectable meals he'd dined on since his arrival. "Weddings seem to be something of a spectator sport in these parts."

Grace laughed. "Come to think of it, we have had our share of bouquets tossed in the past year or so." Still smiling, she glanced at Fiona, who, along with Kerry, was still wrangling over who should be in charge of running Kerry's love life. "And we're not done yet," Grace said.

Smiling, he looked back at her and winked. "Yes, I'm rather counting on that bit." He turned to the other two women, who were openly checking him out and didn't seem the least bit shy about it. "I'm sorry, where are my manners?" he said. "You're the other blushing bride I noticed in the wedding photos alongside Mrs. Monaghan here. Mrs. Maddox, is it?"

He extended his hand toward the older of the two women, who appeared to be somewhere in her early forties yet exuded the same kind of electricity Kerry did, only a bit more audaciously perhaps. She responded to his apology with a dismissive wave of her hand. "Oh, don't mind us, we're just enjoying the show. And the view," she added with a quick once-over. Her accompanying grin was as broad and inviting as her laugh. "Yes, I'm Delia Maddox," she said, taking his hand in a quick, firm shake. "Grace's sister-in-law and —"

"— the ravishing goddess responsible for creating Delia's delectables. The most amazing food in the Americas."

Her pretty eyes twinkled at his nickname for her food, but she folded her arms and said, "Only in the Americas? Hmm, I must be slipping."

"If you ever tire of this place and your sainted husband, just give me the word and I'll whisk you away to Oz, where your magical powers will be duly appreciated."

Delia laughed outright at that and called out, "Hey, Kerry? I vote yes."

All four women laughed, then the last one of the group stepped forward. She was closest to Kerry in build, lean and athletic, though shorter and far more self-contained. She looked both confident and capable, and beyond that he couldn't read a single thing in her deep sea blue eyes. "I'm Alex McCrae." She nodded toward Logan. "The chief's wife."

Cooper's expression immediately brightened. He took her extended hand in both of his, then stepped in and bent his head, speaking sotto voce as he said, "Because you're the only one here who has married into the clan, I'd love a moment of your time, get some pointers on how best to proceed."

To her credit, she smiled, then shocked him by patting him on the arm and saying, "Oh, I think you're doing just fine with your current plan of attack." She leaned in and mimicked his stage whisper. "Really fine."

"Alex!" This from Kerry, who had returned to the group in time to catch the last part of the exchange. *"Et tu?"*

Alex shrugged unrepentantly. "Seriously? Have you seen him? And how you held out against that accent, I have no idea."

Cooper might have been momentarily gobsmacked, but he quickly rallied. "You're angels," he said. "My humblest gratitude."

"Cooper's Angels!" Grace exclaimed, then looped her arms through Alex and Delia's. "We could make T-shirts and everything." She turned and pressed her back against Delia's shoulder, striking a pose that even he knew was part of the iconic *Charlie's Angels* stance. Some things crossed all geographical boundaries. Especially when they were gorgeous and prone to wearing skimpy bikinis.

"Grace —" Kerry warned, but when Alex assumed her Angel position on the other side of Delia, who smiled, shrugged, then completed the little tableau, making even the tall, cool Hannah roll her eyes and laugh, her gaze shifted to him, as if their show of support were somehow all his fault.

He shrugged, tugged on the brim of his hat, then grinned and looked at the three women and, in his best John Forsythe imitation, said, "Hello, Angels," which set them all off, all over again.

Cooper glanced over at Fiona, who was

merely sending her younger sister a smug, see-I-told-you-so smile.

The women, sans Kerry, closed ranks once again, and from the cool, considering look of Hannah to the enthusiastic and plotting smiles of Grace, Alex, and Delia and now the unbridled glee of bride-to-be Fiona, he wasn't exactly sure what he might have just gotten himself into. He glanced back at Logan. "Should I be afraid, mate?"

"Oh, very, very afraid. Mate." Then a slow smile spread across Logan's face, transforming him from stern police chief and protective brother to a far more relaxed and, if Cooper wasn't mistaken, surprisingly relieved-looking comrade in arms. "You know, I just realized I haven't been looking at this the right way at all." Logan looked from Kerry to the group of women and then to Cooper. "Strength in numbers."

Kerry turned to her brother, hands limp at her sides now. "Wow," she said flatly, turning the word into two drawn-out syllables. "Just . . . wow."

"Hey, a minute ago you were jumping all over me for interrogating the guy. Which, you know, think about that. And I'm just saying that maybe, at times, it wouldn't hurt to have another guy on the team."

"You've got all kinds of guys on 'your

team,' " she retorted, making air quotes on the last two words. "Every other person here has another half who is on your man team."

Logan shrugged. "Calder is out at the farm with his horses most of the time, Ben is still getting things up and going out in Snowflake Bay, Ford is out on his damn island, and even when he's not, you couldn't exactly call him a team player. Brodie's either building a boat or sailing one. I'm just saying, it might not hurt to have a little backup right here in the Cove."

Cooper was surprised bordering on shocked by the sudden shift but didn't waste any time pressing the advantage. "Right you are, mate." He glanced out at the harbor, then back to Logan. "Speaking of backup, what does a bloke have to do to hire himself a boat for a lunch date out on the bay?"

Logan pulled out his phone and punched in a number, then turned his back and walked a few steps away as he spoke to someone about getting a boat.

"Traitors. The full lot of you," Kerry said, putting up her hands. "What just happened here? On my very own turf, I might add."

"Wingmen," Grace said.

"It's like the universal bro code," Alex added.

147

"Call it whatever you like," Fiona chimed in. "It's like the fraternal order of testosterone. Don't even think about trying to divide and conquer. Bros before —"

"You've got it all wrong," Delia cut in with a laugh.

"Says the woman married to Robinson Crusoe, the only man in the universe who goes bro-less," Fiona replied.

"No, no, I don't mean it doesn't exist. I'm just saying, when it comes to reclaiming the support of your man, well . . . we're each endowed with a very exclusive arsenal, one that can bend even the biggest and strongest of the male species to a woman's will, rendering him helpless to deny her every need." She eyed Cooper, her smile downright blazing hot and not a little terrifying. "Any. Time. We. Want."

He swallowed a little hard, struggling not to shift his weight. Again.

The only thing more terrifying than Delia's little speech? The dawning realization that she was entirely correct, which spread across the faces of five exceedingly intelligent, beautiful, and apparently cheerfully lethal women.

But if they were using their powers for the good of his campaign with Kerry, he wasn't going to stop them. While being damn sure never to piss any one of them off.

"Well, that might be fine for the lot of you," Kerry broke in, "but given you're siding with Mr. Wingman here, it hardly does me any good. What happened to the whole sisterhood thing? And this after I came to you, hat in hand —"

"You were dragged in," Fiona reminded her. "Laundry basket in hand. Then we had to all but sit on you to squeeze the details out of you. If you want us to be all supportive and on your side, then, you know, you have to actually give us something to side with. So far, all we've heard is how you didn't know how he felt, and then he sent your entire world spinning off its axis with that "

"Fiona —" Kerry said, clear warning in her tone.

But it was too late. Logan had walked back to the group and was just saying he had a sailboat lined up and did they want a captain or were they going to sail it themselves, when he overheard the last bit of Fiona's statement and paused. He turned to look at Kerry, then perhaps a tad more menacingly at Cooper. "With that . . . what?"

Before Cooper could remind him about their recently established wingman/bro code status, Logan's wife slid past him and hooked her arm through her husband's and tipped up on her toes to kiss him on the cheek. "Remember our first kiss?" She gave him a meaningful look to go with what was clearly a very private smile. "So I really don't think you want to go there. Do you?"

Logan cleared his throat. "Right, so . . . as you were," he finally said. "I've got to get back to the station. Keep the mean streets of Blueberry Cove safe."

"Coward!" Kerry called after his retreating back.

"See?" Delia said. "We have our ways."

"Except you're supporting the wrong side," Kerry said.

"Oh, that all depends on how you define 'sides,' " Grace put in. "We're on the side of love." She drew out that last word, making it sound almost like a coo, with Fiona joining her, both of them adding an exaggerated batting of lashes, aimed first at Kerry, then at Cooper. Fiona added a little heart made by steepling her fingers together.

Logan looked back over his shoulder. He was grinning now. "If you know what's good for you, you'll head back to the airport right now," he called to Cooper.

Cooper lifted his hand in a wave. "No worries, mate." He glanced at the group of openly speculating women, then at Kerry, who was shooting emerald green daggers his way, and thought *ummm. . . .* "On second thought," he shouted. "Hold on, I'll join you!" He trotted after Logan, then turned so he was facing the women as he continued jogging backward. "Just getting the boat rental details, luv," he called back to Kerry. "Back in a jiff." He blew Kerry a kiss, then added a wink, chuckling when Fiona grabbed Kerry's arm as she swung it upward in a gesture he seriously doubted was going to be a wave.

He knew she was feeling shoved along a path she hadn't yet decided she wanted to take and he might have been more concerned about her prickly attitude except for one thing. *Sent her world spinning off its axis, had I? Well, all righty, then.* As shaky starts went, he'd keep his focus on that little nugget of truth and build from there.

Whistling a jaunty tune, he turned back and set off to catch up with Logan.

CHAPTER EIGHT

"You say romantic, I say stalker," Kerry grumbled to Fiona as they pushed their way into the Rusty Puffin.

"Please," Fiona retorted, adding an eye roll for good measure. She was a master of those. "Mr. Dead Sexy From Down Under, a hardworking, successful man you greatly admired, with a family you apparently adored, flies halfway around the world to propose to you? Take a poll. That's off-the-charts romantic."

"Right," Kerry said, turning toward her as the heavy door swung closed behind them. "And then I turned him down and he's still here, hounding me. Stalker."

"I hardly think asking you to lunch — a lunch you said yes to, by the way — then hiring a sailboat to take you out on the bay could be considered hounding, much less stalking. That's still firmly in the romantic category. I mean, if you really meant no,

I'm sure he'd be on the next plane back to Oz."

Kerry stopped completely, fists on her hips now. "What makes you think I didn't really mean no?"

"Well, for one, you're awfully worked up over the guy. In that she-doth-protest-too-much kind of way. And secondly, Logan said Cooper told him you two had agreed on him staying the full month he'd taken off from the cattle station, to give you both time to figure out if there was something worth pursuing together."

"He said that? To Logan?" At Fiona's smug nod, Kerry's eyebrows drew together. "What else did Cooper tell him? And how could you even know that? We left the docks together before Cooper came back. We didn't talk to him again, or Logan."

Fiona turned her phone around so the screen faced Kerry. "It's called texting. Maybe they don't have that in Tanzania or on deserted South Pacific atolls, but here in America, we —"

"Okay, okay," Kerry said, waving her hands, still disgruntled. "It doesn't matter. For the record, I said yes to lunch just to keep him from showing up every time my back is turned." She sent a pointed look at her sister. "You know, like a stalker. I didn't agree to an entire afternoon out on the bay with him."

"You didn't agree to that lollapalooza of a kiss either. But that happens and suddenly he's not on the next plane home. Just saying, Ms. Protests Too Much."

Kerry opened her mouth, then closed it again, then folded her arms across her chest. "I never should have told you about that."

Fiona grinned. "I know." She tugged Kerry's arms loose and pulled one through her own, leaning her head on her taller sister's shoulder and beaming up at her, lashes fluttering. "But we're so glad you did."

"Oh, hush," Kerry said, but she didn't push her sister away. And she had to work harder than she should have to keep her scowl in place.

"You're just annoyed because you can't find a way to be in charge and control this whole thing and it's making you jumpy."

Kerry considered that, relented a little. "Maybe."

"And because we all like him. A lot. And you're feeling overly nudged."

"Nudged?" Kerry repeated, eyebrow raised. "How about all but shoved down the aisle? You know, just because you're all schmoopy and wedding obsessed doesn't mean the rest of us live to follow in your

154

pearl-and-lace-encrusted footsteps."

Fiona just batted her lashes again. "Oh, come on. You love the schmoopy. You just don't want to admit it. And you don't have to go all pearls and lace. I'm sure we can find something in a tasteful banana leaf gown for you."

Kerry nudged her sister with a sharp elbow — it was that or snicker — but Fiona just nudged back, and clung to her arm like a kelp bed attached to the seafloor. "And, okay," Fiona added, "perhaps we're just enjoying seeing you so out of your depth. Between that and Cooper's full-on pursuit, I can see it's enough to make anyone a little grumpy." She squeezed Kerry's arm, then added, "Ms. I Can Run Circles Around the Globe But Not Around Mr. Dead-Sexy Accent."

Kerry gave up, as she always did, in the face of Fiona's unrelenting cheer and pulled her in for a quick, if purposely smothering hug. "Don't say anything to Fergus," she whispered against Fiona's hair before turning her sister loose. "He's already stuck his nose in way too far, and you know he'll just worry about me."

Fiona laughed. "You're the only one Fergus never worries about. And don't kid yourself about slowing his roll; he's thrilled

— *thrilled* — finally to have the chance to stick his nose in your business. Do you think anything will stop him from 'helping' you make the right choice? Besides, who knows you better than Gus? He's the one you confide all your little secrets in, so maybe if you won't listen to us, you'll listen to him."

If Fiona sounded the teensiest bit put out by the fact that Fergus had known about the existence of Cooper while the rest of her family had not, Kerry knew it was a fair reaction. She'd have felt the same had the situation been reversed. "We're talking about the same man who thinks he can still run this place by himself," she reminded Fiona, "and clearly that's not the case. So you'll forgive me if I'm not running to him for advice on this one. Besides, apparently Cooper already has him in his back pocket — I know when the deck is being stacked."

Fiona's smile remained, but her eyes took on a more serious look. "Has he gotten any worse? I mean, the two of you have always been your own little tribunal of two, but you'd tell us if he was, wouldn't you?"

"Of course I would. And no, he's fine. Or at least he's improving in all the ways he can. But there are some limitations that appear to be pretty much permanent, most especially in his arm and leg. And with his stamina, I'm afraid the physical toll of doing even as much as he does puts too much stress on him."

"And you think that might trigger another stroke, don't you?"

Kerry knew her expression likely held all the same love and concern Fiona's did at that moment. "Can you blame me? You know what his doctor said about the likelihood of a repeat."

"It's been seven, going on eight months now —"

"I'll probably still be worrying about him when it's been seven years, but more so now. It wasn't that long ago, Fi."

"Well, all I'm saying is, if you were to, you know, take off again on your next adventure, we'd make sure he had this place covered. You know that, don't you?" Fiona lifted her hand, palm facing front. "And I'm not saying it has to be Australia, but, you know, you have been parked here for a pretty long time now. I'm surprised you're not twitchy with the need to get back out there. I know just listening to that accent of Mr. Hot From Down Under would make me a little twitchy. Seriously, Kerry, how did you work next to him for a year and not jump him?"

"Wow, I didn't know you were in such a big hurry to see me out of here," Kerry replied, ignoring the part about jumping Cooper. It wasn't like she hadn't asked herself the same question a dozen times. Or a hundred dozen.

"I didn't say that; I'm just making sure you know we'd support your decision to run off with him, if, you know, that's what you decide to do."

"Since when is this decision up to me? Seems like you all have it all figured out already." Then Kerry's eyes narrowed. "Or do you just want the inside scoop so you can win the pool on when I'll head out again?"

"Pool?" Fiona said overly brightly. "My, my, whatever do you —"

"Oh, don't even bother pretending. I know Barbara's had one running since I came back for Logan's wedding." Barbara was Sergeant Barbara Benson. She was pushing seventy and had been on the force longer than the McCrae siblings had been alive. She'd worked for several police chiefs during her tenure and was currently Logan's right hand. Aside from that, she'd always looked out for the McCraes in her own take-the-bull-by-the-horns maternal way. She wasn't what Kerry would call a mother substitute exactly, but they'd all turned to her with their problems over the years.

"All I'm saying," Fiona went on, ignoring her sister's accusation, "is that you shouldn't let Fergus's condition keep you from living your life. He'd hate that if he knew."

"I'm not staying for Fergus. I mean, I did initially, but it was also Hannah's wedding, and now you're engaged. I wasn't planning on being home all this time, but you guys keep getting married off and I'm here, so I might as well stay until you've all done the deed. Then I won't have to haul myself back here again until you start popping out nieces and nephews." If she felt a surprisingly strong pang in her chest at the thought of being away from the Cove, from her family, and the somewhat startling idea, now that she'd blurted it out, that there would likely be more little McCraes at some point, she ignored it.

"Where were you planning on heading next, then, if not Australia?" Fiona asked.

"Oh, I'll just toss a dart at the map like I usually do," Kerry said, as blithely as she could.

Fiona eyed her closely, as if checking her sincerity. "Well, whenever you do head back out — wherever and with whomever that might be — we'll make sure Gus hires someone to help him with the pub. So, you know, don't let that part affect your decision making or anything."

" 'Wherever or with whomever'?" Kerry repeated with a roll of her eyes.

Fiona beamed sweetly again. "Just saying."

"All kidding aside, I'm not the settling down type, Fi." At the flash of real sadness Kerry saw flicker through her too-optimistic-for-her-own-good sister, she made a show of sliding Fiona's arm out from where it had been looped through hers and dropping it as if she was suddenly contagious. "Don't go trying to spread all your bride cooties on me," she teased, hoping to shift them back to their more comfortable pattern of affectionately swapping insults, and far, far away from delving in to the fears and worries that were truly the reason behind her defensive attitude.

Kerry knew her family and extended family — hell, everyone in the Cove — only wanted what was best for her, wanted her to be happy. She just wanted the space and time to figure out what, exactly, that was going to be, all by herself. "Some of us aren't meant for home and hearth. For white picket fences. Or silly cattle dogs and stone fire pits."

It was only when Fiona's gaze sharpened again that she realized she'd said that last part out loud. A knowing smile played at the corners of Fiona's mouth and her eyes sparked right back to matchmaker life.

"Don't," Kerry warned.

"Whatever do you mean?" Fiona said with false innocence. "I hear what you're saying. And I believe you. At least, I believe you believe you."

"Fi—"

"Are two of my best girls going to stand about inside the door, jabbering on and ignoring their auld uncle?" came a shout from the back of the pub.

They both turned to see Fergus coming from his office toward the bar. He was using his cane, but Kerry noted with relief that he didn't look overly dependent on it.

She started toward him for the traditional hug and buss on the cheek, only to slow a step when she saw that Fergus wasn't alone. A young woman trailed out of the office behind him. She was about the same height as the stocky Irishman, so Kerry hadn't noticed her at first. The woman was of far more slender build than her uncle, but had a wiry, fit look. She had wispy, light brown hair that fell almost to her shoulders, huge, beautiful dark eyes, and a firm chin to offset them, the combination of which gave her the air of someone who meant business. Even so, it wasn't the woman herself who had Kerry pausing. It was the tall, red standard poodle walking obediently at her side.

"Hello," Kerry said to the woman, then looked questioningly from the dog to Fergus. "You know the health department —"

"Dart is a service dog. In training," the young woman said, then shifted to show the credentials hanging from the fanny pack she had strapped on at the waist, so the little zippered leather bag was at her side.

Kerry also noticed now that the black nylon harness on the dog was stitched in yellow with the words *Service Dog in Training* on the brace that ran down the dog's back. "Ah. Well, how cool are you?" Kerry said, smiling at the dog. She loved dogs. All animals, really. "Is it okay if I pet her?"

The woman instantly beamed, which transformed her serious face into something quite arresting as her dark eyebrows arched to offset her deep brown eyes. "Absolutely. The more socialized she becomes, the better. Dart?" She made a hand motion, and the dog relaxed from its alert stance to a bright-eyed, tail-wagging companion dog.

Kerry and Fiona both went over, crouched down a bit, and extended their hands so Dart could sniff them. "What a pretty girl you are," Kerry crooned. "And so smart, too." She gave the dog a good scratch behind the ears, then rubbed her neck. Dart didn't sport a fancy poodle trim but instead had thick, curly red fur, which made her look like an oversize, adorable puppy. The big dog nuzzled her hand in return, her tail wagging now as Fiona leaned in to give her back a nice scratch for good measure. Kerry stood and put her hand out to the young woman. "I'm Kerry McCrae, Fergus's great-niece."

"Madison Diba," she said in return. "Call me Maddy. And yes, he was telling me all about you."

Kerry's eyebrows arched as she glanced over to her uncle. "Was he now?"

"Now, now," Fergus called back from where he stood behind the bar, a few yards away, "no need for all that. Let me get you three girls a drink, and our pretty four-legged lass there a bowl of water."

"Thank you," Maddy said, unzipping her fanny pack. "I have a little pop-up water dish —"

"No need," Fergus said. "I've got an old storage container here or there that will do. Kerry, why don't you see to the drinks?"

"Nothing for me —" Maddy started to say.

Kerry cut her off. "Coke, water, ginger

163

ale?" She ducked under the bar and then leaned over it and whispered, "Trust me, have a sip of something or he'll badger you until you do."

Fiona hiked herself up on one of the stools. "She's right," she told Maddy. "Make mine water, with a lemon." She looked at Maddy. "I have a wedding dress to squeeze into."

Kerry rolled her eyes. "Don't you dare say anything that has the word *bride, bridal, wedding,* or — God help us — *dress,* in her general direction. In fact, you can add *cake, announcements, seating charts* —"

Maddy laughed as Fiona sat straighter, her face lighting up as she said, "Oh, seating charts! Right! With all that happened on the dock, I almost forgot to ask. With Cooper staying on, I'd like to invite him to the wedding. So we'll need to reconfigure a few things."

Kerry didn't even want to begin to contemplate what it would be like to watch her sister say her I dos, then smash wedding cake all over the face of her ridiculously handsome and adorable groom, all with Cooper and his marriage proposal seated anywhere in the same room with her. No. Uh-uh. "See what I mean?" she said sweetly to Maddy before sliding her sister's lemon water in front of her.

"Lemon water sounds good for me, too," Maddy said, smiling as she slid onto the stool next to Fiona. Dart obediently sat next to the stool, then lay down when Maddy gave her a small hand command.

"She looks like she's doing really well," Fiona commented, watching the dog as she relaxed but kept her head up, eyes alert.

"She really is," Maddy said.

"Have you been training service dogs a long time? Interesting profession," Kerry said, sliding both women their drinks before turning to expertly chop a fresh lemon into wedges, then put them in a small bowl and place it between the two.

"It is," Maddy agreed. "I thought I wanted to be a veterinarian, but the schooling was prohibitively expensive, not to mention lengthy." She smiled that arresting smile of hers once again, and Kerry smiled with her. She already liked the young woman. "Then there was that part where I tend to get a little woozy at the sight of blood. Okay, maybe a lot woozy."

"Yeah, that would seriously cramp your veterinarian style," Fiona agreed with a laugh. "Not to mention dramatically narrow the list of services you could offer."

"Exactly," Maddy said, chuckling. "I

worked with the Humane Society and various other animal rescue services all through grade school and into college. I also trained my own dogs to show agility — pound puppies all of them, so that was the only way they could compete. I got into service dog training through a connection I made with one of the rescue volunteers." Her smile grew especially bright at that point.

"Oh," Fiona said, her own smile kicking up a notch as she leaned toward Maddy, a conspiratorial look on her face. "And does this volunteer have a name?"

Maddy lifted her hand to adjust her straw, modestly showing off a twinkling engagement ring. "He might."

Fiona hooted and grabbed Maddy's hand to take a closer look. Kerry just moaned in mock dismay. "Seriously, whatever it is you all are drinking, tell me so I can steer clear."

Fiona just patted Kerry's hand and smiled. "You keep telling yourself that, sweetie." Then she went right back to admiring the antique ring and setting.

"So is that shiny sparkler what brings you to Blueberry?" Kerry asked, busying herself starting the advance prep for when the pub opened later that afternoon. And not looking at engagement rings.

"Yes, actually," Maddy said with a final

flash of the ring. "I'm engaged to Micah Libretti."

Fiona's face lit up as only a fellow bride's would, but Kerry's smile was equally sincere. "Sal's nephew? That's wonderful. Congratulations." Sal owned the only auto repair place in the Cove and had lived there all his sixty-plus years. "His uncle gives us regular updates on Micah's deployment over in Afghanistan."

Maddy nodded. "He's coming home in four months. I just finished out my contract with a state-run service program in Columbus, Georgia — he did basic training at Fort Benning while I was attending Columbus State. That's where we met. So I'm moving here to get settled in before he comes home."

"Another Cove wedding," Fiona crowed, shooting a smug smile toward Kerry. "Oh! I just thought of something else. Did you know that my older sister Hannah actually drove Micah's blue Mustang for a bit when her little Fiat got banged up on her way back into town for her wedding? That accident is how she met her husband."

"I heard about that." Maddy grinned. "I drive a big Ford SUV, easier for transporting dogs and training gear. But I admit I might have jumped on the chance to take care of his 'baby' when he asked if I'd get it back out of storage and drive it some for him."

"Hannah didn't want to give it back," Kerry told her. "I think you'll enjoy it. It's a convertible, so Dart there might enjoy it, too."

Maddy laughed. "We'll see."

"So what brings you to the Rusty Puffin? Or, more specifically, to see Fergus?" This from Fiona.

"Well, I wanted to ask him if it was okay if I brought Dart in during some of the busier times to help with her training. Then we got to talking and, well, I'm going to be helping out here, too." She smiled, clearly pleased by the prospect. "I bartended through college down in Georgia, so it's familiar territory and will give me something to do while I get settled in and get things sorted out with a few of the local rescue organizations and service dog breeders."

"I wasn't aware we had any of those," Fiona said.

"Well, by local I mean from Bar Harbor on up the coast, all the way to Lubec. And as far inland as Bangor. A few hours in any direction."

"That's a lot of driving," Fiona said.

"Not really. I mean, I'm game for it; I like

168

traveling, but once I take on a dog, I'll have him or her here with me. I'm hoping eventually to set up a facility here, train people to do what I do, see where that takes me. I'm in the process of looking into all the certifications and criteria needed to launch my own nonprofit."

Kerry listened to the conversation with one ear, but the moment Maddy had confided her newest job opportunity, Kerry's thoughts had spun wildly off in a different direction. Fergus had done it. He'd hired someone. A very capable, dynamic, confident someone to help out at the pub. He hadn't even talked to her about it. Not that he had to; it was his place. But given how irascible he'd been whenever she'd so much as mentioned the idea that maybe they should look for someone to help out, getting him used to the idea that he couldn't run the place alone, it was somewhat shocking to witness his abrupt about-face. And she hadn't even been part of it.

"Kerry?"

Kerry's attention jerked back to the conversation. She continued cutting up the bowl of lemons. "Sorry," she said. "Got distracted." She motioned to the cutting board with the tip of her knife, then kept chopping, careful not to look at Fiona, who she was certain would read something in Kerry's expression that she really didn't want to discuss. "What did I miss?"

"You're about to miss your sailing lunch date with Mr. Dead-Sexy Aussie. Logan said Fergus had it covered here and I guess he meant it."

Kerry glanced up in time to see Fiona shoot Maddy a grin. Kerry had pretty good instincts about people, as did Fergus. She liked Madison Diba and knew she'd likely fit right in here at the Cove. Marrying one of the town's favorite sons who also happened to be a war hero wouldn't hurt her street cred either. She was bright, outgoing, and just a little eccentric, with her service poodle and all. Still, it rankled, being outmaneuvered.

Fergus banged through the swinging doors, leaning on his knobby wood cane with one hand, balancing a small plastic storage container of water in the other. "He did mean it," Fergus said, picking up the conversation as if he'd been listening all along. And of course he probably had been. "I've got things covered here, lass," he said as Kerry smoothly lifted the bobbing water container from his shaky hand and set it on the bar by Maddy.

Fergus shot Maddy a grin. "We've some

time to go over things before we open the doors this afternoon. And you'll be back this evening to take over," he said to Kerry. "You can hang on longer if you're game, lass," he told Maddy, his Irish brogue thickening as he piled on the charm. "Though I suspect the five o'clock revelers will be enough for your girl there." He nodded toward Dart. "Might want to break her into the nightly melee here a wee bit slowly. You can always put her in the office, or upstairs in our private quarters if —"

"Thank you," Maddy broke in, looking a bit abashed. "That's very kind of you. I don't want to intrude any more than I already am." She cast a quick smile in Kerry's direction, making Kerry wonder if she'd hidden her disconcertment over the speedy hiring as well as she thought she had. "Dart will be fine here or in the office. Not to worry."

"Go on," Fiona said, making a shooing motion toward Kerry with her hands. "We've got things under control here."

" 'We'?" Kerry repeated. "Shouldn't you be out sampling cake or agonizing over invitation fonts? Assuming you don't have clients to design interiors for."

"I have clients," Fiona replied easily, honest joy beaming from her every pore. "Very

171

happy ones. Trust me, after running Mc-Crae Interiors, I can juggle Fiona's Finds and planning a wedding at the same time with my eyes closed."

Kerry gave her sister a hard time — it was what they did — but she was truly happy for Fiona, with both her new business success and her lovely and loving relationship with their longtime family friend, Ben Campbell. Fiona had sold a successful business in Manhattan to return home and start over. She'd just opened a small design studio in a converted cottage near the harbor, focusing on recycling and repurposing antique and vintage items into something fresh and new. Her designs were both eco-friendly and wallet friendly, and the Cove had embraced her return home and her new business with equal enthusiasm.

"Remember you said that," Kerry commented. "When it's go time on the big aisle walk and you're still running around like a crazy person trying to pull everything together at the last second, I don't want to hear about it."

Fiona batted her eyelashes again as she took an extralong sip on the straw in her glass of lemon water. "I'm the epitome of a happy, relaxed bride. McCrae girls don't do bridezilla. Well, Hannah didn't, Alex was lovely, and I'm charming of course." She looked at Kerry over the tip of her straw, smiling sweetly. "We'll reserve final judgment until it's your turn."

"Har, har," Kerry said, but Fiona was high on wedding crack again so she let her run with it.

"Besides, after handling weddings for Logan, Hannah, and the Grace-Delia double do out on that island, this will be a cakewalk. Ha!" Fiona went on, then laughed. "Cakewalk."

"You're a designer? And you do weddings?" Maddy turned on her stool and spun Fiona on hers until they were facing each other. She gripped Fiona's forearms and grinned. "Hello, my new best and dearest friend."

"Oh, brother." Kerry surrendered, tossing her towel on the bar before turning and giving Fergus a hug and a loud, noisy kiss on his ruddy cheek, leaving the two women to bride bond with each other as she whispered in his ear, "We're going to talk about all this, you know."

Fergus's blue eyes were brimming with cheer, not the least bit daunted, as she lifted her head and looked into his beloved face.

"Oh, I suspect we will," he said, then took her arm and squeezed it, all the love and affection he had for the youngest McCrae close to filling his eyes to overflowing. "I've done what I've done to clear the path for ye, lass. Do what your heart tells you to do. I'll nae hear a word of anything or anyone being the cause of holding you back, least of all me."

All of her annoyance at his meddling and upper-handedness was sucked straight out of her with that single proclamation. She should have seen, should have known that the only thing that would have pushed Fergus into taking such a huge step was the thought that he was doing it for her. Which also explained why he hadn't told her or consulted her on the new hire. And why he'd been getting all chatty with Cooper behind her back. Because they both knew that if he'd discussed any of it with her first, she'd have told him what she'd been telling everyone else who wouldn't listen to her: She wasn't marrying Cooper Jax.

She gave him a tight, one-armed hug, kissed the top of his bald head, then leaned back so she could look him in the eye. "I love you. I know you want what's best for me, but I'm still figuring that out. And I want to do that for myself. When I need help or advice, you know I'll come to you, right?"

He took her comments as she'd taken his: to heart. But while his love for her shone in his eyes, he wasn't looking exactly abashed about the whole thing. "Indeed I do, lass. But you'll have to indulge an auld man for doing what he knows is best by those he loves. Ye ken?"

"I do." When he brightened at her saying those two particular words and winked, she narrowed her gaze, but knew he could still see the same love brimming in her eyes. "Don't get any ideas, laddie," she told him, adopting his brogue with perfect pitch. "We've got enough folks spouting those words around here. It's to the point now where even if I wanted to get married, I would resist just to keep from running with the herd."

He chuckled and she gave him another quick kiss, then pushed through the doors into the kitchen.

Fifteen minutes later she was up in her loft bedroom, freshly showered, standing naked in front of the hulking antique chifforobe, debating what to wear on her sailing date. "What *do* you wear for a man who kissed you like he was making babies?" Go the demure route, so he knows you're not there to continue indulging in that kind of behavior? She snorted. Yeah, she couldn't exactly pull off chaste and demure. Audrey Hepburn in *Roman Holiday* she was not.

So maybe something more her style, something loose fitting and comfortable that she didn't mind getting wet? She looked at the clothes jammed in the wardrobe and laughed. Yeah. Pretty much everything she owned fit under that heading. Femme fatale were not the words generally used when describing her.

A slow smile curved her lips. Well. Not usually anyway. *Hmm.* "Should you? Or shouldn't you?" she pondered, thinking about an impulse purchase she'd made some years back, in a beautiful music- and flower-filled street market in French Polynesia.

Smiling at her reflection, she could feel her skin start to tingle with anticipation as her thoughts turned to how she would like to spend her time with Cooper on the high seas of Pelican Bay for this long, hot, sunny afternoon.

He thought he wanted to marry her because that's the kind of man he was. Home, hearth, family, and roots. Really deep roots. He couldn't imagine anything else. Kerry, on the other hand, still thought maybe they just had a really bad itch that they'd never got to scratch. She'd told him as much, so there was no leading anyone on, no subterfuge. She wanted to scratch that itch and he was hoping she'd realize it could be more than that.

And, okay, so maybe they both might want to scratch it more than once. Or a whole lot of times. But they had an entire month to indulge themselves, to go ahead and just do whatever they wanted to do. Perhaps it was best not to waste any time, head right on down that path now. Then, once they'd burned that need out of their systems, he'd see past the horny haze of pheromones and realize she'd been right all along. She really wasn't wife material after all. But at least when he headed back home again, they'd have a month of memories to look back on with fondness. And maybe a little lingering desire. But that wouldn't be so bad, would it?

"Well," she murmured, knowing damn well she was rationalizing because she wanted Cooper Jax like she wanted air to breathe, "I suppose there's only one way to find out."

Her smile shifted to one that might have been a little predatory, bordering on carnal, but once she'd allowed herself to consider this new course of action, the rest of her had leaped so enthusiastically on board with the idea, there really was no point in pretending otherwise.

She very deliberately shoved all thoughts of weddings, marriages, roots, and home from her mind. Her home, his home, and any possibility of a future where their home might be one and the same. This afternoon was for exploring needs and desires that were far more immediate in nature. And intimate. They needed to answer the big question the two of them had danced around for the entire year they'd spent together. And that was to find out just what would happen if they simply gave in to desire, got naked, then got on with the business of finding out what it would be like simply to have each other. In the most carnal and primal way a man and woman could. Maybe the rest of the questions would answer themselves after that. Or not. But this one needed answering first.

So let's just put that one to bed straight off, shall we?

She wiggled her eyebrows at her reflection. "And put us to bed while we're at it." She laughed, and it felt so good, so . . . freeing. Why had she let herself get so worked up about all this? Why hadn't she just gone and taken the dive, doing what she did best? She was an inveterate adventurer who knew, better than anyone, that the only way to discover what was around the next bend was to keep heading down the trail until you found out.

She dove into the wardrobe, a woman on a mission now, flinging clothes over her shoulder, digging all the way to the back. "Aha!" she barked in triumph, tugging out the cute jungle-print, sarong-style sundress she'd bought because she'd felt daring that hot afternoon in Bora Bora. There was a big beach festival that night, featuring food and dance and probably more liquor than was advisable, and she'd decided she was going to cut loose and have herself some fun. And she'd wanted to look like a woman when she did it.

Her grin grew as she recalled how that night had ended up going in a far more Kerry typical kind of way. She'd wound up, as she recalled, heading out with some locals in dugout boats to night fish on a river tributary only they knew how to reach. They'd eaten their catch huddled around a fire on a remote, secret beach, under the moon and stars, while the island natives regaled her with big tales — emphasis on tales — of their mighty fishing prowess. It had been a magical night. The dress had been shoved into her duffel, but there hadn't come another time to wear it.

"Until now." She shook it out. The fabric was soft, silky, and the bold pattern hid the wrinkles fairly well. She studied it, wondering if she dared, then grinned as she pictured Cooper's face when he saw it. It would be worth any discomfort she might feel — she really wasn't a dress person — just for that one moment. It covered the essentials. Barely. She pulled it on, tugged it into place, and checked it out from all angles. Snug didn't begin to define the fit.

Determined not to chicken out, she faced front, fluffed up her red curls, and smiled. "You're going to do this. Besides, if you do wear this" — she tugged the bodice up a bit higher over the newly created swell between her otherwise very average-size breasts — "you probably won't have to keep it on very long." She turned, tugged down the hem in the back, where it barely cupped her derrière. "So there's that."

She quickly dug around until she found a pair of flat sandals that wouldn't land her overboard if the water got rough. Thinking of the temperature difference out on the water and not wanting to freeze her sarong off, and, okay, maybe to give her a little something more to cover herself up with, she reached back in and grabbed the only thing she had: a faded old hoodie sweatshirt. "Next time, buy a cute wrap to go with the dress." There was nothing for it now, though, so she wrapped the sweatshirt around her tanned shoulders and tied it Audrey style, slid on a pair of sunglasses, and struck a pose in front of the mirror. "You femme fatale you."

Snorting a laugh, she grabbed the only headwear she had. Not exactly a jaunty, Audrey-approved scarf, no. It was an old canvas fishing hat. "But whaddya gonna do? I yam what I yam." With that, she bounced down the back stairs before she could change her mind and climbed quickly into her truck before anyone else could see her.

She might not be getting married anytime soon, but if she was lucky, she was about to have some afternoon delight on a sailboat with a dead-sexy Australian hunk of a man who'd kissed her like she was the last woman on earth.

Her body felt all shivery and alive as she gunned the engine of the old truck. "Sorry, Audrey, it's not a Vespa, but it'll get me where I'm going." Her cheeks were warm and her body felt like it could set off sparks as she pulled out of the lot, leaving a bit of gravel spurting in her wake. "And where

I'm going, I'm planning on getting very, very lucky."

CHAPTER NINE

Cooper wasn't sure she'd show. He'd gone after Logan to get the boat info, and when he'd returned not two minutes later, the women had all departed. He'd gone back into the inn, but there was no sign of Kerry. Grace and Delia had simply grinned and wished him good luck.

Luck. He'd need more than luck to get Kerry to give him a real chance. He hadn't handled a single thing right since stepping on American soil. He'd thought to charm his way in, but clearly that had been just as boneheaded a move as showing up at her family-owned pub and all but proposing to her in front of everyone she'd known since birth.

"Yeah, you're a real sharp one you are, mate," he muttered as he paced the dock. He hadn't a lick of experience in a boat of any kind, so he'd hired the boat captain Logan had recommended along with the boat. He wasn't looking for anything more than some time out on the water, away from everyone else — save the captain — to relax, enjoy each other's company, and hopefully fall back into the natural rhythm they'd always had together. Where that led he wasn't sure and, for today anyway, he didn't particularly care. He just needed a starting point, that was all. Something to build on. Maybe the presence of the boat captain would prove he didn't have any ulterior motives. He just wanted them to have some time alone.

A clearing of a gravelly throat pulled him from his thoughts. He turned and looked at Thomas, the boat captain, who was seventy if he was a day.

"I think that's your party there," the older man said, nodding toward the gravel lot at the end of the dock. If he seemed a bit uncomfortable, Cooper chalked it up to the rather taciturn older man being thrust into what, based on the bits and pieces of the conversations Cooper had overheard while eating breakfast at the café that morning, was the biggest gossip story to hit the Cove in ages. Maybe the boat captain had been secretly hoping Kerry wouldn't show and he'd be excused from chaperoning duties.

Cooper was too relieved that Kerry had

come to get distracted by what the captain was thinking or feeling. He turned around, a welcoming grin on his face, then went completely, utterly still. Even his heart seemed to have stuttered to a stop. *Holy jumping mother of — what in the hell was she wearing?* He'd just been hoping she'd show at all and assumed he'd have to cajole her out of being annoyed with him for his high-handedness. Again. Only she sure didn't look annoyed.

She looked . . . like an edible tray of ripe, luscious fruit. With him being the only guest invited to the bountiful buffet. *Sweet Jesus.* How was he supposed to keep his hands to himself with her wearing nothing more than a glorified bandana?

She drew closer, and her smile turned a shade smug. She was clearly enjoying his all but cartoon character worthy, goggling reaction. And well, hell, what did she expect? He was a red-blooded male whose bed had remained strikingly empty since her departure. Since long before then, truth be told.

"Hi, Thomas," she called to the boat captain as she closed the remaining distance between them, still smiling brightly. If she was uncomfortable in her little getup in front of the older man — a man, Cooper supposed, she had to know, given everybody

185

knew everyone in such a small village — she didn't show it. Instead, she said, "Did they rook you into being our captain today?"

The old man's cheeks were beet red in a way that had nothing to do with decades of harsh weather. He nodded somewhat tensely. "Did indeed, Miss Kerry. Good to, uh, good to see ya," he managed to choke out, trying to look anywhere but at the expanse of bare leg and curvy cleavage.

Cooper would have felt sorry for the man, but he was too busy trying to get his own voice back.

Kerry walked over to the boat and nimbly hopped aboard without waiting for assistance, tipping up on her sandaled toes so she could buss the old man loudly on his cheek. He went from red to scarlet, making Cooper fear old Thomas might drop dead right there on deck from a heart attack.

She patted the captain's arm, smiling confidently as she said, "Well, you officially have a paid afternoon off. I've got this. And don't worry, I'll take as good care of her as if she were my own."

The older man looked from her to Cooper, relief and concern waging a battle on his craggy face, before he looked back to her, his gaze aimed somewhere past her left shoulder now. "Miss Kerry, I don't think —"

She patted his arm again. "Come on, Tom, you know I've been sailing since before I could walk. I could run these lines in my sleep. But if it makes you feel any better, we're just going to putter out to the edge of the harbor and drop anchor for a nice lunch, then putter back. No sailing."

Thomas looked back to Cooper, still clearly concerned, but relief was winning the war and there was a decidedly hopeful look in his faded blue eyes. "Mr. Jax, Chief McCrae was pretty clear about my taking the helm, and —"

Cooper climbed back on board, though perhaps not quite as nimbly as Kerry had. He could ride a horse blindfolded, but getting his sea legs might take a moment or two. "No worries, mate. I trust the lady. We'll be fine." *And alone. So very, very alone.*

Under any other circumstances, and given the intent behind Kerry's wardrobe choices, he'd be thrilled with that particular outcome. But when he added in the borderline feral smile Kerry shot his way the moment he'd agreed with her plan, he swallowed hard, wondering just who was being high-handed now. "Enjoy the afternoon off, Tom," he said, thinking, *in for a penny, in for a pound.*

"No, no fee," Thomas said. "Wouldn't be right."

"We've kept you from booking another fare," Cooper said, "so —"

"I'm retired; I just agreed to help because —"

"Because my police-chief brother thought his thirty-one-year-old baby sister needed a chaperone." Kerry beamed at Thomas, who flushed all over again. "It's okay, Tom. You were a peach to agree to do this, but trust me, we're fine." She slipped her arm through Cooper's but didn't so much as glance his way. "I know my brother and Cooper would want you to keep whatever they paid you. Enjoy your afternoon. Go buy your lovely wife, Gladys, some pretty flowers, take her out to lunch. It's a beautiful afternoon for it, don't you think?"

Cooper had to stifle a laugh when the old salt blanched at the thought of an afternoon spent with his wife, then turned beet red again when Kerry winked at him. Apparently his aging heart had taken all it could; he made his good-byes and climbed back onto the dock.

"Just have her back before the tide goes out," he said from the pier. "Tie her up here. I'll move her over to my slip later."

"Aye aye, Captain," Kerry said with a jovial salute, slipping her arm from Cooper's and stepping over to the steering console and its big, beautifully restored teak wheel.

Tom cast off the ropes mooring the boat to the dock, tossing the ends in to Cooper, who caught them and quickly spun them into a neat pool on the deck. Ropes he knew a little something about.

Kerry waved as Thomas ambled back down the dock, then turned a key, and somewhere in the bowels of the two-masted boat an engine purred to life.

"This beast has a motor?"

"Well, we don't typically sail it right up to the dock."

He nodded. "I suppose that makes sense."

"First time on a sailboat?" she asked, as casually as if she wasn't standing there, gripping the wheel of a sleek, forty-foot sailing vessel while looking like sex candy on a stick.

"First time on any boat," he told her.

She turned that smile on him again, and his body leaped to attention, while his mind leaped to wondering just what it was she had in mind. Looks might be deceiving. But he was beginning to hope they weren't.

"Looks like you'll be getting a few firsts in this afternoon, then." With that little bombshell dropped, she calmly looked back to the water as she navigated the boat away from the pier and through the other vessels tied up along the maze of docks and piers, some of them sailboats but more of them working ones.

With nothing else to do, and fairly certain if he stared at her in that tropical print napkin any longer he'd simply lunge at her, he made his way over to the picnic basket and cooler and stowed both in one of the big storage bins Thomas had showed him earlier.

Once that was accomplished, with nothing else to do but be a passenger on a date he was apparently no longer in charge of, he went with the new flow, leaned against the rail and let the steady breeze riffle his hair and the sun warm his skin as he watched her quite capably maneuver them out toward the open harbor waters. Once they were away from the docks, there were still boats moored at anchor dotting their immediate landscape, but she nimbly eased the big boat through that bobbing and floating maze as well, and fairly quickly they were past all that and out on the open water. Alone.

The rumble of the engine was loud enough, combined with the brisker wind out on the open water, that the combined noise precluded easy conversation unless he were to go stand right beside her at the helm. He thought it might be more prudent, while she was steering anyway, to keep his hands and the rest of himself over by the rail. Instead, he took the time to ponder this apparent new game plan of hers . . . and tried to figure out just what he should do with it. He knew what he wanted to do with it, and it had nothing to do with the savory stash of Delia's delectables neatly packed into that picnic basket, or the bottle of wine Grace had tucked into the cooler as he'd headed out of the inn again. Though maybe a glass of the chilled white sauvignon wouldn't be such a bad start to the afternoon.

The wind continued to pick up as they eased out to the edge of the harbor, molding the silky jungle print fabric to her firm, athletic frame. Even in flat sandals, her tanned legs looked like they went on for miles, what with that short skirt hugging the firm curve of her backside, barely flirting past the spot where the curves ended and the back of her toned thighs began.

He casually crossed his legs at the ankle and shifted to give his body's response to her barely there outfit some room in the rapidly tightening fit of his Daks, glad he'd untucked the shirt. Back on Cameroo, she'd generally worn loose-fitting, unisex work trousers and equally loose-fitting cotton or chambray shirts over white T-shirts — standard Cameroo gear — along with heavy leather work boots or black rubber barn Wellies, depending on the tasks at hand. He'd seen her bare legs from the knees down in the knicker-length khaki shorts she favored in the hot months, along with her bare shoulders when she'd rolled the sleeves of her T-shirts up and over them when the sun was high overhead and the air sweltering.

He'd spent quality time imagining what the rest of her body looked like underneath all that baggy khaki and cotton. He knew her legs were strong and lean from watching her ride, as were her arms from the heavy work that station life demanded. Her backside was trim and, from the lack of curves in the front, so were her breasts, but while he wouldn't have described her body as exactly boyish, neither had it ever struck him as being particularly curvy, much less voluptuous.

Seeing her now, though, all bound up in tightly wound, flimsy, stretchy silk, he realized how desperately wrong he'd been about that. Her bum was trim, aye, but curved and toned, perfect for a man to cup his hands around when he pulled her close between his own thighs. And don't get him started on her breasts. He doubted that sarong came with padding, which meant the soft, full swell of cleavage there in front was all natural . . . also the perfect fit for a man's hands. His mouth watered as he imagined pert, dark nipples, growing taut as he rubbed his thumbs over them, budding even more tightly as he slowly tugged the fabric down under the swell of flesh beneath. He'd slide his hands around her waist, cup that beautiful backside of hers, and pull her in close so he could lean down and taste each perfectly tight, plump nipple, taking his time to savor them, until her head tipped back and she offered herself up to him, pressing her hips into his, and —

"Cooper? You feeling okay?"

At Kerry's shouted query, he blinked his eyes open and found himself staring straight up at the sky, his hands gripping the rail so tight his knuckles were likely white.

"If you're feeling queasy —"

"No," he said, choking back a bark of a laugh. *About ready to climb out of my skin and on top of yours, maybe.* "Just enjoying the moment," he called back over the

193

rumbling engine, speaking truthfully enough. He subtly tried to clear the gravel from his throat, looking anywhere but directly at her, and added, "I can see why you love it out here." Also true.

The water was a gorgeous, surprising shade of turquoise, the color so deep and rich it almost looked too beautiful to be real. The sky above was a never-ending expanse of mirrored, brilliant blue, and the steady breeze filled the air with the sharp tang of salt and brine, accompanied by the snapping sound of the heavy canvas sails as they went taut, then slack, then taut again when the wind rippled through them. Frothy whitecaps topped the chop of the rougher waters out in the bay ahead, while the joyous shrieks and high-pitched calls of seabirds split the air as they coasted on air currents, dipping and diving above, occasionally plunging into the water and coming up with dinner dangling from either side of a clenched beak. It was all like something out of a soaring seafaring novel, as picturesque as anything a storyteller or a movie director could have dreamed up in his mind's eye.

Cooper caught her smile from the corner of his eye and wasn't sure if the knowing gleam was one of agreement, or if she suspected where his mind really had been. He casually uncrossed his legs and turned to face the water directly, watching the far horizon bob up and down as he willed a certain part of his body to stop bobbing at all. *All in due time,* he thought. *Or not,* he silently added, still not entirely sure she wasn't playing him, as a revenge of sorts, for all his high-handed maneuvers leading them up to this point. He couldn't say he'd blame her for it. He had been running a bit roughshod in his manhandling of her daily routine, her whole life, really, since his arrival.

His attention caught on the sight of Brodie's massive historic schooner, sitting low in the water off to their north. He motioned toward it. "Any chance of a drive-by?"

She shook her head. "I don't want to get that far out. We don't have that much time before the tide rolls out."

He nodded, not having thought about that when he'd planned their little excursion. The extreme highs and lows of the tide would create problems getting a boat the size of the one they were on all the way back in to the dock. He understood now why all those larger boats had been anchored out in the deeper waters of the harbor, and why most of them had smaller inflatable skiffs tied on to the back, as did this boat, he knew, though it was currently strapped to a back launch deck. Much easier to zip those in to the docks or the shore when traveling and back out again, he supposed. "How long do we have?"

"A couple hours."

Was he imagining the amusement he heard in her voice? The hint of suggestion? *Do you think she wore a dress so small you could tuck it into the pocket of your trousers and leave room to spare because she wanted to catch some rays?*

He suspected his mind had tripped along to exactly the place she'd hoped it would. The only question that remained was why. He sincerely doubted she'd suddenly changed her mind and was ready to run back to Oz with him. So . . . what then? A wild fling on the high seas? Or at least on the relatively tame waters of Half Moon Harbor?

Logic told him that was not the way to get things started between them. He wanted her so badly at that moment he would happily have peeled that dress off her with his teeth. And no amount of mind over hard-on was going to talk his body out of what it wanted either. But to what end? If they

196

jumped straight from unwilling to even consider his proposal to what he quite suspected would be the sexual highlight of his entire life, what came next? He knew the likely answer was more of the same.

He doubted a few short weeks would be enough to sate even the tip of his hunger for her. So they'd tear up the sheets and immerse themselves in every carnal delight they could dream up until they exhausted themselves. And then it would be time for him to leave. With nothing of what they needed to talk through, allow themselves the time to discover, having even been broached. He wanted them to partner each other in all ways, not just the naked, sweaty ones.

So . . . no. It might kill him, but, for now, he was going to keep his mind on talking to her, enjoying her company unencumbered by her vast pool of family and friends, just the two of them, renewing their relationship one on one, only now with so much more on the table for consideration than simply friendship and a working relationship.

The sound of the engine cut off abruptly, and the resulting silence, save for the snap of the wind in the sails, was filled a moment later with the sound of heavy links being unspooled, indicating the anchor was being dropped. Apparently electronically, because it wasn't visible anywhere on deck. He remained at the rail, his back to her, realizing there was another part to this, too: While he was pushing to see if they could have it all, she was apparently willing to settle for having some kind of temporary physical relationship with him.

It wasn't only that he felt a bit insulted by that but that she'd never, ever struck him as the type to settle for anything, and certainly never someone who had a casual attitude about sex. Quite the opposite in fact. The number of women on staff at Cameroo was in the single digits. So adding a smart, beautiful, strong woman to the staff was akin to painting a bull's-eye on her back for every single, and likely not so single, man out there. Yet she'd kept to herself and, as far as he knew, hadn't so much as flirted with any Cameroo employee, much less anything more than that.

But now . . . now she was willing to take what she could get? He couldn't square that with the woman he knew, the one he'd fallen for.

He focused on the pitch and roll of the water moving the boat up and down, adapting pretty easily to the movement, as it turned out. Years spent on horseback had perhaps made him more naturally capable of achieving balance with steady motion. He tried to focus on that. *Remaining steady. Balanced. In all things.*

"So somebody said something about lunch?"

He turned to find her flipping up the thick red canvas cushion that was tied to the top of the long storage bin he'd stowed their lunch in earlier. She opened the lid, caught his gaze, then surprised him by straightening and letting it drop closed again, making him wonder exactly what she'd seen on his face. She braced a hand over her sunglasses to keep her red curls from tossing about over her face now that the wind was behind her, as well as to shade her brilliant, emerald green eyes from the sun.

"Not hungry yet?" he asked, trying for a smile, a little humor, wanting them to at least start off as he'd planned. Light, casual, taking some time to catch up on what they'd been doing the past year, ease in to whatever might come next. In the next moment he could have kicked himself for all but handing her the exact opening she was likely looking for. Not that she needed one. The dress had already done that for her.

He let go of the rail and reached down to flip up the lid again. She might have her own ideas about how this lunch date was going to go, but so did he. Besides, it was either grab the cooler and picnic hamper or grab her.

"Why don't we start with some wine?" he said. "Grace recommended it, said it was from a local winery."

He admitted it had made him feel good when her friends and family had decided to welcome him, or at least been open to the idea of his trying to pursue a relationship with Kerry. Which was saying a lot, he knew, given he'd begun his pursuit with the proposal of marriage. After his surprising discovery that no one save Fergus had even known of his existence prior to his arrival, he was grateful — and thankful — they hadn't simply run him out of town for the bold way he'd shown up and declared himself.

Stay on topic, mate. Focus. "We also have an assortment of Delia's delectables," he added, nodding toward the picnic hamper. "Hand selected by the chef herself. And Tom said there's a blanket in the other bin." He smiled at her, and wondered how he'd be able to pay proper homage to Delia's amazing lunch basket when the only thing he really wanted to savor was Kerry. In or out of that dress. *Delectable indeed.* "So,"

200

he said, clearing the roughness out of his throat. "Where should we set up?"

There was a narrow galley belowdeck and, he knew from Tom's brief tour earlier, there was also a small cabin tucked up in front, with a snug queen-size bed wedged inside and a small shower between the two. All completely outfitted, ready for its next occupants. He tried like hell not to think about that.

He knew she'd been about to say or do something when she'd closed the lid of the bin, but whatever it was, she let that go. He had no doubt she'd get back to it, if it was important to her.

"Foredeck," she said, motioning with her free hand to the expanse of white fiberglass and sealed teak that formed the raised, flat, front end of the boat, where the thick masts soared upward, rigged out under full sail. "You okay to maneuver up there? I can take the hamper."

"No worries," he said. "I've got it." Given the way things were going and the war he was waging with his body, better to keep his hands full for as long as humanly possible.

With only a bobble or two, they both made their way to the relatively flat surface of the topside front end of the boat. Ducking under the sails to get between the two thick masts, they pinned down the heavy blanket using the hamper, the cooler, and their bodies, to keep the breeze from flapping it straight off into the water.

Cooper set about taking the containers out of the hamper, careful not to pay too close attention to the way the barely there skirt of her sundress rode up even higher on her world-class legs. She rested on one hip, bracing her weight on one hand, miles of smooth, tanned leg casually stretched out to her side, crossed at the ankles. The fact that he was still very aware that they were parked directly over the snug bunk below didn't help matters at all.

Kerry made appreciative noises over the foods Delia had packed, wasting no time in helping herself to what she explained were called hush puppies — little breaded and fried bits of cornmeal heaven, as she described them — which were still steaming in their wrapped foil, airtight container. He'd always liked watching her eat, the way she savored every bite. It was one of the things that had endeared Kerry to his family as well. She didn't mince or pick at her food; she dove in and didn't apologize for having a hearty appetite. Goodness knew, as hard as she worked, there was no question she'd earned it.

At the moment, however, he thought watching her pop hush puppies into her mouth, closing her eyes as she relished every bite, might actually kill him. A little smear of the tartar sauce she'd been dipping them into had caught and clung to the corner of her mouth, requiring superhuman levels of restraint on his part to keep from clearing the blanket in a single lunge so he could take care of that creamy little dab. With his tongue.

He turned his attention to the wine, thinking, at that moment, he could probably rip the cork out with his teeth, and wondered how in the hell he was going to follow his own edict to keep his hands to himself for the duration of lunch, much less the entire boat ride.

Kerry groaned in satisfaction as she unwrapped a mini lobster roll and sampled it. "Here," she said between half-closed teeth as she finished her first bit. "You have to try one of these or you can't say you've really been to Maine."

He did as she asked, nodding in agreement but unable to think that anything, even the deliciously rich lobster salad and yeasty bread roll, had anything on the tasty morsel he really wanted to try. *So much for her being the one willing to settle.*

And maybe it was that fact still niggling him, or his own wavering on the matter, but he abruptly decided that, whatever their personal agendas might be, several hours of self-torture wasn't how he wanted to spend his hard-won time alone with her. He set down the container of fresh blueberries she'd been sampling and had offered to him to try next and pushed the wine bottle back through the open cooler flap into the ice packed inside before looking directly at Kerry. "I'm a bit confused here."

Kerry slid the finger she'd been licking out of her mouth with a little pop, her green eyes twinkling mischievously. "About?"

So that answered one question. She really was going to pursue her quite deliberate little plan to drive him straight out of his mind. And his clothes. And hers. He gestured to her, the motion of his hand indicating the entirety of her being. "What's all this, then?"

She looked down at herself, then back at him. To her credit, she didn't dissemble or feign innocence. "Overkill, I know." She was still smiling, but her expression was open, honest, her words sincere, when she said, "I guess I just wanted to make sure you knew I wasn't being ambiguous on the matter. I know you think there's something lasting to be had between us. Just as I've said that I think maybe it's more a case of the two of us having an itch we never scratched. You're here for a month and, well . . . I figured that would give us time to see which one of us is right. I know what you want and you know what I think, so no one is leading anyone on, no hidden agendas." She gestured to herself. "Not much of hidden anything, really."

"A bit calculating, don't you think?"

If his bald honesty in the face of her more charming playfulness bothered her, she didn't show it. She answered him just as squarely. "No. I think it's simply being honest and owning up to the reality of the situation. As I see it anyway. You said you'd regret it if you didn't at least come here and ask me what you wanted to ask before I left. Well, I've thought a lot about what you said, and about what I'd regret, now that you're here, and we have this chance to explore things. And at the moment, what I'd regret is letting you leave and not finding out what would have happened if that kiss we shared hadn't been interrupted."

"And . . . let the chips fall where they may?" he asked, somewhat surprised to feel a little anger push in alongside the desire and frustration. It wasn't her fault if she didn't feel what he felt. Except . . . he'd been the other half of that kiss. He'd felt the depth of her response, had seen the look in her eyes when he'd lifted his head. Had heard the truth in her voice when she'd said she wouldn't have turned him down if he'd started this when she'd still been on Cameroo.

Her smile softened a bit then, though the openness and directness of her her gaze was still there. "I'm not being cavalier, Cooper. Although I know it probably sounds — and looks — that way. I know emotions are involved here. And not just yours. We had a great working relationship and a really good friendship. I know I haven't shown it since I left, but I did care about you — do care — about all of you. It's just —" She broke off for a moment, seeming to gather her thoughts. Or her courage. "I don't get involved," she said in something of a rush, leading him to believe it had been the latter. "Not on a family level, not on a personal level. So getting so close to you and your family was new to me. And while I'd like to think I'm better than that, the truth is, I did what I usually do; I ducked out, moved on to the next thing, and didn't look back." She held his gaze. "That's who I am; that's who you're trying to get involved with."

"Kerry —"

She lifted a hand, stalling him. "But while I moved on, I didn't forget you. Any of you. Try as I might," she admitted, looking apologetic, but straightforward as well. "And now you're here and I'm suddenly forced to confront all that. How I felt then, how I feel now. This" — she gestured to the two of them — "is new to me. I have no idea of the right way to handle it. And clearly my track record isn't so great at handling anything that requires commitment of any kind. So I'm moving blind here, feeling my way while trying not to string you along."

She ducked her chin briefly; then, when she lifted her gaze again, she held his even more directly than before, as if beseeching him to crawl inside her head and understand how she was feeling, what this was doing to her, and maybe help explain it to her while he was at it. Whether or not he was going to like the rest of what she had to say, he respected her for confronting the subject, and him, head-on. No bullshit, his starfish. She was as frank and honest as she'd always been. It was one of the reasons he'd come halfway around the world to see her again. He'd never met anyone like her.

"The way I see it," she went on, "our

friendship, and our working relationship, were solid foundations we built over time. Now you're here wanting more, and the way we started that next step was with a kiss. So I feel like we've done just about everything two people can do in getting to know each other except . . . finish that kiss. It seemed to me that the logical next step, the next piece of information we needed to know, was what comes next when we let that kiss go to its natural conclusion."

She did smile then, and her emerald green eyes blazed as she let down a guard he didn't know she'd still had erected, letting him see for the first time the rest of what she was feeling. "Or at least that was my rationale for finally letting myself have what I fantasized about having, all those months I worked next to you."

He opened his mouth, then shut it again when her words sank in. "I — what did you just say?"

Her smile remained, but there was a new light flickering in the depths of her eyes now, one that somehow managed to look bold, excited, and endearingly nervous all at the same time. "You weren't alone, Cooper, in wanting . . . what you wanted. At least the physical attraction part anyway. I should have been more forthright about that when you showed up at the pub, or afterward. But at least try to see this from my perspective. Suddenly, out of the blue, the man I lusted after all those months was standing, quite improbably, right in front of me, in his full, Technicolor gorgeousness, looking even better than the guy I was sure I'd exaggerated and romanticized. Right there, in the flesh. And before I could even begin to get a grip on that, you went all going down on bended knee on me, and — it was all so much, too much, to even begin to process."

She let out a short, disbelieving laugh. "Maybe if you'd just dragged me into your arms and not given me a chance to think, I might have surrendered right there on the spot, and the rest of the Cove be damned. But instead you're all sincere, with your big, beautiful heart hanging on your sleeve, all earnest and lovely, and I so didn't deserve anything like that, not after the way I left things between me and your entire family. I didn't have the first clue what to do with that. With you." Her smile turned decidedly rueful. "So, naturally, I resorted to form. I shut you down, told you to go away. If I couldn't run away, I was going to make damn sure you did. I mean, it was one thing to leave Cameroo, then insult you and your family by not keeping in touch. It was another thing entirely to do it again, right to your face."

"I hate to interrupt," he said, trying like hell not to grin, then drag her into his lap to do what he apparently should have done the moment he'd laid eyes on her again. "But I haven't heard a word you've said since that part where you've been lusting after me for two years."

Desire flashed in her eyes, undoing him further, but she held him off. "I need to finish; I need to say all the things I should have then. And I apologize for the getup, for the overkill. But that's the rest of what you need to know. Apparently we were both having our own private lustful thoughts, but you have to understand, you're proposing marriage, and I didn't even know you ever noticed there was a woman underneath the barn clothes and beat-up old Akubra. So I hope you'll forgive me, but it's taking me a little time to play catch-up." She sat upright and tucked her feet under her legs. "I really don't want to lead you on, even though I know this dress makes it seem otherwise. But lust . . . lust is at least an emotion or feeling I understand. I don't understand any of the rest of what you want. I've done nothing to show you I could handle anything more than maybe indulging in our physical attraction, and everything to prove to you that I would be a miserable disaster at anything that required more dedication that that. You asked me what I would have done then, if you'd made it known how you felt, and I was honest with you. But how I would have responded then, and what I want to do about it now, here . . . with life as it is now . . ."

She lifted a shoulder in a helpless little gesture that jerked a little knot in his heart, though her gaze still didn't waver. "So I thought maybe we should start with that first part. The lust part. The part I have some passing clue what to do with. But only if you understand that that's all I know I can offer. It's not that I don't or wouldn't maybe have an interest in taking things from friendship to something more . . . involved. It's not about respecting you enough or about worth. The only one unworthy here is me. If I was still on Cameroo, I think we can both safely say that if you'd made a pass at me, it wouldn't have taken us long to take that first kiss to its natural conclusion. So when I came here today, I thought, why do it differently, just because we're here, not there?"

"Kerry —"

She lifted her hand again, briefly, apologetically. "I'm sorry; I know I'm all over the place. Just . . . let me work this all the way through. I'm figuring this out as I go, and there's a time element involved on top of all of it. I don't want to be making more stupid mistakes, and I don't want to hurt you. Or me. We're adults. We want each other. Can that be a place to start? Or is it all or nothing?"

Cooper straightened and had to work harder than before to keep his hands to himself. But for entirely different reasons now. She was laying herself bare to him. No artifice, no excuses, just straight-up, in your face, this is what I am, love, and, fair warning, it might not be enough. She was breaking his heart and proving he could want her even more than he had before, all at the same time. Because he knew she was being as honest as she was able, and while he might want to tell himself a fairy tale about how their coming together in some fiery ball of lust and desire would somehow transform her into the dedicated, loyal partner for all eternity he wanted her to be . . . he knew it *was* a fairy tale.

And he wasn't ready to accept that yet. He'd waited too long, risked so much in taking this chance; he just wasn't going to up and quit on it. Or her. "And then what?" he heard himself ask, forcing the words past the gravel in his throat.

Now she frowned. "And then what, what?"

"Your plan is that we romp around a bit, get it out of our systems, then what? You're thinking we'll both just pack up our toys and return to life as usual? Thanks for the ride, have a safe trip home?"

She shocked him by not being hurt by his swipe.

No. Not his Kerry. What she did was wiggle her eyebrows, all but willing the suggestive twinkle into her eyes, and a bit of playfulness into what had become a very revealing, vulnerable moment. "You brought toys?"

He knew he should respond in kind, allow her to shift the mood, but he couldn't.

She reached out and took hold of his arm, her fingers still sticky from blueberry juice.

"Cooper, I wasn't trying — I don't want to hurt you. That's what this whole conversation was about. I don't want to get hurt either. We're two consenting adults. I honestly thought —"

"That if we rolled around a bit, had a few laughs, and shared a climax or two, we'd, what, get it all out of our system? I'd realize that I came all this way because what I really needed was to get laid? Because I hate to burst whatever bubble you're building around this, but if all I'd needed was that, I'm fairly certain I could have taken care of it back at home."

Now she did look abashed, and a little hurt. Maybe more than a little.

Now who was handling this all wrong? That would be the same one who'd been handling it wrong since he got here.

He swore under his breath, then said, "I'm sorry. That was out of line. I'm . . . I understand you're being frank with me. And I appreciate that more than you know. Now I'm the one left trying to pull it together. I know I caught you badly off guard just showing up like this, with all these grandiose ideas I apparently have about what the future could hold for us." He straightened a little and took her hand from his arm, held it in his own, then just said what was in his heart. "But I've had quite a long time to think on it, and I know what I want. Along with that, I guess I know what I'm willing to take. And what I'm not. I think more of you than, well, than this."

She ducked her chin then, and he hated that more than anything. He let go of her hand, tipped her chin up until their eyes met. "Don't misunderstand me. I want you," he said quite sincerely. "I want you so bad my teeth ache. You've gotten to me, hook, line, and sinker. I want to drag you down to that little bunk below by your hair and take you until we both howl at the moon."

He watched her eyes widen, then darken with desire. Her throat worked, and it was all he could do not to yank her directly into his lap, peel that thing off her, and take her right there on top of the boat, in full view of anyone who happened to sail by.

"But if I do that, the very last thing I'll want to do is let you go. And if you think that a few tumbles will cure us of this hunger we have for each other . . . well then, I think I should be getting back to Australia. Because clearly what I want of you, need of you, isn't at all what you want or need of me."

CHAPTER TEN

This wasn't going at all how she'd imagined when she'd taken a risk on wearing the sundress. So much for her attempt at playing femme fatale.

"Cooper," she said, her voice hushed, her throat dry as she tried valiantly to ignore the mass of loudly demanding hormones her body had become when he'd laid bare his desire for her. Just the feel of his fingertips, lightly pressing under her chin, made her struggle not to wriggle in her seat. She wanted him to press those broad, firm fingertips on a few other spots on her now quivering body. "I honestly wasn't trying to insult you. Or me. I told you, it's not about your worth but about mine."

She trailed off, shivering a little under his steady regard. His beautiful blue eyes were simultaneously blazing with desire and with frustration that he couldn't simply will this situation to resolve itself, will her to be the woman he wanted and apparently needed her to be. She wanted to reach up and touch his face, soothe his frustration away. She took a steadying breath instead and held up under his gaze. "I wish I could give you more, promise you something, but I can't do that when I don't know if I'm capable of doing anything more than living in the moment. Despite my long stay here, I have little doubt I'll be packing up and heading out again. To put it bluntly, aside from our physical attraction, I honestly can't imagine what it is about me that would make you do this, take this trip, declare yourself like you did. So —"

"So you thought I'd get you out of my system by having you? Or us having each other?"

She stiffened, then pulled herself upright, removing her chin from his touch. "I know this might be hard for you to believe, but for all I'm a well-traveled woman, my adventures have rarely landed me in this particular spot, wanting this particular kind of adventure. I don't simply offer myself up to the —"

"I know that," he said quietly. "I do. Your integrity, your sense of self, is one of the many things that attracted me from the start. I guess that's why this — what you're doing, feels so . . ."

"Yeah," she said, quietly now, letting the tension of the moment ebb away. They were both frustrated, both wanting what they wanted and realizing there might not be any way to get it. "I know." She looked away, let the briny breeze lift the hair from her neck, toss the soft tangle of curls around a bit, caress her overheated skin and overly sensitive nerve endings. It didn't help. It only served to make her want his hands to be the thing caressing her skin, soothing her electrified nerve endings, easing them past this seemingly insurmountable obstacle. She finally looked back at him and surprised them both with a little smile. "I guess we're even, then. I didn't handle this right at all. I'm sorry."

A flicker of a smile ghosted over his handsome face, but the inscrutable look in his eyes remained. She realized she wasn't used to not being able to read him, which only proved how well she'd truly come to know him during their time working together. She also learned that she hated it, hated feeling closed out; hated, specifically, being closed out from him.

"For the record," he said at length, his voice still a bit gravelly, "when I asked you to lunch, it was to get some time alone with you, away from everyone else, so we could talk freely. It wasn't for —"

"I know it wasn't," she broke in. "I really do. And I'm sorry for trying to make it into something else. Cooper —"

Now he lifted his hand. "No worries. I should have accepted your explanation with a bit more grace. Or maybe I shouldn't have said anything at all and just accepted your offer. Who knows? But . . . you were being honest and, at the very least, I owed you the same."

She shook her head. "No. I'm glad we cleared the air." She smiled then, hoping the sadness clutching at her heart wasn't reflected in her eyes. She'd expected to feel crushing disappointment when he left, but this . . . this was entirely different now that they'd talked, bared their souls, been as honest as two people could who were trying hard to get what they wanted without hurting each other.

So no one gets anything, then.

She motioned to the spread of food. "Is it too late to enjoy some lunch?"

"No," he said, not looking as relieved as she'd hoped; but then, it was what it was. Both of them would have to find their way past their personal disappointment on their own. "Not at all." He reached for the wine again as she took the rest of the containers out of the hamper and began setting out a more organized spread. "Although," he said, easing the cork up and out as his grin flickered back to life, like a long-awaited ray of sunshine after a storm, "I don't suppose you have anything else to wear."

She gave a little spurt of laughter at that, relieved that he wasn't going to make it harder on either of them, and was perversely that much more turned on. His eyes widened when she grinned and held up a finger, then scrambled back aft and retrieved her canvas tote. She came back wearing the faded hoodie and ancient fishing hat. "Better?" she asked, plopping back down on the blanket and modeling her new look.

His gaze skimmed over her legs, then back up to her face, his own eyes glittering now. "Not in the least."

She swallowed. Hard. When he surprised her by not looking away, her palms began to sweat. Then he shocked her speechless by reaching behind his neck, grabbing the back collar of his shirt, and pulling it over his head and off. A life spent on a cattle station had given him a deeply golden, well-muscled torso. One she'd thought about often, though, it turned out, her imagination hadn't remotely done justice to reality.

Even though she'd been on Cameroo Downs for a full year in a wide variety of different situations, this was the first time she'd ever seen him with his shirt off.

He grinned for real at her dumbfounded expression, then began filling his plate as if he'd done nothing more than take off his hat. More at ease than she'd seen him since she'd arrived at the dock.

"I suppose I deserve that," she said, shaking her head in a silent touché.

He just winked at her, then went back to filling his plate with another lobster roll, a few more hush puppies, and a small mound of blueberries.

She laughed — what else was there to do? — then shook her head as he handed her a glass of wine. She lifted it in a toast. "To good food, good company, and a few hours of solid torture on the high seas."

Chuckling, he lifted his glass, tapped hers, then held her gaze over the rim as he took a sip. She was now intimately acquainted with his reference to aching teeth and need.

You're in so much trouble, Kerry McCrae.

Not because she still wanted him to drag her down to that bunk by her hair — though, at the moment, it was her most fervent desire — but because she was starting to remember all the other hundreds of

221

little reasons why she'd fallen for him in the first place.

They both looked at the world with the same dry humor, which allowed them to discuss any manner of things without getting too worked up if they felt different about this topic or that. When issues did arise, they also had the same need to confront them head-on — no letting things fester — but along with that came the same ability to speak their minds while being respectful of the other's opinions, then moving quickly forward. It was one of the reasons they'd worked so well together in a demanding and fast-moving environment.

Only rather than wanting to move forward now, she wanted to go back a step or two to see if maybe there was some way, any way, for them both to get what they wanted.

She quashed even a hint of that inner debate before it could get so much as a toehold in her mind and pulled the cooler closer, hoping to find something to distract herself from that dangerous path. Inspecting the contents, she gave a little hoot of delight and pulled out the small tub of homemade whipped cream. "I'm betting there are some sweet biscuits in the hamper," she said, waving the small tub at him.

"I think so, but what do you do with —"

He didn't finish the thought but dug out the container and handed it to her.

"Just sit back and watch the perfection that is Delia's version of blueberry shortcake take shape before your very eyes." On a small plate, she constructed the dish, breaking apart the biscuits, then dumping a scoop of blueberries on top, adding a dollop of whipped cream, then drizzling some of the blueberry juice from the container on top. "It's even more heavenly with a scoop of freshly churned vanilla bean ice cream on top, but this will do." She scooped up a bite for herself, closed her eyes as the sweet and buttery flavors mixed in with the crush of ripe fruit, then pushed the plate at him. "Go ahead. I dare you not to clean that plate."

"You know," he said after finishing off the rest in two bites, a deep groan of satisfaction rumbling from his throat as he savored the last bits, "if she wasn't married, I'd toss you over in a heartbeat and steal her away Down Under, where I'd keep her enslaved in the kitchen."

Trying not to laugh, Kerry held up a hand. "Leave your sordid little kitchen fantasies out of this. Also? Good to know where I would have stood in the overall hierarchy." She took another biscuit from the container and built another shortcake plate, then lifted it up to her chin, smiling sweetly at him over the small dollop of whipped cream. "Oh, did I happen to mention that Delia shares her recipes with her closest and dearest?" Then she dared to stick out the tip of her tongue to lick the blueberry juice drizzle off the top of the whipped cream.

His eyes flared, and she thought she might have pushed things too far. The rush of anticipation and hope that she'd done just that should have been a big, flashing neon warning sign. But when he grinned and lifted the plate from her fingers, then mirrored her own action, making her squirm in her seat, she realized she was having far too good a time to take heed. "Hey," she said, "get your own plate of decadent temptation."

She went to grab her plate, only to have him pull it out of reach. "I believe I just did," he said, turning his back slightly to her and lowering the plate to mouth level.

Laughing, she shifted the hamper and their other plates aside and pushed up on her knees, recklessly reaching for the plate. He tried to move away, but he'd just been lifting it to his mouth when she swiped out, sending the contents sliding off the plate and all over his chest. His bare chest.

Kerry's eyes went wide and her mouth made a small *o,* before she burst out in a chortle of glee. "Serves you right, mate," she said, her accent dead-on. "Take a girl's dessert. That'll show ya."

He turned on her, rising to his knees so swiftly and smoothly she had no chance to scramble back, which had the unfortunate result of pressing his bare, blueberry, biscuit, and whipped cream–covered chest up against the front of her hoodie. "Get between a man and his biscuits and bad things can happen, luv," he warned, his eyes glittering once again, matched by his devilish grin.

Ensnared by him as neatly and completely as if he'd taken her in his arms, Kerry swallowed hard, realizing they'd both raced right up to the edge of something they might live to regret, especially given his earlier declaration of his intent where she was concerned, and his unwillingness to accept anything less.

"Cooper —"

She was cut off when he pressed the business side of the empty paper plate against her nose, leaving a dollop of blueberry juice and whipped cream on the tip of it, before he crumpled up the plate and stuck it in the cooler. All while never once taking his eyes off her. "Looks like we both need a bit of a cleanup," he said, his deep voice taking on that gravelly edge she'd only heard once before. Right after he'd kissed the daylights out of her.

"I'll start." He leaned forward and very deliberately nipped a bit of the cream off the tip of her nose. Every erogenous zone in her body felt like it was being teased by the hot licks of a wildfire, right on the verge of burning out of control. "I wonder which of us would get cleaned up first." Then he lifted a finger and took a swipe of blueberry from the base of her throat and nipped it between two rows of gleaming white teeth, which he kept bared as he chewed the juicy bit and swallowed. "Race you," he said, his scorching gaze leaving absolutely no ambiguity about where he knew this was headed.

"I thought you said you didn't want —"

"Oh, I want. I told you that."

"But —"

"Maybe you were right," he conceded, then plucked another blueberry piece off her. "We've talked it to death. Maybe it's time to try action."

Her nipples were so hard they hurt, and the streaks of deep purple blueberry juice running down her skin had nothing on the juices he was creating quite naturally inside her.

"Maybe you had a point about getting the arse end of the elephant in the room to ease up a bit so we can focus on all the rest."

She was so wound up, so pent up, she was surprised she wasn't shooting sparks. Her ability to snort a short laugh just then was a tribute to just how many things he could make her feel all at once. God, she'd missed him. "You have such a way with a metaphor, mate."

"Sorry," he said, looking and sounding anything but. "I'm a little distracted at the moment." He leaned in, removed a swipe of cream from her cheek. With his tongue.

She shuddered almost violently in response.

"You're falling behind," he murmured in her ear before nibbling a biscuit crumb from her hair.

She might have moaned, just a little. Possibly her head tipped back a hair, of its own volition, to allow him greater access to her neck. "I haven't decided if I'm going to play."

He straightened just then, shifting so there was only a hairsbreadth between them. "You made that decision when you wore that man-eating scarf to lunch."

She giggled then — and she wasn't much of a giggler — but he had her on such an electrified, erotic high at the moment, she couldn't help it. "The only one doing any eating at the moment is you."

He took another sip of juice, this time from her chin. "I believe I invited you to join in. It's like one of those all-you-can-eat buffets you Americans are so fond of." He straightened again and held his arms out to either side, shamelessly offering his stripped-down, blueberry-shortcaked torso. "Might I recommend the whipped cream bits? They're especially delicious."

She couldn't help it; she looked hungrily at his dessert-covered chest and abs. Like a woman starved and stranded at sea. Her gaze rose slowly to meet his. But before she could reply, or attack and devour him, a boat horn sounded, making them both start. An amused voice carried the short distance across the water. "He surrenders, Kerry! Don't make him walk the plank!"

Kerry pulled back as if she'd been physically poked, swinging her gaze across the water to where another sailboat was passing by, getting ready to leave the harbor for the bay, sails fully unfurled. It was Jim Stein, with his wife, Carol, an older couple who were long-time friends of Fergus's but well known to the whole McCrae clan. She felt her cheeks flaming in embarrassment and was grateful they were far enough away not to see the particulars of what was going on. Of course they could plainly see Cooper was shirtless, but she still had on the hoodie and fishing hat, so how inappropriately could they be behaving, right?

If only they knew. Five more minutes and her old friends might have gotten a completely different eyeful. Hell, five more seconds.

She waved, flashed a thumbs-up, then waved again as they sailed on, leaving laughter in their wake. With her teeth still gritted in a smile, she said, "This will be all over the Cove five seconds after they get back. Sooner if they have radio signal." She turned back to Cooper, who was grinning shamelessly, hands linked behind his head now, as if preparing for his plank walk. "Very funny," she said, trying to ignore how the posture made his biceps flex and showed off the definition in his six-pack. She couldn't help but note that some of the blueberries had slid all the way down to the waistband of his cargo shorts, leaving streaks of blue on his skin, like arrows pointing to where she should go to resume their little game.

She realized she was staring when her eyes slid a little lower still and — she jerked her gaze back to his, realizing he'd made her blush again. She typically wasn't much of a blusher either. But she didn't usually find herself playing food Twister with a half-naked man. Rather than finding a mocking smile waiting for her, the curve of his lips was amused, maybe even a little affection-ate. Like she was being cute or something. She'd show him cute. Then she met his eyes and saw there was nothing amused or even borderline condescending to be found there. *Incendiary* was the word that came to mind.

She started to speak, then realized she had to swallow, whet her suddenly dry throat, just to get a single word out. Apparently all the moisture to be had in her body was pooling elsewhere at the moment. "I — I think we should head back in. Tide is start-ing to move."

"Your friends there were just heading out."

"They're probably not coming back in tonight." *Thank God.* "They cruise the inlets and coves all the time. That boat sleeps at least eight."

At the mention of sleeping, his gaze flared and raked over her quite deliberately. She felt it as intimately as if he'd put his hands on her. Or his tongue. Again.

She needed to move around him and back to the console, start pulling up anchor. Preferably while he put away the picnic food so as to remain out of temptation's reach while they got themselves back under control again. Only she couldn't seem to take that first step. She was all caught up in his heated gaze. "Cooper —"

"Kerry," he said, and that rough-edged tone was back in his voice again.

It would be easy to forget their brief interruption and return to what they'd been doing. Or, more to the point, she thought, what they'd been about to do. Because she had no doubt if she'd let any part of herself touch his skin, they'd have been baring a whole lot more of it shortly thereafter. *You say that like it's a bad thing,* her little voice whispered.

"We shouldn't," she said. "Not because we don't want to. But you were right. There would be nothing mindless about it, and you were also right that it wouldn't clear things up but hopelessly cloud them further. Because I don't think one time —" She broke off when his gaze went from incendiary to full-blown firestorm. "Cooper," she repeated, only this time it sounded like a desperate plea. She just wished she knew which thing she was really pleading for him

231

to do. Take his own earlier advice to stay hands-off until she was more certain of what she wanted? Or put his hands on her and remove responsibility for the decision altogether?

Then she remembered the tide. She hadn't been using that as an excuse. "We really should head back in."

Cooper lowered his arms to his sides, a slow, dead-sexy smile curving his chiseled lips. "You're right. Go lift anchor and I'll pack up the food."

Had she dreamed he'd just agreed to do what she'd asked? Was he going to make it that easy? And if so, why was she feeling suddenly all let down? *Get a grip on it, mate,* she schooled herself. She also noticed he hadn't exactly leaped into action either.

"I'm sorry," she said.

His brows drew together now. "For . . . ?"

She waved her hands, motioning at nothing in particular. "This. Coming out here, confusing matters further. Leading you on when I said I wouldn't."

"Were you?" he asked, quite soberly. "Because you seemed quite serious about it there, until I stupidly talked you out of it."

"Yes. I mean no. I mean yes, I was serious about getting physical. But —"

"Then no apologies necessary. I took care

232

of dashing that hope all by myself."

"Except —"

He pressed a finger against her lips. "Enough talking about it, Starfish," he said. "I'm going to pop down belowdeck and rinse myself off, if that's okay."

She nodded dumbly, wondering how this day had gotten so . . . well, so weird. And so uniquely unfulfilling. Maybe that was his goal: to make her want him as much as he wanted her. If so, mission accomplished.

"Leave all this," he said, motioning to the picnic blanket. "I'll get it when I come back up." He motioned to her. "Why don't you give me the hoodie and I'll at least get the bigger bits and bobs off it?"

At any other time she'd have made some brazen comment or done something bold and daring while unzipping it and taking it off. It made her wish they were still teasing and laughing and poking fun at each other. And not about to climb out of their respective skins for want of the other. She wondered what it would be like to have both of those things with him at the same time. *Bliss.*

She shrugged quickly out of the hoodie, hating that her fingers shook, certain he'd noticed. He never missed a thing. He plucked it nimbly from her hand, careful not to touch her. "Back up in a jiff," he said. Then he was gone.

Still kneeling there on the deck, Kerry folded her arms over her chest, feeling a sudden chill on her skin that had nothing to do with being exposed once again to the salty breeze. "What am I going to do about you, Cooper Jax?" she whispered, letting the wind snatch the words away.

She wanted him but couldn't risk taking the life he offered, knowing she likely wouldn't stick with it. Nor, she thought now, could she take knowing what it felt like to lie in his arms, to feel him move over, push himself deep inside her, then let him leave her life forever.

Better, then, that they'd been interrupted before doing something foolish and impulsive they could never take back. Walking right up to the edge wasn't the same as leaping off. They could still save themselves.

Every inch of her body aching with need, confusion, and not a little disappointment, she quickly stowed the food back into the hamper, shoved the cork in the wine and put it back in the cooler, then bundled everything up, slid the straps over her shoulders, and banged it all back aft. She shoved the hamper and cooler into the storage bins, then wrapped the blanket around herself, knowing it wasn't her bare shoulders that made her feel exposed but tucking the blanket close to her front with her arm anyway. She got the anchor going, keeping her hands busy and her mind off a naked Cooper in the tiny shower cubicle below. *Or you could just get over yourself and go after what you want.*

"God, just shut up already," she snapped.

"I beg your pardon?"

She turned from her spot at the helm, where she'd been white-knuckling the steering wheel, to find a freshly showered, damp-haired, and once again clothed Cooper. His shorts were also damp where he'd washed off the shortcake bits, but she didn't let her gaze linger there.

"Just muttering to myself," she said.

He nodded, accepting her explanation. Though he looked good natured enough, his customary grin was nowhere to be found. Maybe he'd had the same come-to-Jesus talk with himself in the shower that she'd had with herself abovedeck and come to the same save-yourself conclusion.

"I hung your hoodie up over the shower stall door. Unless you want it back?" he added, noting the blanket wrapped around her shoulders.

She shook her head, sighing in relief when

she heard the anchor bump its way home. She turned and started the engine. "I already got the picnic stuff stowed. We're good to go."

"I don't think so," he said from a spot somewhere right behind her. Somewhere very close behind her.

She went still, her heart instantly banging inside her chest again, but stayed right where she stood, the teak floorboards vibrating under their feet as the boat began drifting forward, not yet in gear.

"Cooper —"

"Shh," he said, then gently put his hands on her shoulders until she let go of the steering wheel. With her arms still at her sides, he turned her toward him. "None of this has gone as we planned. Whatever that plan was." He shifted one hand from her shoulder to tip her chin up so she looked directly into his eyes. "But let's at least get this much on the table. I heard everything you said. Despite the obstacles, the odds, or anything else we think is stacked against us, the fact is, I want you, Kerry McCrae. And you've said you want me, too. Talking it to death and second-guessing what might or might not be between us isn't the answer." He let his thumb trace over her bottom lip, which quivered a little under his touch. Her shoulders relaxed and her lips parted as she was utterly incapable of not responding to him.

The color of his eyes flared, like the blue flame of a newly struck match. "The one thing I think we both can agree on, however, is that we're far from done yet."

And without waiting for her to dither about it, or shut him down, he dipped his head the rest of the way down and kissed her.

CHAPTER ELEVEN

He felt her tremble as he took her mouth slowly, fully. The vulnerability in her eyes just before he'd claimed her mouth once again roused all his protective instincts, and not a few of his more primal ones. She didn't otherwise touch him or reach for him, but he felt her body gradually relax under his touch as he deepened the kiss, her shoulders softening, her stance wavering a little as the boat rocked. This time it was him making that sound deep in his throat when she opened to him, took his tongue deep, and then finally, mercifully, kissed him back.

He slid his hands into her hair, framing her face as he pulled her into the shelter of his body, silently urging her to touch him, pull him the rest of the way in, wrap her arms around him. And hold on tight.

He felt her hands come up to rest on his hips to steady herself as she gasped when he left her mouth and buried his head in the sweet curve of her neck, kissing her there, maybe a gentle nip or two as he tried to keep from going faster, taking more. Taking all.

Her nails briefly pressed into him, finding his skin under the soft cotton of his shirt. But in the next breath, before he completely forgot he'd only meant to kiss her, meant to get them firmly back to square one, the one where they'd both been on the same page, she gently but firmly pushed at him until he lifted his head.

He only resisted when she tried to push him away completely. Her back was to the console so he let her go but gathered the edges of the blanket in his hands, holding the fuzzy thickness closed over her chest, his knuckles brushing her collarbone, keeping her from moving completely out of his reach. He didn't know if she'd ever allow herself — or them — to be in each other's arms again. And he simply wasn't ready to let her go. He'd only just reconnected with her. And despite everything they'd said to each other, he still couldn't shake the feeling she was right where she belonged. And so was he.

"There's something here," he said, searching her gaze. "Something beneath all the pheromones dancing about whenever we're within reaching distance of each other. Something beyond this . . . this crazy hunger."

"I know," she said in a hushed whisper, the words barely reaching his ears over the sound of the wind and the snap of the sails.

He leaned his head down until his forehead brushed hers. "I want both," he said. "The friendship and the hunger."

Her eyes were luminous pools of the deepest sea green as she looked into his, and he thought he could fall into them and never surface again and die a happy man. "Explore them with me," he said, "and let's see where it leads. That's all I'm asking."

He waited this time, for some indication she accepted his request, needing to know she was consciously willing and not merely allowing herself to be swept away in the moment. He had to have that much from her.

The vulnerability in her eyes were edged now with real fear, and it jerked at something deep inside him, making him wish this wasn't so hard for her. He knew what he was asking, the risk she'd be taking letting herself get more involved with him. He believed her when she said her emotions were involved, too. He was drowning in a sea of them right now. This wasn't about a roll in the hay to slake their lust. If she accepted him, all of him, once they'd had each other, they would be on a new path regardless of where it ultimately led them. "There's no going back to what was," he whispered. He leaned in, kissed her again, gently, briefly, closing his eyes as her soft lips parted beneath his. "But I'm hoping we'll never want to," he said against her lips. "Because it's going to be that good between us, we wouldn't stand for anything less than having it all."

She answered him by sliding shaky hands to his hips, letting him keep the blanket wrapped around her as she gripped the waistband of his shorts as she might a rope tossed to a drowning woman.

"Kerry," he breathed, the word a groan of pleasure as she moved a step into him.

He slid the blanket from her shoulders, flipped it around his own, then pulled her in, wrapping them both within the warm, soft folds as she pressed her lips to the side of his neck.

"Kiss me, Cooper Jax," she whispered, her voice hoarse with need, with want, against the spot just below his ear.

"Kerry," he said again, feeling her tremble in his arms, feeling his own control growing shaky.

"No promises I can't keep," she said, then pressed a kiss to his jaw, and another to the indentation beneath his cheekbone.

And now he might be the one shaking a little. She was saying yes.

His heart swelled, even as his body leaped to full, aching attention. He knew this wasn't a promise, merely a start. It was all he could ask from her, and more than he'd thought she'd give him. "We're both taking risks here, Starfish," he murmured against her hair, pulling her more deeply into the warmth of their blanket cocoon. "I'll do my best to make sure you don't regret it. All I ask for is an honest effort."

"That I can do," she said, then nipped his chin. "Now," she said, sliding her hands from his hips and up between them, over his chest and around his neck. Her fingers wove into the damp, wavy curls that lay on his neck, then raked up the back of his scalp. "Kiss me."

The touch of her hands on him, her nails on his skin, made his body feel like it had been plugged into one of Cameroo's electric fences. Apparently time for talk really was over.

Fingers still wound in his hair, she tugged his head down, then pulled his bottom lip between hers, suckled it, nipped it before letting it go so she could tease the tip of her tongue along the seam between his lips.

If he thought he'd been hard a moment ago, he was fairly certain he could cut diamonds now. "Danger, danger," he murmured when she nipped his chin again. "Playing with fire there, Starfish. We might not make it down to that sweet stateroom-size playground if you're not careful."

She leaned her head back then, and gone was the vulnerability, the ambivalence, the fear. In its place, his Kerry was back, eyes flashing, confident, at the ready.

An honest effort. Dear sweet heaven, it looked like she was bloody well going to give him that.

"You didn't say anything about being careful." She slid her hands from his nape to his shoulders, then slowly down over his pecs, with no sign of stopping.

Possibly a coronary to go with it. And they were still fully clothed.

She slid one hand through the slit in the blanket and groped behind her on the console. A moment later, he heard the sounds of the anchor dropping.

"We're going to miss the tide," he managed, leaning his head to the side to give her access to the side of his neck, the lobe of his ear, both of which she nipped, then suckled, then kissed, as he strained to hold on to the last shreds of his control.

"I believe we are, yes," she said, her voice throaty now, needy, as she continued her trail of completely unnecessary but deeply appreciated seduction along the open collar of his shirt. Here he thought he'd be the one leading this first foray, trying not to overwhelm her with his half-starved need for her. Apparently she hadn't been kidding when she said she'd been lusting for him, too. He grinned then, even as he groaned when she skimmed flat palms over his chest, brushing against his nipples, pebbled hard now from her slow and utterly thorough dismantling of his restraint.

"Do you — should you radio . . . anyone?" he said, gasping slightly when she nipped at one nipple through his shirt.

"Mm-hmm," she murmured, leaving a trail along the side of his chin with her tongue.

He turned her around inside the blanket so her back was to him, then tugged her up against him, sliding his arms around her waist and keeping the blanket around them, the opening now in front of her. He leaned down and gently bit the side of her neck, then whispered, "Well, you might want to take care of that right swift, luv, because you're about to be ravaged."

She moaned when he nipped her, wriggling a little, giving a delightful giggle at the last part, which made him grin. Kerry wasn't typically a giggler. He now had a vested interest in seeing her become one. She'd clearly let go of all the worry, the tension, the fears about what might happen, and was doing exactly what he was doing: grabbing on to what they had right now and leaving the future to settle itself.

"Ravaged, am I?" she said, tipping her head back against his shoulder to look up at him. "Are we playing pirate on the high seas, then?"

"Aye, my saucy seafaring wench, 'tis true. I've boarded yer lovely vessel to see what treasures you have worth pillaging." He leaned down, nipped her earlobe, then tugged the blanket so it snugged tightly over her breasts as he tucked her backside against his hips. "It appears I'll need to board yer personal vessel to discover all your riches."

She laughed at that outright, then wiggled against him quite deliberately, making him grit his teeth. "Careful now, wench, or you'll be spilling my doubloons all over the deck."

She let out a choked laugh at that, then bumped him back with her hips, and it was his turn to groan as her firm derrière came into contact with an even firmer part of him. "Why don't you and your doubloons go on belowdeck so I can catch my breath long enough to send out an all's-okay to Thomas without him thinking I'm doing what I'm about to be doing? It was mortifying enough to have to brazen it out in front of him when I showed up in this — what was it you called it? A glorified napkin? I've always thought of him as kind of a secondary grandfather. I'm not sure which of us was more in danger of that heart attack." She glanced over her shoulder with a dry smile. "I think my femme fatale days are over."

"Oh," he said, tossing the blanket toward a side bin so he could run his flat palms down the center of her back, then frame the swell of her hips, which were tightly wrapped in that glorified napkin. "I don't know about that," he said in all sincerity. "At least the fatale part."

Her laughter was pure Kerry, deep, throaty, inviting, but he could see the little thrill in her expression at his compliment. She had to know she'd been born an Amazon warrior queen, and men around the world had likely knelt in homage to her feminine powers, but it was nice to see that what he thought mattered to her pleased her. She'd always pleased him. He would make sure she never doubted that.

"Well, don't get used to it," she informed him. "You know as well as anyone that I'm far more at home in baggy pants and ancient T-shirts."

"Far be it from me to ask you to don anything that makes you uncomfortable. In fact . . ." He turned her back around, pulled her in close, then leaned down and kissed her quite thoroughly on the mouth. Her breath was hitching just a little when he lifted his head, his lips hovering over hers, and said, "Just so you know, I'm good with you wearing nothing at all."

The corner of her mouth curved upward. "You're so generous like that."

"What can I say?" he said, smiling against her lips before kissing her again. "I'm Australian. We're all about no worries."

"Mm," she hummed, eyes flashing again as she smiled back. "Lucky me." She surprised him by shoving him back a step. "I'm going to hold you to that. Now, this saucy seafaring wench needs to make sure our anchor's holding and send Thomas a quick note so he doesn't send out the Coast Guard to rescue us."

Cooper made a mock sad face. "That would be bad."

"Not to mention embarrassing." She made a shooing motion. "So why don't you go scope out the stateroom, Captain Hook?"

"Hook, is it?"

She reached up and casually slid her fingers in his sun-bleached locks as if she did it all the time. As if the touch of her fingertips on his scalp didn't make him wilder than he already was. "I don't think you could pull off a convincing Blackbeard, sorry."

He tugged her in close, getting a surprised gasp and a laugh from her. He put his mouth by her ear and in his best pirate voice whispered, "Ye best be hopin' I didn't come by my nickname due to an unfortunate genetic anomaly, luv."

"Well, I suppose that depends on which way the hook curves." She closed her eyes and smiled, then grinned and pushed him away again. "Belowdeck with you," she ordered, all Amazon queen now to his swarthy pirate, then as he finally ducked through the opening and began climbing down the short, metal rung ladder to the galley belowdeck, he heard her call out, "And no pirate worth his salt uses words like *anomaly.*"

He laughed at that as he hopped off the steps and turned to face the galley, feeling as if he'd just woken up on Christmas morning and found a winning lottery ticket in his stocking. He stepped into the small kitchen space, then stopped again as he realized he actually had no idea what to do next. Had they both come belowdeck, half-falling and bumbling down the short ladder in the midst of tearing each other's clothes off . . . well, what happened next would have rather taken care of itself.

Instead, he'd been charged with being first in the door to set the stage, so to speak. So what did that entail exactly? He hardly thought she'd expect to come down and find him, clothes shucked, sprawled on the bed, lying in wait for her. And it wasn't as though he had the supplies needed to concoct a scene of seduction, complete with burning candles and rose petals.

"Aye," he said, a low, rumbling Hook now as he looked about and sized up his options. He ducked back to have a quick look at the bed. He folded back the navy blue bedspread. Sheets in order, pillows — check. *This is ridiculous.* He was a thirty-two-year-old man who felt like a schoolboy on his first real date. One on which he was going to get really, really lucky. Better to go back topside, he figured, and get them back to the half-falling-half-climbing-down-the-galley-stairs, ripping-their-clothes-off scenario he'd initially envisioned. He'd do well enough in that instance.

He turned around and bumped straight into Kerry, who stood just behind him, wrapped once again in the blanket. He took one look at it, then lifted his gaze to hers and grinned. "We're quite a pair, we are, Starfish. One minute all but tearing each other's clothes off with our teeth, the next, with five seconds to actually plan something, you'd think neither of us had ever done the horizontal folk dance."

She spluttered a laugh. "Horizontal — ?" She couldn't finish, still shaking her head. "What makes you think that? I —"

"Am covered head to toe in blanket again," he finished for her with a nod at her hands, presently clutching it closed in front of her as if the now nonexistent wind might rip it from her hands at any second. "Whilst I stand here and wonder how best to get you horizontal. Lure you in with my piratical gleam?" He leveraged himself into a full-on back flop onto the high-sided bed, arms akimbo. "Lie here sprawled in my birthday suit, hoping you'll be overcome by lust upon spying my trusty —"

"Sword?" she supplied.

Now he barked a laugh. He rolled up to a

seated position and scooted to the foot of the bed, beckoning her closer. She shuffled between his legs, blanket still held tightly in the front.

He lifted his gaze to hers, liking the way the sun slanted through the small portholes on either side of the narrow stateroom, casting her skin in a golden glow and making her red curls dance as if the tips were sparklers. Her green eyes slowly darkened, while his gaze remained on hers as he reached up and gently tugged the blanket loose from her grip. He urged her forward by pulling on the edges of the blanket until she was standing between his thighs. "I've had one rather insistent fantasy over the course of this beautiful Maine afternoon," he said, hearing the rough edge come back into his voice, his hunger for her making his mouth go as dry as Cameroo in April.

Her lips curved upward, and that gleaming light flickered to life in her eyes. "Does it involve pillaging?"

"Aye," he said, a bit of the pirate back in his voice. He let the blanket slide from his fingers, then put his palms on her hips, wrapping his fingers around her so the tips pressed gently into the firm curve at the top end of her bum. His thumbs rubbed over her hip bones, pressing against the tight

251

wrap of her dress.

He felt a little shudder go through her and had to dig deep for what little restraint he had left. He kept his gaze tipped up and on hers. "I stood by the rail as you steered this big beast through that maze of bobbing boats in the harbor and imagined what it would be like if I walked over to stand behind you, to wrap my hands around your hips." He did sink his fingertips into her softness a bit then, and was rewarded with a little gasp from her. Her parted lips called to him like a siren, but he remained where he was.

"I wanted to slide them up, cup your breasts, find out if they'd fit as perfectly in my hands as I've imagined." His actions mirrored his words, and he felt her intake of breath as he slid his palms up, over her rib cage. She didn't stop him, and his gaze shifted to his hands as he slowly circled her breasts, all pushed up and bound tightly within her dress . . . and, indeed, perfectly shaped for his hands.

Her body twitched under his hands as he ran his palms up and over her nipples, and she let out a little moan. He could feel them grow harder, pushing at the silky, gathered fabric, pushing against his hands. "I wanted to slide my fingertips under the top edge, here," he said, curling his fingers until they slid under the inside edge of her bodice, "and tug it down, slowly, so the soft, silky fabric would rub over your nipples, making them stand up, full and pink and hard, just for me."

She took a swift intake of breath as he began to do what he'd described. He kept his attention focused solely on what he was doing, wondering why in the hell he thought torturing himself further was a good idea. By the time he got rid of her clothes, he might not be able to get his own off, or ever father children, but then he glanced up, saw her eyes were lit like the fire of glittering emeralds, and decided he'd gnaw his clothes off if necessary.

He drew the silky fabric slowly downward and could feel her body trembling as the first hint of the rosy, dark skin circling her nipples was exposed. He slid his fingers to the side so they wouldn't touch her most sensitive skin, making her groan a little. He glanced up, found her gaze focused laserlike on his fingers, her bottom lip caught between her teeth.

He watched her as he slowly drew the silk over first one plump, hard tip, then the other. She let out a short cry, her body jerking slightly as the full, dark buds were revealed, the cooler cabin air caressing their now bare tips. She was shaking, her legs visibly trembling as he urged her a step closer, putting her nipples right in line with his mouth.

"Cooper," she said, begged, the word nothing more than a rasp.

"I will," he promised. He left the tight fabric bunched under her breasts, keeping them pushed up, keeping her nipples jutting toward his waiting tongue, and slid his hands back down to her hips. "Mmm," he murmured, "where to begin my plundering." He blew a warm breath over first one nipple, then the other, making her shiver and let out a small cry of need. Her hands were still down at her sides, her fingers curled into tightly fisted balls, as she willed herself to stand still and wait for whatever he'd do next.

He slid his hands around so his fingers cupped her backside, sliding the tips until they brushed the slender dip between her cheeks, the dress enhancing that enticing crease. Her moan started softly as he brushed his fingertips down along that silky seam, then turned to a low keening wail of want when he brought his lips right up to the tip of her nipple but only brushed across the tip in the barest of kisses.

Her trembling increased, and he cupped his hands more firmly, let his fingers dip more deeply between her cheeks, his palms holding her firmly in place, both in support and urging her to let him continue. He ran the tip of his tongue along the soft curve under her breast, bringing the tip up to the edge of her nipple, before moving to her other breast. He pressed his fingers in, slid his hands a little farther down, until they cupped the fullness of her cheeks. He urged her closer still, letting his fingertips brush the bare skin of the backs of her thighs, just below the hem of the dress as he circled one nipple with his tongue. She was shaking now, shuddering when his lips brushed across the tip of her nipple, moaning as his fingers caressed the topmost part of the back of her thighs, flirting with the edge of her dress, inching it up a tiny bit, then a tiny bit more.

When he took her other nipple fully into his mouth for just a moment before letting it slide out with a small pop, she cried out. Her hands came up then, and she pressed her balled fists into the tops of his shoulders for support, the movement dipping her nipples lower, closer, allowing him to gently pull the other one between his lips, tease the tip with his tongue, while finally pressing one finger between the apex of her thighs, sliding the tip along the silk panel that ran between them. The damp silk panel.

Now it was his turn to groan, deep in his throat, as he continued to suckle, lick, and nibble on her sweet, plump tips and urge her legs apart a little, so he could stroke her fully. The moment his fingertip ran over her other most sensitive bud, she cried out, slumping into him as her knees buckled, letting him support her weight as her climax ripped up and right through her. *Her first climax,* he thought.

"Cooper," she said between small whimpers, shaking harder now. As the waves continued to rake her, he ran his finger along the edge of the elastic of that now wet silk panel between her thighs, wanting more, needing to give her more. He didn't know if her cry was begging him to stop or begging him for more. He was going to go with more until she told him otherwise.

Sweet Jesus, she was so responsive, so delicious to arouse, it made him want to see how far he could get her to climb. And how many times. He teased his finger under the damp silk and found her to be even silkier, so wet for him, because of him. She stayed leaning against him and he toyed, licked, and suckled her nipples more firmly now as she moved against his fingers, trying to get him to slide them where she wanted — needed — them most.

He could feel her body tense as he slowly took her up to the edge again, sliding his fingers along that delectably wet, silky part of her, teasing around, near, and right, right there, while pulling her now puffy, sweet, dark buds between his lips, first one, then the other, until she was keening again, climbing closer, closer still.

She was moving against him, gasping between small whimpers, saying his name. "Please," she whispered raggedly. "Please."

"So polite," he said, his lips pressed to the space between her breasts. She tried to move, tried to get his fingers where she wanted them, his mouth back on her beautifully engorged, tongue-slicked nipples. He kept his fingertips close, urged her just the tiniest bit closer, then let go with one hand so he could grip the back of her neck and pull her mouth to him. When she instantly opened for him, taking the plunge of his tongue with a deep, welcoming groan, he slid his finger inside her at the same time. Then took her shuddering, shaking orgasm into his mouth as she cried, shook in his arms, clenching her strong thighs to keep his finger deep inside her while sucking on his thrusting tongue in the same pulsing motion as she held his finger inside her hot, wet depths.

As her rocketing shudders peaked and began to subside, she tried to push at his shoulders, tried to shove him back on the bed, but he wasn't finished. "Not yet," he said as she dragged her mouth from his, her skin damp, flushed, her eyes a little glassy and so dark he thought he could come right then and there from the hunger still raging in their glossy green depths. He didn't give her time to regroup. He was flying on instinct now because nothing in his life up to this moment had prepared him for this, for her, for the peaks he knew they'd both reach before this interlude was over. Already well aware he'd be planning the next one before his eyes closed to rest and regroup. In fact, he hoped to be forever planning their next romp. And their next one.

He placed his palms on her hips, gripped her, steadied her, then turned her around so her beautiful, shapely bum was right there for him to admire. She lifted her hands to her hair, raked her fingers through her damp curls, trying to get herself steadied for whatever he was going to do next, then left her arms folded over her head, her hands dangling down, clutching at the hair at the nape of her neck. The pose was decidedly erotic, though he doubted she realized that. He pushed the snug hem of her skirt up over her hips and tugged the zipper down the back so the front of the dress drooped down to her waist, freeing her breasts fully. No bra, he already knew, as the dress had provided all the support needed there. He thought it only right, then, that the panties should go as well.

He pushed them down her hips, leaving the dress, pressing his hands to her thighs when she started to wriggle so it would shimmy down, too. "Not yet," he told her. That dress, bunched up above her world-class ass and gaping down in the front, exposing breasts he would happily pay homage to for the rest of his natural life, her hair a tousled mop, and her eyes filled with a need he'd created, all combined to create the most carnal, primal female he'd ever been blessed to see.

He slid one hand around her thigh and slid his fingers between her legs, making her gasp as he toyed with her now screamingly sensitized bud. He moved softly, slowly, while his other hand slid up to toy with and gently squeeze one nipple, then the other, until she was shaking again, only with nothing to hold on to. She was slippery wet and her musky scent was driving him mad. When he didn't think either one of them could take another second of this carnal torture, he turned her around, urged her arms down until she braced herself on his shoulders; then he bent down and drew the wet, hot center of all that delicious wet musk into his mouth, suckling hard as he slid first one finger, then another, as deeply inside her as he could.

She screamed as she came this time, bucking against him as he slid in and out, keeping the pressure on that soaking wet nub with his tongue until she literally collapsed over him, sending them both back onto the bed. She was sprawled half on him, half off, mostly naked, exceedingly wet, still shuddering, and very aroused while his hands went immediately to his waistband, fumbling now as he hadn't since he'd put his hands on her, trying to get his damn zipper open. She'd wriggled out of her dress while he finally managed to get off his pants, shoes, and shirt, grabbing his wallet at the last moment and taking care of that bit of business.

"Cooper, I'm —"

"We'll talk it through next time," he said, realizing quite belatedly they probably should have had that particular talk before the first time, so protection was the order of the day this go. He couldn't even allow himself to think about next time, and even the merest possibility of removing that last and final layer between them, or he'd never make it to this first time.

He levered himself up along the bed toward the headboard, then pulled her into his arms, kissing her, discovering her all over again, only now they were both doing the kissing, seeking, and exploring. For the first minute anyway; then he had her on her back and she had her legs wrapped around his hips before either had to ask the other if now was the time. He was positioned over her, every atom in his DNA urging him to fulfill the most primal of directives, only he paused, between one heartbeat and another, and caught her looking up at him as he looked down at her.

She whispered, "Cooper, please. Yes."

He grinned, lowered his head, and took her mouth in a slow, deep, erotic mating of tongues as he slowly pushed into her. They each let out a long, low groan of blissful satisfaction as she took every hard, aching inch of him and held him tightly there while one word echoed through his mind, over and over.

Home.

CHAPTER TWELVE

Kerry woke to the feel of the steady dip and swell of the sailboat, lulling her back into sleep. Goodness knew her body was more than willing. She rolled to her side, facing the porthole, tucking her hands under her cheek and allowing herself a small private smile. *Mother have mercy,* she thought; she'd learned things about her body she hadn't known there were left to learn.

She could hear the rise and fall of Cooper's breathing as he slept on, sprawled on his back behind her. He didn't snore, and that was yet another count in his favor. *Like there's any room left in the plus column at the moment.* She stifled a little giggle at that. But her little voice wasn't wrong. She'd spent some serious quality time fantasizing about her former boss while she'd been working with him, and more hours than she'd cared to admit since coming back home. If she'd combined every last fantasy she'd dreamed up, multiplied it by infinity, then squared it, she wouldn't have come close to the reality that was making love with Cooper Jax. Mainly because she hadn't known it was possible to dream that big. *Big,* her little voice echoed. *My, my, yes. And wasn't that another nice bonus.* She lay there, her smile more a smug grin now, happy not to be shushing her little voice for once.

She was well aware she should be using this private pocket of time to sort through her thoughts, figure out what the answers were to all the questions that were bound to come rushing in the moment he woke up and they had to face the new chapter titled "What Comes Next." But it felt too good to simply lie there and wallow a bit in the afterglow of what had been a rather spectacular way to spend, as Cooper had put it, a beautiful Maine afternoon.

Given the slant of the sun through the porthole, they were now edging into evening, which meant she needed to go topside to see about getting them back to the docks. She refused to think about the ribbing she was going to face for having been out on the boat so long. Not that Delia's delectables weren't worth an extended lunch break, but it was unlikely anyone would think they'd spent that entire time at anchor marveling over lobster rolls and hush puppies while staring at the distant horizon line.

At the mention of food her tummy rumbled a bit, and she thought about going up and getting the hamper and cooler from the storage bin. A nice little feast in bed with Cooper sounded like a fabulous way to spend the next hour. She buried her face in the mattress and snickered, knowing damn well that with sustenance, it was highly likely they wouldn't climb out of bed again until sunrise the next morning.

"What's so amusing, wench?" came a gravel-throated voice from behind her, followed by a gentle swat across her sheet-covered backside.

"Just plotting my mutiny, Captain," she said.

"Mutiny?" he said, pulling the sheet, and her, closer to him. "I thought I'd convinced you to join my merry little band of thieves." He tugged at the sheet she'd grabbed in her fist, rolling her neatly over and right up against his side. "You don't want to be the pirate queen of the high seas?"

"You're a merry band of one who can't sail a boat, so —"

He silenced her with a kiss.

When he finally lifted his head, she sighed and let her head loll back on his arm. "Well, when you put it that way . . ."

He rolled on top of her, making her squeal. "I'm happy to put it another way, if that'll help persuade you."

"Sheath your sword, pirate king. Your wench needs some sustenance before she can allow you to have your pirate ways with her again."

"I thought I was sheathing my sword," he said, then laughed when she hooked her leg over his and rolled him to his back. "I see you've been paying attention to my pirate tricks."

"Indeed I have," she said, looking down into his handsome face and twinkling blue eyes. She didn't want to think about the next chapter, not now, not yet. But there it was, staring up at her, framed in tousled blond hair and five o'clock shadow. *This could be your life, Kerry McCrae. Just say yes.*

"In other news," she said, sliding off him to sit on the side of the bed, drawing the sheet around her, trying like hell to push those thoughts away for now, "we need to pull anchor before the sun gets any lower."

"Aw, because that would be . . . bad?" he said, tugging at the sheet.

She couldn't help it; she laughed, and the glow simply refused to fade. She tugged the sheet free from his grasp and stood, albeit

265

on wobbly legs for a moment or two. Summoning her most haughty pirate queen manner, she made a show of draping the end of the sheet over her shoulder and shaking loose her bed-head curls, knowing she likely looked more like Medusa than anything remotely regal. "Your merry band of one here is going topside to get us underway." She made the mistake of looking at him, sprawled in all his gorgeous, naked indolence across white sheets, beams of the lowering sun streaking across his golden skin, making it look even more burnished than it already was. *Dear Lord, she wanted to have him all over again.* Even hungrier now that she knew what awaited her when she did.

Taking full advantage of her hesitation, he propped his arms behind his head and crossed his legs at the ankles, a grin equally as indolent as his pose sliding across his handsome face. "You were saying, my queen?"

She scooped a pillow off the floor and threw it at him. "Incorrigible."

Chuckling, he caught the pillow with one hand and tucked it behind his head. "Well, I'm pretty sure that's near the top of the list of preferred character traits in the pirate handbook."

She laughed, then dodged to the door when he made a sudden, nimble grab for the edges of the sheet.

"Is there enough time for us to have a bit of supper out in the galley before getting underway?" he asked.

She didn't want to tell him her thoughts had run in the same direction, only she'd pictured them dining right there in bed. They probably had another hour or so before they really had to go. "I think we could swing that. I just want to get us back in before dark."

He glanced to the porthole. "Good point," he said, then looked at her and wiggled his eyebrows. "Care to take a quick shower?"

"You've been in that shower; you know we won't both fit in there."

"I'm sure I could find some way to scrub your . . . back."

At even the merest suggestion of him putting his hands on her, her previously tired and spent body happily flipped the On switch. "I'm sure you could," she said, sighing a little at the thought of what a little slippery, soapy fun would be like with Cooper. *What wouldn't be fun with Cooper?* her little voice wanted to know.

He rolled off the bed and stepped to the doorway, pulling her sheet-clad body easily but gently into his arms. "You shower first," he said, kissing her nose, then her mouth. "I'll go get the hamper and cooler. We'll dine like pirate royalty, then get ourselves back to the dock before the boat turns into a pumpkin."

She giggled at that. "I think you've got your fairy tales a bit mixed up."

He smiled, shook his head, and pulled her in close. "No, I've got everything exactly right." He kissed her again but stopped just before they sank into something deeper and more primal. "Thank you for this," he said quietly as he pressed a kiss to the side of her neck. "For giving it a go. I know it's not all as simple and easy as it feels, and it's not a fairy tale." He lifted his head and smiled into her eyes. "But it's damn well close."

She smiled back, thankful for the confirmation that he was feeling what she was feeling, and grateful that he was aware that a few hours of fun and laughter didn't mean everything was magically solved. She nodded, then tiptoed up and kissed him. "Thank you back," she whispered.

He held her and they stood that way for a long moment, content in each other's arms and, at least for her part, trying hard not to think about what would happen after they left the boat. He finally kissed the top of her head, then gently nudged her toward the shower. "Take your time," he told her.

And she did. Afterward she made the bed with fresh linens while he took his shower. She pondered the best way to handle the laundry situation after they got back to dock. If she thought she'd been a bit pink cheeked to have Thomas see her in her glorified napkin dress, it didn't come close to the potential for mortification when she delivered him a stack of freshly washed sheets and towels tomorrow. "Yep, that'll be fun." But if that was the price for the day, then it was one she was willing to pay.

Two hours later, with the last streaks of sun splashing red and orange behind the tall pines that backed the harbor, she guided the boat smoothly in along the dock, and Cooper hopped out and handily tied them off. She grinned, seeing he might have used a knot that was more cowboy than nautical in origin, but it worked all the same.

Their day had ended well, she thought. Tranquil and easy. They'd shared a lovely meal of leftovers and wine in the tiny galley, kept all the food on their plates this time, and spent a relaxed hour basically catching up. He'd filled her in on the goings-on at the station, regaling her with stories of Big

Jack's sixtieth birthday bash, complete with music and dancing, Ian's apparent long-distance love affair with a girl with whom he'd gone to college, and the family's attempts to wrangle her an invitation to the station. Sadie had adopted another injured wallaby, who was wreaking all kinds of havoc, and Marta had threatened multiple times to turn the creature into kangaroo stew.

Kerry smiled, thinking about them again as she turned off the engine and began going about the business of lowering the sails and stowing things for the night. It had felt good to hear the stories, made her heart lighter, even as the tales tugged at her more than a little, making her realize just how deeply she really did miss them all; missed the station, too. While she knew that hadn't necessarily been Cooper's intent in telling those particular stories, she also knew he wouldn't be disappointed if they helped her make her decision about where she was going to go. She still wasn't thinking that far ahead. Not yet. It had been a wonderful day and she wanted to simply hold on to its pleasures a while longer without attaching anything bigger or more portentous to it.

Cooper had the hamper, cooler, and bundled towels and linens stacked up on the deck by the time she finished battening everything down. He gave her a hand up to the pier. "Thank you for captaining your own lunch date," he told her with a smile.

"My pleasure," she said, smiling back. If she'd thought it would be at all awkward or tense, returning to reality, it wasn't. But they were still out on the docks, still in their own bubble. She was quite certain it would burst soon enough, so she took their last few moments and enjoyed them while she could.

"Oh, no," he said, his smile spreading to a grin as he winked. "The pleasure was all mine. Well, maybe not *all* mine."

She might have blushed a little. "True enough," she said, nudging at his shoulder as delight spread across his face when he realized her cheeks were a bit pink.

"You're a wonder, Kerry McCrae," he said, dipping his head, kissing each warm cheek, her nose, then her mouth. The first kisses were sweet, the last one utterly carnal. He did that to her. Made her feel cherished one moment and utterly desirable the next.

She might have been breathing just a bit unevenly when he lifted his head, a gleam of an entirely different sort in his eyes now.

"I'd ask when I could see you again, but I suppose I need to let Fergus have at least a bit of your time. And I don't want to press."

She barked out a short laugh at that. "You? Press? No," she said in mock surprise.

He chuckled, too, his grin not remotely sheepish, then leaned down to scoop up hamper and cooler, leaving the lighter laundry bundle for her to grab.

They stopped at his car first, stowing his load in the trunk. "I'm happy to take the laundry," he said. "I'm sure I can find somewhere to —"

"No, I'll take care of it," she said, maybe too quickly, just imagining Delia and Grace's faces when he asked them where he could find a good Laundromat. The gossip mill would get all this juicy new grist soon enough but no need to willingly feed it.

"Well, I'll be happy to return them to Thomas, spare you the trip."

"The walk of shame, you mean?" she said, then laughed as they paused by the passenger's side of her truck so she could stow the laundry bundle on the front seat. "Actually, I plan to get them washed and back on the boat before he comes to move it tomorrow."

Cooper considered that, then nodded. "Sound plan." He smiled. "Need a ride? Maybe a sunrise breakfast?"

Smiling, she nudged him as they walked

around to the driver's side. "Look at you, making it a whole five minutes before pressing." She wiped a pretend tear from the corner of her eye. "I'm so proud."

Chuckling, he snatched her up close to him and kissed her senseless before she knew what was happening, turning her squeal of surprise into a soft moan of need in a matter of seconds. "You forget," he said moments later, his voice a bit gruff, too, "I know how to handle that saucy lip of yours now."

"I should be so affronted by your smug machismo," she scolded, then let him pull her in for a nice, tight hug as she rested her cheek on his shoulder. "And yet . . ." She sighed, smiled, and slid her arms around his waist.

"And yet indeed," he said quietly, rubbing her back. "We're a pair, we are, Starfish." He kissed the top of her head in a gesture of affection she was quickly coming to love, then eased them apart.

She took a small step back, but he kept hold of her arms. "Time well spent," he said. "I'm happy to have had it. All the parts of it."

"Me too," she said. "I — I'll let you know. Talk to Fergus, see what works best. Fiona's wedding is right around the corner and I have obligations —"

"Shh," he said gently. He squeezed her arms, then slid his hands down until they linked briefly with hers before letting them go. "No worries. We'll take time as it comes. I'm just happy you want the time."

"I do, Cooper. Like you said, it's not so simple and easy as it seems, and you're being very understanding. That means a lot to me. So I want you to know, I do want more time. With you."

He flashed her a quick grin, but for the first time that afternoon, since they'd gone belowdeck, he also let her get a glimpse of just how much he wanted that to be true. And rather than make her panic, it made her entire body feel warm. And more than a little bit of her heart.

"Good," he said. "Then we'll go with that."

He held her truck door for her, made sure she was all up in the seat and belted in before closing it — twice, until the handle caught — then leaned in to give her a kiss on the cheek before backing up a few steps.

He tipped his fingers to the hat he — for once — wasn't wearing, making her picture him in it all the same, smiled, and said, "G'day, Starfish." Then walked back to his car. She turned the key and noted that he waited for her to exit the parking lot before he did, and they turned in opposite directions. She headed up the hill toward the pub and he headed down along the harbor road to the inn.

"What are you going to do about him, Kerry McCrae?" she whispered into the encroaching darkness. "What are you going to do?"

Any time she might have had to ponder that question was mercifully erased when she stepped into the chaos that was a summer Saturday night at the Rusty Puffin.

It felt as if she'd been gone a month.

How was it possible for a person's life to change so utterly in the span of twenty-four hours? she thought as she ducked up the back stairs with her laundry bundle. She got that load going in Fergus's ancient washing machine, then quickly changed into jeans and a Rusty Puffin T-shirt before looking at herself in the mirror. "Dear Lord," she murmured, picking up her hairbrush, then setting it down again. She had opted not to wash her hair in the tiny boat shower and consequently looked like she'd been in a wind tunnel, then rolled around in bed for a few hours. "Which, actually . . ."

She couldn't stifle the smile and, because she was alone, decided she didn't have to.

She'd be going down into the lion's den soon enough and would face enough knowing smiles and out-and-out social commentary on her love life to make her wish she was back out on Thomas's sailboat. But for now, the happiness was still all hers and she decided to savor it.

She dunked her head under the shower spray until it was good and wet. The one thing about her curly hair that she did love was that it was wash and wear. At least it was to her. She rubbed as much water out of it as she could with a towel, swore her way through a quick detangling with a big comb, then shook the curls loose once more and proclaimed herself as ready as she'd ever be.

"Yeah," she said, nervousness starting to creep in as she went down the indoor stairs to the kitchen. "Right."

Doon was in the kitchen that night, an old Irish ex-pat who'd buddied up with Fergus a few years back and helped out when Fergus needed a hand. He'd been a cook in the Irish army and handled the griddle on a busy night as easily as if he was at home cooking dinner for the family. He was tall, lanky, the opposite of Fergus, but shared the same shock of white hair and faded blue eyes as her great-uncle. And the charming grin.

At his surprised smile at her sudden appearance, she tipped up on her toes, kissed his ruddy cheek, then stole one of the potato skins he'd just put in a red plastic basket and winked at him, scooting through the swinging doors as he good-naturedly scolded her quickly retreating back.

From the noise level that had crept upstairs while she'd been changing, the pub was exactly as she'd expected. Packed to the gills and music thumping from the jukebox, with thirsty people crowding the bar. A bar, she quickly realized, that was being handily and quite competently covered by Miss Madison Diba.

Kerry quickly tied on an apron and eased in beside her. "Need a hand?" she asked with a quick smile, raising her voice to be heard over the ruckus.

Maddy shot her a returning smile. "What, and share any of this fun and excitement?" she replied while handily setting three glasses on the bar, pouring a beer into one and filling another with soda from the spray hose, while taking an order from another patron pushing his way toward her. "Well, okay, if you insist."

Kerry laughed and dove in. "Where's Gus?" she asked as she slid an order from

Doon down the bar and set a round of ales on a tray to be delivered back to the pool tables.

"In the back, in his office. Dart is with him. He looked a little tired so I told him Dart was getting a bit overwhelmed and needed a time-out, asked if he'd mind taking her back." She shot Kerry a smile. "That was thirty minutes ago."

At Kerry's brief look of worry, Maddy added, "Dart would bark and keep barking if something was wrong with Fergus."

Kerry immediately relaxed. "That's . . . awesome actually. Maybe we should think about getting him a trained companion dog."

"He's great with Dart," she said, not disagreeing.

"He loves all animals and they love him back. He's a sucker for a stray cat but ends up finding them all homes, says he can't be bothered."

"Well, how about I keep an eye open, and if a likely candidate comes my way, we can always do a trial run. Make him think he's helping me by training a newbie?" She shrugged, then slid another mug down the bar. "Whatever you think is best of course; just shooting ideas."

"You rock, Maddy Diba," Kerry told her

quite sincerely, then grinned. "We'll talk."

"Great!" she replied, matching her grin. "And maybe you can tell me all about the hot Aussie you spent the afternoon with." She shook her hand next to her chest. "I heard he's pretty hubba-hubba."

You have no idea, Kerry thought, and in the face of Maddy's charming, infectious smile, couldn't squelch her own. "It was a passable way to spend an afternoon."

Maddy hooted a laugh. "I'll bet."

Then they both dove back in, and Kerry made her way to the back of the pub with her tray. She wasn't surprised to see Hardy and some of the other guys from Blue's crowding one of the tables. She delivered her tray to the table next to theirs and went to snake her way back to the bar, but Hardy had noticed her and stepped in her path. "Well, look who's back from her sailing date looking all windblown and smug. Big day on the high seas?"

Kerry knew she'd have to deal with a lot of this kind of flak but didn't really want to start the ordeal with Hardy. Although, she thought, maybe it was better to get this dealt with up front. He'd said it smoothly enough, and seemed to be simply razzing her, with no other agenda in his eyes, but she treated him as if there was, just in case. "Oh, Hardy, you say the nicest things," she teased right back. "It was a lovely day for a sail," she added, then smiled brightly and, as it happened, quite sincerely. "Thanks for asking."

Her sunny response did seem to catch him a bit off guard, leading her to believe maybe there was more behind the dig than simply one friend razzing another. But the moment passed easily, and he actually smiled and nodded, which surprised her, given it was a bit out of character for him. Whatever the reason, she didn't care. She was perfectly happy to let it go. But he didn't step aside when she went to move past him. That was more in character. She swallowed a sigh and looked up at him again. "Need a refill?"

"No, we're good," he said, missing her thinly veiled impatience completely. Yep, that was the Hardy she knew. "So what's the lowdown on the new hire?" he wanted to know.

Ah. All became instantly clear. Hardy had moved on to new prey. And while that was a yay for Kerry, it was a boo for poor Maddy. She'd have to warn her. "You mean Madison? Sorry, Hardy, she's taken. Happily engaged to Sal's nephew, Micah."

"Engaged isn't taken; it only means she's been reserved," he said, a cocky grin spreading on his face as he glanced over the heads of the crowd to where Maddy was tending bar. "Reservations can get canceled."

"Hardy —"

But he wasn't listening to her. He'd been called back to his table by his buddies to take his turn.

"Oh, boy," she muttered and wound her way back to the bar. She ducked under the bar and worked her way back down until she was beside Maddy again. "Warning," she said, keeping her voice as low as she could. "Mr. Tall, Dark, and Cocky at the back pool table? You might want to keep an eye there. I told him you were engaged —"

"Don't worry. We've already had a chat."

"Well, you may be having another one, as he doesn't seem all that put off."

"I'll be fine, but thanks for running interference."

"He seems well meaning enough," Kerry told her, "but he's not the sharpest tool when it comes to the word *no*. You'll have to say it repeatedly for it to sink in."

Maddy nodded while setting bowls on the bar, then filling them with pretzels and nuts. "Have I mentioned that I grew up working in my much older brother's dojo?"

"Dojo?" Kerry repeated. "As in karate? Judo?"

"Tae kwon do," Maddy said. She shot a

knowing grin Kerry's way.

"Ah," Kerry said, understanding dawning. "And what color would your belt be, *jongyeonghaneun yeosong*?"

Maddy laughed. "I don't know if I'm an honorable woman," she said, surprising Kerry by understanding her very rough Korean. "But my belt, it is black." Maddy sketched a quick martial arts bow, making both women laugh. They glanced toward the back of the bar at the same time, only to find a grinning Hardy looking their way.

"See? He's the guy who assumes women are always talking about him," Kerry said.

"Well, we are," Maddy replied. "He can't know we're discussing how best to dismantle his manhood if he so much as thinks about laying a finger on me." She said all this with a serene smile.

Hardy lifted his beer in a salute, presumably to Maddy, before downing the rest in a single gulp, as if beer consumption somehow proved his manly man prowess.

"Poor Hardy," Kerry said with a mock sigh. "But then, he never did seem big on wanting to have children. Just ask his ex-wife." She ducked her chin as both women shared another laugh before continuing with their work.

After that, the rest of the night didn't seem

all that arduous. Maddy was happy to return Kerry's wingman favor, and between the two of them, they managed to distract, deflect, or defend much of the ribbing being thrown Kerry's way and actually had a much better time doing it than Kerry would have imagined.

Kerry had gone back to check on Fergus more than once, happy to find him still dozing on the couch in his office each time, an alert Dart by his side. Maddy said she'd wake him up when she went back to get Dart after closing so Kerry left the two to lock up and discuss how the night had gone, but not before letting Fergus know that whatever he'd offered to pay Maddy, it wasn't enough. That had gotten a smile from Maddy and a brief grumble from Fergus, who, she knew, would give her a lecture later about not being so quick to spend his hard-earned money.

She was smiling as she climbed the stairs to her room, plumb worn out in every possible sense of the word but feeling as good as she'd felt in a very long time. In fact, it had been about a year since she'd felt even close to this good.

She put the laundry in the dryer and barely made it through shrugging out of her clothes before face-planting in bed and mercifully sleeping like the dead until her alarm went off at the crack of dawn.

She smacked it silent, wondering why in the hell she'd set it so early, then remembered. The sheets and towels. "Time to pay the piper," she groused but wasn't really all that annoyed. All she had to do was let herself think about her lunch date and it was hard to stay grumpy.

Her mood brightened further when she went down the back steps to her truck, clean laundry all folded neat and tidy and tucked into a basket, only to discover a small starfish perched on the dashboard, a note tucked underneath.

She'd managed to make it all the way until morning without letting herself really think about what she was going to do about the situation with Cooper, coasting instead on the good mood the day had left behind and riding that wave through the crazy, busy work night and on into dreamland.

She slid behind the wheel and picked up the delicate starfish and the folded piece of inn stationery. She was smiling as she unfolded the note, so charmed and delighted there was no use even pretending she wasn't.

His handwriting was the same she'd seen on the dry-erase boards they kept in the stables and work buildings, neat and tidy, listing things to be done, passing on information as needed. The message, however, was purely personal.

G'day, Starfish. I've a date with a horse this afternoon. If you're free, I thought you might like to chaperone. You're quite good at that, as it happens. Fortunately, this time I'll actually know how to steer my ride, so your duties will be more limited. Might free you up to enjoy a ride of your own. And yes, I meant on horseback. Mind out of the gutter, pirate queen. Of course if you've time for dinner, I'll be happy to discuss dragging it back there later. As ever, your swashbuckling merry band of one, Hook

If she'd been charmed by the existence of the note, she felt downright swoony over the actual contents. *He truly was too much.* A tease and a flirt, yes, but in ways that made her feel strong and feminine and desirable. He was also a man who knew what he wanted and wasn't making any bones about going after it, yet doing it in such a way that thoroughly dismantled any defense she might mount as to why she shouldn't let him get away with it.

"Lunch with a man and his horse," she murmured, then giggled. "Or a pirate and his horse. What kind of pirate rides horses?" She folded the note and tapped it against the steering wheel. "Well," she murmured, "I guess there's only one way to find out."

CHAPTER THIRTEEN

"I appreciate your passing the word to your husband. It's very kind of him to extend the invite." Cooper smiled, looking forward to seeing the pretty little spread Kerry had described, which Calder and Hannah were developing along the banks of the St. Croix River. "I hope I'm not intruding on his work. I'm happy to pitch in if I can."

"No worries," Hannah said, then smiled at her inadvertent use of his Australian colloquialism. "And you're on vacation so we aren't going to make you pitch hay."

Calder smiled. "Truth be told, I wouldn't mind a bit of hard labor. Feels odd not to be putting in the hours."

"Your body is probably thanking you."

Cooper looked down at his booted toes at that, not wanting Kerry's sister to spy even a hint of just how spent his body had felt when he'd woken up that morning, much less why. "Big Jack — my dad — would tell you that taking so much as a day off makes a man soft." As soon as the words came out of his mouth, he realized the double entendre, then realized she wouldn't get that it was a double entendre and decided maybe he'd just stare at his booted feet all day long. Then he thought he caught just a hint of a knowing smile on Hannah's lovely face before she too decided to check out her footwear for an extended moment. Cheeky, like her sister, he thought. And sharp, like a defense attorney. The afternoon had barely gotten underway, too. *Sweet Mary.*

Another few minutes of this and he wouldn't be surprised to see Logan pulling up with the paddy wagon, ready to haul him off for putting his hands — and a whole lot more — on his baby sister.

"I told Calder about the work you do at Cameroo Downs," Hannah said easily enough, mercifully breaking the brief, awkward silence. "And that you were hoping to get out here during your stay to see how we do things. Of course what we have is minuscule compared to what you do, but he thought you might like to see his work with the at-risk and abused horses he's been rehabilitating. Our riding school hasn't been open that long. We only have one instructor so far, and a half-dozen students signed up to start, but we're happy with it, hoping to expand as the word gets out."

"Kerry told me a bit about that yesterday," Cooper replied, relieved to be back on safe ground. "It's good work you're doing there," he said. "For both the horses and the kids. I understand the students are children who have disabilities. I'm sorry, how did she phrase it — ?"

"Special needs," Hannah supplied. "And yes, they do."

"Don't we all, in a way?" he said with a brief smile. "That's a wonderful thing he's doing. You've a good man there."

"Yes, I definitely do," she said, sharing his smile, her eyes filled openly with joy and love for her newly wedded spouse.

"I want you to know I appreciate the warm welcome, Hannah."

She laughed briefly at that. "Well, mine might have been slightly cooler there at first, but —"

"You've a younger sister to look after. As do I. No need to explain." He leaned back against his car. "I like knowing Kerry has a protective clan standing watch for her."

"She needs watching over," Hannah said with another short laugh. "Actually, that's not fair. She's a strong, smart, capable woman. We worry because we love."

He nodded, grinned. "Family support, in all its colors, is one of the things we share and is a large part of why we are who we are. You're her foundation, her support. You've let her go off and be who she is, championed her free spirit. It's no small thing, that. I think about my sister, Sadie, taking off like that and . . ." He shook his head, chuckled. "I'd like to think we'd be so understanding as you all have been with Kerry, but —"

He broke off at Hannah's more full-bodied laugh. "Understanding? Is that what she told you? Well, if you count living in a constant state of fear that she'll end up in a scrape she can't get out of as being supportive, then yes, we are that. But she has put us to the test from time to time. To time," she added wryly.

"Yes, she mentioned that you've gotten her out of more than one little to-do. She said she turns to Logan for advice on travel logistics, her sister Fiona for advice on how best to handle certain social situations, and you to bail her out when things get sticky."

Hannah gave him a somewhat surprised, considering look. "She told you that, did she?"

He nodded. "I'm sure she turns to you for other things," he quickly added. "I didn't

290

mean to imply —"

"Oh, no need to apologize," Hannah said with another short laugh. "You've got it absolutely right. Trust me, I wish she'd turned to me for the social advice. And the transportation advice. Maybe then I wouldn't have had to bail her out so often. I was merely surprised she admitted as much to you."

Cooper grinned. "If you're worried about what other family tales she's told, I'd like to tell you not to worry, but —" He chuckled when Hannah looked momentarily surprised, then waved his hand. "No worries. It's all safe with me." He patted his palm over his heart. "You can trust that."

Hannah narrowed her eyes at him in mock severity, a smile still hovering about her mouth when she said, "I'll hold you to that, Mr. Jax."

His responding grin was unabashed. "Yes, Counselor, I imagine you will. I'd be disappointed in anything less."

The sound of Kerry's truck bumping over the curb into the small gravel parking lot next to her sister Fiona's new design shop drew both his and Hannah's attention. She parked between Hannah's little red Audi roadster and Fiona's peapod green Prius, making Cooper smile as he thought how the vehicles the sisters drove reflected them pretty accurately. Hannah all cool and sleek, Fiona both cute and pugnacious, and Kerry, who wasn't so concerned about looks but on getting where she was going and getting as many miles out of the adventure as she could.

She hopped down, slammed the door twice, then had to reach in the open window and hold the handle while she bumped it closed a third time. "Hulking piece of rust," she grumbled, then gave it a little pat on the wheel well as she scooted out between her truck and Hannah's car. "Can't let the car gods hear you dis their minions," she said when she caught Cooper's amused look. "They'll strand you in the desert as sure as look at you. Besides, she might be a hulking piece of rusted metal but she's my hulking piece." She stopped when she reached her sister and gave her a one-armed hug. "And to what do I owe this pleasure? Cross-examining my afternoon date, are we?"

"Maybe," Hannah said, hugging her back.

"Oh, good." Kerry grinned, rubbing her hands together. "What did you learn?"

"Hey, now," Cooper said, chuckling. "What makes you think I'd give anything up?"

"Oh, she's good," Kerry told him. "She once talked a tribal chief in Papua New Guinea, out of marrying me to his youngest son."

Cooper looked at Hannah, who just raised an arched brow but didn't refute the statement.

"Well, then, I suppose I'm even more in your debt," he told Kerry's oldest sister. "Unless of course the tribe believes in polygamy."

Kerry looked affronted. "You'd share me? Well, well, good to know." She folded her arms. "So glad we're having this little chat."

"Oh, no, Starfish, no such luck. You'd be stuck making do with only me. You see, I know a guy who could fly us out of there on his helicopter, and I'm guessing your erstwhile tribal spouse wouldn't go anywhere near one of those flying birds. I'd spirit you off and —"

"And leave my poor first husband broken hearted and alone? Do I get a say in this?" She looked to her sister. "You're drawing up my pre-nup, right?"

Cooper brightened and clapped his hands together, which earned him an arched brow from Kerry. "Well, while I'm not too thrilled about your attachment to Number One, speaking as Number Two, I will say I'm happy to hear we're in the negotiation phase."

"Husband Number One is a lot younger," she said consideringly. "And while he doesn't have as many head of cattle as you do, he does come with an entire village, and if something happens to his other six brothers, he'll be chief one day." She smiled sweetly. "Just saying."

Cooper flashed her a smile that might have been a little too private with her sister standing right there, but what the hell. "Keep in mind, Number Twos traditionally try harder. So I have that going for me."

Hannah looked from Cooper to Kerry, then at both of them, before finally looking at Kerry. "Seriously, marry him before he wises up."

"Hey," Kerry replied, mock wounded. "And why do you say that?"

"You speak the same language."

"Says the woman who communicates with her husband using old movie quotes that nobody gets but the two of you."

Hannah smiled, really smiled, and it transformed her often more serious expression into something truly radiant. "Yes, that's exactly who's saying that." She looked at Cooper. "I have a feeling you and Calder will become fast friends."

"Thank you," Cooper said, "for both sentiments."

Kerry frowned. "Wait. Why do you say that? About Cooper and Calder?" Then understanding dawned. She turned to Cooper. "Your horse date is at Blue Harbor Farm?"

"*Our* horse date. And yes, the very same. I had expressed interest in seeing the place so Hannah's husband was kind enough to extend an invite. I thought it might be a nice outing for both of us. You do like your brother-in-law?" He glanced to Hannah for confirmation but was already certain the family all got along. Kerry had told him as much the day before, while they were dining on cold hush puppies and broken biscuits in the boat's galley, completing what had been, hands down, the best afternoon of his entire life.

So far.

"Of course," Kerry responded, and he could see her trying to figure out why she should be wary of the proposed setup but coming up empty-handed.

"All good, then," Cooper said. He extended his hand to Hannah. "Thanks again. Will we see you out at the farm later?"

"I'm meeting Fiona, Grace, and Alex for our last dress fitting, then yes, I'm planning on heading back out that way."

Frowning, Cooper turned to Kerry. "Do you need to go take care of that, too?"

Hannah snorted, and it was so unlike his impression of her, he grinned and decided he liked her even more. "That one?" Hannah said, pointing at Kerry. "Of course not. She's like an Olympian runway model. Drop a dress over her head and pow, instant bridesmaid. No adjustments necessary." Hannah smiled sweetly at her sister. "She's been quite obnoxiously built like that since birth."

"Good thing because I had to wear hand-me-downs from the living mannequin here" — she nodded at her oldest sister — "and va-va-voom shrimp boat in there." She sketched a curvy figure with her hands while jerking her chin toward Fiona's shop.

"A too-tall mannequin maybe, one whose ankles always show in long dresses and with arms that are always a bit too long for the sleeves."

Kerry smiled and played a little imaginary violin, which Hannah swatted at before they both laughed. Hannah gave her a quick hug. "I'd better get in there. You want to pop in and say hello to the rest of the bridal party?" Hannah asked Cooper.

"When I've been given a free pass from

the wild and crazy fun that is dress fittings and seating-chart scheduling?" Kerry answered for him, smiling sweetly. "He passes on that. Call us when it's time to test that lemon-blueberry wedding cake she's considering and we'll be right over. I vote yes, by the way. Yum."

"Be careful," Hannah warned, still smiling as she headed toward the white picket gate, prettily framed by an arched trellis, through which led a stone pathway across the yard to the front porch. "One of these days it will be you fretting over seating charts and invitation fonts, and when you come begging us for help, we will take great pleasure in reminding you of how much you *loved* helping us when it was our turn."

"You know," Kerry called back, "with an attitude like that, maybe I will run off to Australia."

Hannah turned and back walked a few steps. "If it means you're eloping and I get to wear one less bridesmaid dress this year, I'll be happy to book your flight."

Cooper watched the back and forth, enjoying every volley — as were the sisters — while being equally thankful his father had only managed to produce one female offspring.

Hannah was smiling as she blew an exaggerated kiss to Kerry, then waved to Cooper. "Have fun at Blue Harbor. Tell Calder I'll call him when I'm on my way home."

Kerry turned and pretended to catch the kiss on her backside. "Thanks so much! Kisses and hugs!" she called back smartly before turning to Cooper, her smile dry but her deep, honest affection for her sister still shining in her eyes. "I bet you're standing there thankful that Sadie doesn't have sisters."

"Got it in one," he said with a grin, thinking he'd like to see that kind of shining affection in her eyes for him. He'd seen desire, hunger, vulnerability, uncertainty, and was thankful she'd lowered so many of her walls for him. But it was good to have goals. Maybe they'd get one step closer today. "Should I have mentioned our destination in my note? I assumed the horse mention would be a tip-off. You and your brother-in-law seemed to get on well from the stories you shared yesterday so I didn't see any harm there. There's no hidden agenda, I assure you."

"Cooper, it's okay," she said, looking amused. "I adore my new brother-in-law. Calder's an all-around great guy and, even better, he makes my sister deliriously happy and a lot less uptight. Win-win all around."

"Good, then we have a date." It should seem odd, he thought, having to plan dates with a woman he'd all but lived with for over a year. But it didn't. He liked the whole idea of courtship, of wooing her, and should even count himself lucky that it had all happened as it had. If he'd made his feelings known before she'd left, he'd have been planning dates on Cameroo Downs, which would have narrowed the list of potential romantic outings substantially. "I understand it's about an hour from here, so — you have the time?"

Kerry nodded, not looking so wary now about the plans. "I mentioned yesterday about Fergus hiring new part-time help? Well, her name is Maddy, and if I was worried about keeping my day job, she would be trouble because she's completely awesome in the truest sense of the word. I worked with her last night after I got back, and she fit right in like she'd been born and raised here. Well, behind a bar anyway."

"She's working tonight, then?"

Kerry nodded. "It's Sunday, so we're not open as late. We have a pretty good after-church crowd, and some after-supper regulars for pool and darts, but things wind down by ten and we're locked up by eleven usually. Maddy wanted the time when it was quieter to get her dog some experience —"

"Hold up. She's training her dog? To what? Serve beer and pretzels?"

"Didn't I mention? She's a service dog trainer. She's working toward opening up her own facility here, but she's got a wedding to plan —" Kerry made a face when he hooted a laugh, then wiggled his eyebrows.

"You've got to find out what they're drinking, luv. I'll make it for you special every morning."

"You're adorable," she said dryly.

He tipped his hat. "It's what I do, ma'am."

"Anyway," she said, giving him a warning look, "it was too crowded last night to give Dart — that's the dog — a service dog training session so she's hoping to do that tonight, which means —"

"I've got you all to myself, do I?"

"Well, if by 'all to yourself' you mean you, my brother-in-law, my sister, and a dozen rescue horses, then yep, you sure do."

"I thought I mentioned something about dinner."

"Oh, that. Well, you also told me to get my mind out of the gutter so I thought we'd dine with Hannah and Calder this evening," she said blithely, smiling at his surprised look. "Although they are still in that mooshy-gooshy newlywed phase so it might get a little uncomfortable. Fair warning."

He pushed off his car, then, and walked toward her. She didn't back up or do anything to obstruct his progress so he kept walking until she was forced to back walk a few steps, until the trellis over the gate blocked her from going any farther. "Nice touch," he said, noting the trellis was actually constructed from bicycle wheels welded into an arch, the flowering vines weaving in and around the spokes.

"That's Fiona," Kerry replied, only her voice was a bit more breathless now that he was deep inside her personal space.

"I'll look forward to seeing more of her work," Cooper said, bracing his hands on the arch of the trellis overhead. "But at the moment it occurs to me there's something we forgot to take care of in all that back and forth with your sister."

Kerry frowned, surprised. "Oh? Well, she's right in the house. If it's important, we can go get —"

"Not that," he said. "This." And he leaned down, caught her mouth with his, and kissed her. Not a short peck hello but a welcome-back, I've-missed-you kind of kiss. He was gratified when, instead of pulling away or using the possible prying eyes in the shop behind them as an excuse to demur, she sighed a little and sank willingly into the kiss. Her green eyes were dark and shining when he lifted his head a few moments later. "G'day there, Starfish," he said quietly, thinking he'd never tire of looking into them.

"G'day yourself, Hook," she replied, a quick grin flashing across her face when he must have looked a little too delighted by the nickname. "I'm looking forward to your having to explain that one," she added. "Take the heat off my nickname for a bit."

"Starfish? What do you tell them when they ask?"

"I tell them the truth. That you think I'm a big starry fish in my wee little pond. Which, you should know, is generally met with either a serious eye roll, a shake of the head, or, most often, both."

He pulled her into his arms and spun her around. "I can't help it if they're all blind to your many charms."

She swatted at him to put her down. "Oh, I don't think they're the ones with the vision problems." She surprised him with a rather sincere kiss on the cheek when he set her back on her feet. "But it's sweet that you think so."

He grinned, shook his head, and opened

the door. One of the things he was enjoying most about their unusual courtship was learning just how big a softy she was under that tough, smart-alecky exterior. He liked that he brought that out in her. Quite a lot actually. "Your carriage awaits," he said, gesturing her to the front seat.

She promptly held out her hand so he took it in his, thinking she was making a show of him helping her into the car, only for her to pull her hand back. "No, I meant the keys. Or are they already in the car?"

"I'll do the driving," he said. "No worries." He grinned. "You drove last time."

"Well, it's going to be a tight fit, then, seeing as you're handing me in to the driver's side of the car." She laughed when he shook his head and sighed in self-disgust. "That's what that big round thing is for," she added, still snickering when she pointed to the steering wheel.

"Har-har," he responded dryly, with a hint of pirate in the tone. He walked around to the passenger side, opening the door, then motioning her over with an exaggerated flourish of his hand. "I'll bet you had a time or two going to the wrong side of the car the first time you drove in a country with opposite lanes than you were accustomed to driving."

"Who, me?" she said, full of innocence. Except for that little flash of mischief in her green eyes. He liked making her do that, too. She scooted around to the other side and climbed in. When he was in and buckled behind the wheel, she confessed, "Actually, my first time was in Glasgow, Scotland. I'd just turned nineteen. I landed at night, rented a car because I was driving up to the Western Highlands to check out the Outer Hebrides, and decided to stay the night first in the city to get some sleep before embarking on my adventure. My hotel had a parking garage with the narrowest spiral drive winding up to each parking level. I had rented a stick shift and was trying to work the stick with the wrong hand but the pedals with the right feet, while seated on the wrong side of the car, managed to get halfway up, then realized I was going up the down drive when another car whipped around and almost hit me head-on." She shot him a dry smile. "And if you think driving up that tight spiral was a challenge, you should have seen me try to back all the way back down. It's a miracle I didn't smash every bumper and fender on the darn thing."

He chuckled, shook his head. "You know, I think about the things you've done, wandering any and everywhere by yourself, and it still blows my mind. I know every member of my family has asked you at one point or another if you were ever truly scared or found yourself in a seriously dangerous situation, but I guess, for me, the thing I marvel at is how fearless you seem to be about it all. I mean, I know you got into some risky situations, but that never seemed to factor into your decisions on where to go next or which new job or adventure to give a go."

He had already started heading them out of the Cove as he talked and was glad they had a little time alone, where talking was all they could do. After the huge step they'd taken the day before out on the boat, he was worried it would either make her retreat once she had time to think about it or worry that that was the only thing he'd want to be doing with her. So he'd opted for a family day excursion. Partly to reassure her that his interest was far broader than simply getting her into bed — though, admittedly, he'd thought of little else since climbing off that boat — and partly because he did want to meet her family, spend some quality time with them, see her with them, in hopes of making sure he was doing the right thing in asking her to come back to Australia with him.

When he'd made the decision to find her, that hadn't been a concern because she'd spent her whole adult life traipsing about; pulling her away from family — or anything else, for that matter — hadn't been on his list of worries. Getting her to stay in one place, however, had been.

Now he felt like she was caught between two opposing forces. The wanderlust siren song that inevitably called her to go forth and seek out the new, the different, the exciting. And her home and family, whom, it seemed, she was surprised to find herself wanting to cling to. He didn't need to see anything further to know they were a tight-knit, supportive clan. But before, she'd used their strong bond as the foundation she could spring from with confidence. Now, the strong bond seemed to be calling on her to stay. Her family had all reunited in the Cove, and maybe she felt it was time to settle down, too. She'd said as much to him, just as she'd said she wondered when the siren call would come again.

Limbo, he thought. Or purgatory. Unable to trust she could stay, but not being pulled to leave either . . .

And then he came along, offering her a third option. One that meant everything to him. One he hoped could come to mean everything to her.

"Cooper?"

He jerked from his thoughts. "Sorry," he said. "I — wandering thoughts. It's not the company, I assure you."

"Wandering to where?" she asked, easily enough but also seriously.

He glanced at her, then back at the road, debating on whether this was a topic they should broach again. Or whether he should just keep giving them time to build a shared future together. Suddenly the few short weeks he had seemed like no time at all.

"To how similar our family backgrounds are in some ways," he said, which was true enough, if not all of what he'd been pondering. "I was mentioning that very thing to Hannah. That we both share the love and strong support of family."

He could feel Kerry looking at him.

"What?" he finally asked, not sure he really wanted an answer.

"My family worries endlessly about me, and I've given them reason to, from time to time, but yes, they do support me, no matter what. As I do them." She paused for a moment, then said somewhat in a rush, "Would your family support you if you decided you didn't want to be a cattle baron and run the family dynasty?"

"Cattle baron, am I now?" he said, his chuckle a bit uneven. He hadn't expected this particular line of questioning, though he supposed he should have. "I suppose if my heart were pulling me in a different direction and, ultimately, if I were truly serious about it, my father would support my choice. Of course it helps that he's got Ian, who is dedicated and has big plans for the place." He grinned. "Just ask him."

Kerry laughed at that, and he knew she was remembering the many, many nights at the fire pit, listening to Ian's endless plans on his future vision. "He also has Sadie," Kerry added. "Unless Big Jack is so old-school that he can't picture a woman running the family empire."

Cooper shot her a quick smile. "I think we both know that Sadie's not meant to live her whole life on Cameroo Downs. I can't even — don't want to — think about the time when she'll be wanting to head off, but I'm fair to certain she will."

"What makes you say that?"

He glanced at Kerry again. "I've seen the way she looks at you, Starfish. She's got a bit of the wanderlust herself. You're her hero."

Kerry ducked her chin, but she was smiling. When he looked at her again, she was staring through the front windshield, a mix of wistfulness and guilt on her face.

"I didn't say that to make you feel bad."

"I know," she said. "But I do, all the same." She shifted in her seat so she was angled more toward him. "Whatever happens between us, I'd like it if — do you think she'd still want to hear from me?"

He nodded immediately. "She's got a huge heart, as you know, and she misses you greatly. She'd be over the moon."

"She's counting on you to bring me home, isn't she." She didn't make it a question.

"They all are," he said quite honestly. "But they won't hold it against you if your heart says otherwise. They — we — wouldn't want you there if it's not where you want to be." He looked back to the road. "You've two families who support your life choices now, you know, regardless of their own wants or desires."

He didn't look at her then, well aware that he'd added to the guilt and fear she already was feeling. He supposed, if he were being brutally honest, she'd earned a bit of the guilt where it concerned not staying in touch with Sadie as she'd promised, but the rest . . . well, it was all water under the bridge now.

"I appreciate that," she said in a quiet but

steady voice. "More than you know. More than I knew."

They drove on in silence a bit longer; then he decided to just put it out there. "I know life isn't easy for you these days. Any of it. Even without my being here, adding more options to your plate. I wish I could tell you what you should do, what would make you most happy and fulfilled. I know what I'd like of course, but I need you to know, ultimately, what I want is for you to do what you need to do. What's best for you." He smiled, tried to lighten the suddenly serious mood. "That doesn't mean I won't do my best to convince you I'm your best bet."

"I know," she said, sounding grateful. "And I appreciate that, too, a great deal." She looked at him, and he could feel the weight of her consideration. "I wish I knew what was best for me. I wish I could have my cake and eat it, too. Be here with my family, run off with you, know I could take off at any time if the call of the wild gets too loud to ignore, all without hurting anyone I leave behind. It was always clear-cut before. It wasn't a matter of would I be going, just when and where. I had the love of my family, who understood and supported my lifestyle and, quite frankly, I made sure I never had the love of anyone else to worry about."

"Did you ever think that would change at some point? Did you — do you — see yourself with a family of your own?"

"I suppose," she said, then quickly added, "I know that sounds ambivalent or uninterested, and I don't mean that. But given how I've lived, and that nothing has happened to make me want to change that, I started thinking maybe I wouldn't." She grinned. "I'd just be the cool aunt who brought home amazing things for my nieces and nephews and had wonderful stories to tell."

"Would that have been enough?" he asked without judgment, truly curious, and she seemed to take it that way.

"I don't know," she responded honestly. "If it stopped being enough, then I'd have to figure something else out. But while I was still wanting to travel, and my hunger to see more of the world was still the strongest driving force in my life, I did make the conscious choice not to tangle anyone else up in it who might ultimately want different things." She looked at him. "I'm sorry for that," she said. "And, at the same time, maybe I'm not. I don't know."

"Sorry for what?" he asked, honestly confused.

"For tangling you up. Complicating

things. I shouldn't have stayed in Australia as long as I did."

"But you did," he reminded her, not unkindly. "And maybe that was saying something." He glanced at her, and she was truly listening, open to what he was saying. That was another thing he loved about her. She was strong willed and opinionated but still open to ideas other than her own. "I mean, if having a family was ever going to be part of your life, the transition had to happen somewhere, and likely that meant somewhere on your many travels something would change the way you saw things. Unless you got sick of adventuring and decided to up and go home and cast your bait in the pond there."

She snorted, wrinkled her nose. "Casting my bait? Ew."

"Well, what do you expect from a cattle baron pirate?"

She giggled at that, and he was relieved to feel the tension ease. Not tension between them so much as tension over the future and what hung in the balance.

"I guess you're right, though," she said at length, and seemed really to be giving his comments serious thought. "The shift would have to start somewhere. I guess I thought it would be like you said, though.

I'd get tired of life on the road, go home, and figure out my next step."

"You never thought maybe you'd find someplace you didn't want to leave and make that your home?"

"Do you mean was I ever looking for that?" She shook her head. "No. I had a home so it was never about that."

"But you said you actively made sure no new place became home either."

"Well . . . yeah." She paused, then said, "It's true, I did my best not to get involved too deeply with anyone because I knew myself, knew I'd get the itch to leave. I didn't want to hurt them or hurt me. But it wasn't some sort of protective measure."

He wasn't so sure about that, but he left it alone. "Did you ever feel lonely?"

She looked honestly surprised by that question. "You mean —"

"Not sex," he said. "Though I guess that's a fair question, too. But I'm not asking you to kiss and tell. What I meant was, did you ever feel lonely for the lack of strong bonds."

"I have my family —"

"Yes, true. But I mean something more immediate than that. People actually in your life, day in and day out, that you feel connected to, look forward to sharing things with, small and large."

She thought about that for a long time, then finally said, "I didn't let myself see it that way. You can't miss what you don't have."

"Did you leave friends behind, school chums, that sort of thing, when you took off? I mean, you spent the first eighteen years of your life in one place, and a small-town place at that. Surely you left behind some lifelong friends when you headed out."

"Yes, sure, I had friends back then. But I think it's a lot like anyone else after graduation. You all tend to scatter, head off to different colleges, take different paths, grow apart. I know some folks, like Logan with Ben, find a way to hang on to childhood friends no matter what. But it didn't happen that way with me, and . . . I don't know. I took off so young, I didn't really look back. I was too excited to get started on the future."

"And it never seemed overwhelming, just up and taking off to parts unknown all by yourself?"

"Not really. I mean, I couldn't see everything all at once and I had my entire life ahead of me so I just picked one adventure at a time. I started by tossing a dart at a map in Fergus's office." She smiled. "I took that dart and map with me. That was how I

314

picked most places I went. I mean, I had some things on my bucket list, if you want to call it that, and places I'd hear about on my travels that sparked an interest, but . . ." She lifted a shoulder. "It wasn't so mapped out as all that. I wasn't on a deadline."

"Have you kept a journal?"

She gave him a quizzical look. "You're really hung up on my being solo. Not everyone needs a buddy or pal to confide everything to." When he ducked his chin briefly at that, she hurried to add, "Cooper, I didn't mean — " She sighed. "You're trying to understand how I can wander through life alone so you can figure out, or maybe help me figure out, if I can ever be the type to actually want someone by my side. And I don't know. I hadn't felt that need." She reached out, put her hand on his arm, and pressed her fingers in. "I never found a place I didn't want to leave or a person I wanted to confide in. At least until I stumbled on this cattle ranch in the tropics of Australia."

He looked at her then, knowing his confusion and want and, yes, maybe a little hurt and disappointment, too, shone in his eyes. He didn't try to hide them. She was baring everything to him in a far more intimate way than she had on the boat yesterday. She deserved the same from him. "Would you have left if the wedding invite hadn't come?"

She let her hand slip back to her lap. "I don't know." She looked at him. "It's as simple and complicated as that. I felt itchy, but only because I wasn't feeling itchy. I had come to care about all of you. My experience on Cameroo was entirely different from any I'd had, as far as making connections, enjoying my work, not getting bored, or simply getting the itch to move on and see something new, try something different."

"Did that worry you? Did you ever think maybe you'd just stay, ride it out, see what happened? Was that an option for you?" He didn't ask defensively, though it took a bit to keep the edge from his voice. He was all but grilling her so he couldn't go and get upset if he didn't like the answers he got. But he was human, and this wasn't any easier on him than it was on her.

"It might have been."

"If?"

He heard her take a steadying breath and felt himself bracing for her response. "If I'd felt about you the way I felt about the rest of your family. Like you were a brother or something."

"But?"

"Looking for a little ego stroke?" She swatted at him then, tried for a playful laugh, but the serious undertone remained. "But I had feelings for you. Well, lust and feelings. We had a friendship, then I had lust. And I really didn't think, even if you were interested in me, that was something you'd pursue, given your position as employer and me being temporary. So . . . I don't know. . . ."

"But when you came back here to Maine you didn't head out again."

"I didn't go back to Australia either," she reminded him. When he didn't say anything for some time, she said, "What are you thinking? I've been pretty frank so go ahead, be honest with me."

"Okay," he said. "I guess I can't help but think that you didn't head back out on the road, you didn't come back to Australia either — but you also didn't write, keep in touch. And not because you were out in the jungle somewhere, unable to drop a postcard in the mail. You were right here, with all the modern technological conveniences at your fingertips. But you didn't send a single e-mail. Not even to Sadie. And I can't help but think that maybe that means we were all a lot more important to you than you wanted to admit or keeping in touch, at least with her, would have been no big deal. You also haven't even mentioned us to anyone here, as far as I know, other than your uncle. Which, given how long you stayed and how much we'd come to mean to you, seems odd to me, too. So . . . maybe the only way you thought you could get over us was to put us firmly in your rearview mirror. Only then . . . you never started looking ahead again either."

She said nothing, and a quick glance showed she was staring out the side window of the car, her hands in her lap, fingers twisting and untwisting.

"Or maybe we really were easily left in the past, and the change in you is more because you got home and your entire family was living here, all together, for the first time in your adult life," he said, giving her an out. "And it makes you want to stay, even though you don't know what, precisely, you want to do here yourself."

He paused, then said the rest of what he was thinking, what he was feeling. "And maybe you stay because it's the closest thing you can have to what you had started building with us, and remain safe while having it."

CHAPTER FOURTEEN

Kerry leaned on the fence and watched Calder show Cooper the ropes, literally, while working with one of the rehab horses he'd had at the farm for a few months. Cooper of course picked things up quickly, and Calder eventually handed the lunge line over to him, nodding approvingly as he continued working with the big brown gelding.

"He's good."

Kerry startled, turned to find Hannah approaching the ring. "I didn't hear you drive up."

Hannah was still in the slacks and silk blouse she'd been wearing when Kerry had seen her earlier, but that didn't stop her from propping her high-heeled foot on the lower fence rail and leaning next to Kerry. "Penny for your thoughts," she said, apparently seeing something more than admiration for Cooper's animal husbandry in her sister's eyes.

But then, her former defense litigator sister rarely missed much.

"I wish I could sort them all out," Kerry said, sharing a small smile. "I'd be happy to give you a go at them."

"He seems like a good guy," Hannah said easily, but maybe nudging just a tiny bit.

"Oh, he is that," Kerry agreed quite readily. "I don't think I could ask for better."

"So . . . what's the holdup?"

Kerry turned her attention to her sister. "Oh, maybe the fact that the longest I've stayed in one place for the past twelve years would be the year I spent on his cattle station and the year I've spent here."

Hannah nodded at that, then asked, "Do you love him? Or . . . are you falling in that direction?"

"I — I . . ." Caught off guard by the directness of the question — her sister's forte — Kerry didn't know how to answer. "In some ways I love all the Jaxes," she said haltingly, putting those particular feelings into words for the first time. "I mean, like the family they'd started to become to me. I think — know — given more time with them, that feeling would only have grown deeper."

"And Cooper?"

"It's not about love, Hannah," she said, avoiding that particular topic. She turned to her sister. "I love all of you, and the new members of our family, but that doesn't mean I feel the need to stay by your side. I've always loved you, but that hasn't kept me from traipsing all over the place. So whether or not I love him isn't the question, really."

"Would it be so bad, to stay in one place? I mean, you loved it there, didn't you? Fergus said —"

"Seriously, I'm never telling him anything ever again," Kerry grumbled.

"He wants to help you. We all do. I mean, you have to understand, it's hard for us. We know you were happy there, and weddings and strokes notwithstanding, you've surprised us all by sticking around such a long time. Now here's this amazing guy showing up, proposing marriage to you — who, let me tell you, is also not hard on the eyes — or the ears, for that matter. Wow, with the accent." She nudged Kerry's shoulder, gave her an affectionate smile. "What's wrong with you already?"

Kerry nudged back, and they shared a small laugh. "I know, I know. I wish I could explain to you what it feels like. I . . . I have loved all the things I've done, some more than others of course, but no matter what it is I'm doing, at some point I get a little bored or a lot restless. I know there's still so much more out there to do, to see. I — I don't know how else to describe it. It's not that I don't want to stay, don't love you enough, or Cooper or his family either. It's just . . . I start getting fidgety, looking at the horizon." She leaned her head on Hannah's shoulder and bumped hips with her. "I want to be solid and dependable and loyal like the rest of you, and in my heart, I *am* solid and loyal. I love you all more than life. But —"

"But you can't do that and sit still forever at the same time," Hannah said quietly. "I guess I understand. As much as someone who hated even booking a flight from DC to Maine could understand."

"I know it seems selfish as all hell."

She reached up behind them and tugged on one of Kerry's curls, much as she had when Kerry had been little. "No," she said. "Selfish would be agreeing to run off with Cooper, promising him the world when you were pretty sure you wouldn't be happy staying in one place with him in the long run. We're all responsible for figuring how best to live our lives, to feel fulfilled, happy, satisfied, and to be as good at taking care of

those we're responsible for as we can be."
She leaned her cheek on top of Kerry's
head. "You've stayed true to who you are,
never letting anyone believe otherwise or
leading anyone on. If you're happy with
your path, continue on along it. You know
we'll support you."

"I'm not leading him on," Kerry said
softly. "Am I, Han? I mean, I've been honest with him. But at the same time, I'm
here, spending time with him, giving him
the chance to change my mind."

"Can he?"

"I don't know."

Hannah lifted her head, waited until
Kerry looked up at her. "Do you want him
to?"

Kerry didn't think or analyze; she simply
gave her instinctive, gut response. And nodded. "Yes. I think I do."

Hannah grinned, seeming surprised but
happy. Truly happy. "Well, then, good." She
squeezed Kerry's shoulders. "Good."

Kerry groaned. "I should never have
answered you."

"Yes, you should have. Maybe it's the only
way you'll hear it, to hear yourself say it out
loud like that. At least now I know you see
what we all see."

"Which is what?" Kerry asked warily,

straightening away from her sister and leaning once again on the fence rail.

"That he makes you happy." She lifted a hand to stall Kerry's reply. "Maybe not for all eternity, but then, none of us can know that about anyone. What's important to recognize is that he makes you happy now. So live in that space for a bit. Try it on, wear it around town. Sleep with it at night," she added with a little twinkle. "Who knows, maybe in a few weeks the idea of heading back out into the world alone won't look so appealing to you."

"Maybe," Kerry said, though she wasn't sure how convinced she was. She just knew that she really, really wanted to be convinced. Which was a start, she supposed. "A few weeks isn't a lot of time."

"Have faith," Hannah said. "You'll know how you feel when it comes time for him to leave."

The thought of that day made her belly clutch and her heart rise to her throat. *So that's a sign, maybe.* She ignored her little voice, and the clutch. Of course she wanted Cooper. Who wouldn't? But promising him a life together? Marrying him?

Hannah leaned down and whispered in her ear, "You know, maybe it doesn't have to be all or nothing. Who says you can't have a trial period Down Under when his trial period ends here?"

Kerry nodded but was no longer sure of anything. Between Cooper's barrage of thought-provoking questions on the drive up and Hannah's cross-examination and leading questions, Kerry wanted nothing more than to crawl off in a corner somewhere alone, where she could examine her head and her heart.

One thing was certain: She was probably past the point of making sure no one got hurt. Because she already knew that not seeing Cooper ever again, not feeling his body on hers, his mouth on hers, hearing him laugh, making him laugh, arguing, talking, finding notes tucked under starfish on her dashboard in the morning . . . never having all that again? Might well kill her.

But how did she dare reach for what she wanted today and damn the consequences of what would very likely happen in the future? Would the greater pain they'd all suffer then be worth the memories and what they'd get to share leading up to that point?

"Do you have your keys?" Kerry abruptly asked.

Hannah looked surprised, then alarmed. "Kerry, don't go and do —"

"I just need to take a drive. Clear my

head. Think. Cooper is in his element here and likely will be for a good long while. If he asks —"

"If?" Hannah said, lawyering up again, clearly not on board with Kerry's sudden wild hare.

"If he asks," Kerry repeated evenly, "tell him I've gone for a drive and will be back for dinner." She looked Hannah square in the eyes. "I promise. I just need some space. I have a lot to think about."

"It doesn't all need thinking out today," Hannah reminded her.

"If I don't get a handle on it now, it's only going to pile on and be that much more complicated and confusing. I don't want to get pushed or overwhelmed and do something I'll regret." She took the keys Hannah begrudgingly handed her. "Thank you. I won't put a scratch on her, I swear."

"It's not her getting banged up I'm worried about," Hannah said.

Kerry impulsively pulled her sister in for a tight hug. "Thank you," she whispered. "For loving me despite what a confusing pain in the ass I can be."

Hannah hugged her back, then let her go. "I do love you," she said to Kerry's retreating back. "But if you're not here by dinner, I'm going to tell Cooper to run, run fast."

Kerry tossed a smile over her shoulder. "Good luck with that. I already tried."

"He loves you, Kerry," Hannah said quite seriously now. "But he's not a puppy dog who'll hang around and wait forever. If you don't love him, let him go so someone else can."

Kerry patted her backside in response but then looked over her shoulder, first at Hannah, then beyond her to where Cooper was working the horse in the ring, all traces of teasing gone from her face. "As soon as I figure things out, he'll be the first to know." She looked back to Hannah. "That much I can promise." Then she headed for her sister's little red sports car without looking back again, and tried not to break into a run.

CHAPTER FIFTEEN

Cooper sat on the end of the inn's private dock, his bare feet dangling above the water of the harbor, listening to the seabirds overhead and the steady sounds of Brodie sanding wood in his boathouse, perched out at the end of a network of piers belonging to his shipbuilding company.

Cooper knew that was the source of the sound because he'd taken his coffee and walked out there earlier, just as the sun was coming up, to see what was going on. He'd found Brodie hand sanding the hull of a sailboat he was in the early stages of building, using an old-fashioned hand lathe on the wood. Cooper had questioned him about it, surprised that he wasn't building the boat up in the big boathouses on land, and using something more high-tech to get the job done. Brodie had just smiled and told him that some boats required a more personal touch and a more personal space.

Cooper understood that. Some women needed the same.

Cooper hadn't really been surprised when Kerry had taken off for a drive. Hannah had apologized, explaining that they'd gotten into a rather serious conversation on life and love, and she felt like she'd maybe piled on a bit too much. Cooper had assured her that if anyone was to blame it was him, for doing much the same on their drive out. Everyone was so determined to help Kerry figure out what would make her happy, they weren't giving her much room to simply be happy.

He realized his deadline wasn't helping matters and had told her as much on their drive home. She'd been in a good mood when she'd come back to the farm, her red curls all wind tossed and her face warm from the sun from putting the top down on Hannah's little sports car. She seemed refreshed, relaxed.

They'd both gotten on horseback and spent some time in the ring with Calder putting her and Cooper and the horses through their paces. Dinner had been casual and fun, burgers on the barbie, served out on their back deck, with stories shared and more laughter than anything else. Kerry had been a lively participant in all of it, and he'd enjoyed seeing her with her family and how honestly and sincerely she'd welcomed Calder into the fold.

The McCraes were a solid bunch and would no doubt lay down their lives for one another, but they also put a priority on happiness and finding one's way in life. Both of her sisters had recently made huge, life-altering decisions, not only in deciding to marry but in packing up their respective successful lives elsewhere and coming back home again to start over with new hopes, new dreams.

So he knew they meant well in encouraging Kerry to give his proposal serious consideration, and that they'd support her no matter what she ended up doing. Just as he hoped she knew he would.

But despite the pleasant afternoon and evening spent with the Blues, Cooper wasn't fooled into thinking Kerry had sorted everything out. Or anything, really. Both because she'd been relaxed but quiet on the drive home, letting the afterglow from dinner be enough company as the stars winked to life overhead. And because he'd told her he'd stop pushing so hard and not to worry about when he was heading back to Australia, that if they wanted to continue to figure things out, they'd find a way, and there was no hard-and-fast deadline. He'd told her he'd let her set the pace, decide when they'd next spend some time together.

That had been three days ago.

He knew, because Grace had told him, that Fiona's final wedding plans were kicking in to high gear. It was now Wednesday, and the wedding was a week from that coming Saturday. So he'd been patient and remained true to his word. But he wasn't going to lie and say he wasn't frustrated. Not so much by the time that had passed but by the complete radio silence that had accompanied it. Maybe he shouldn't have been surprised. He knew she regretted not keeping in touch with Sadie, but then here she was retreating in exactly the same way again, when she didn't have to. She certainly didn't seem to be a changed woman.

If you have to change her to make things right, maybe you shouldn't be here in the first place.

He wished he could ignore that niggling doubt, but there was truth to it. Not that he wanted to change her per se. She'd started doing that all by herself, staying on in Cameroo well beyond her planned end date. Staying on at home past the time, continual weddings notwithstanding, that her presence was truly needed. He'd only wanted to see if maybe he could provide an alternative that would be equally as fulfilling to her as her nomadic lifestyle.

Footsteps vibrated the dock lightly, mercifully pulling him from the endless merry-go-round of his thoughts. He looked up, half-expecting to see Grace coming out to check on her guest, or possibly Logan, breaking it to him that Kerry wanted him gone and couldn't find the heart to tell him in person.

So it was a surprise, when he looked up, to find it was Kerry. The instant whoosh of relief he felt was immediately tempered by the smooth expression on her face. Maybe she'd found the heart to do it herself after all.

He didn't realize how tightly he'd gripped the edge of the pier until he pried one of his hands loose to reach up and offer her assistance. She sank effortlessly to the dock next to him, no assistance needed, and slid her feet over the edge of the pier so they dangled next to his.

"You look like someone stole your pirate ship," she said, squinting into the sun as she briefly looked at him, then back to the water.

"No, it's moored just down the harbor. I seem to have misplaced my pirate queen, though." He bumped the side of his foot

332

into the side of hers but otherwise kept his hands to himself.

"Oh, she's been navigating the choppy waters of Bridal Bay, trying not to drown in the froth of lace whitecaps or get dragged under by the pearl-seeded kelp beds."

He smiled at that. "I've heard that particular channel can be a tricky one to navigate. Lots of something olds looming out there in the deep, blocking the easier paths to the something news."

She darted a quick look at him, but seeing his smile, she rolled her eyes, then nudged his foot right back. His smile eased into a wider grin. The tension, however, didn't lessen one whit. Judging by the stiff set to her shoulders, hers hadn't either.

"I wrote you a note," she began, and if he thought he'd felt tension before, he wasn't too sure he wasn't about to lose his breakfast after that little announcement. "I didn't know if your phone worked here, and even if it does, I don't have the number. Same goes for e-mail. I could have left a message at the inn, but then I might as well have posted it on the bulletin board outside the town hall for the whole world to read." She lifted a shoulder. "So I thought I'd take a page from your book — a very charming one, I might add," she said, glancing up at him from the corner of her eye. "But the doors to your car were locked, and I didn't put it under your windshield wiper for the same reason I didn't leave a message with Grace." She let out a little breath. "But I did write you a note. I just wanted to go on record. Because I know what I did with Sadie, and you're probably thinking —"

"I'm thinking that unless you're about to tell me to bugger off back to Australia and never darken your door again, I'm about to be all those things I promised not to be and kiss you senseless right here on the dock, in front of God, the seagulls, and anyone else who happens to be watching, and damn the consequences."

Maybe he'd said all of that in a bit more of a rush and with a bit more heat than he'd intended. Okay, a lot more heat. Probably so, given the goggle-eyed look she was giving him.

"I was trying to apologize," she said, relief and humor easing into her eyes and curving her lips.

"You didn't answer my question." He thought he might snap off the end of the pier, he was gripping it so hard.

In response, she ducked her hand into the pocket of her shorts and pulled out a folded and now somewhat crumpled piece of paper. "Here. Read for yourself."

He took the paper, realizing he was acting like a complete yobbo, and knew then that perhaps he wasn't nearly so cool and level-headed about this whole endeavor as he'd led her to believe. The truth of it being, he only really wanted her to figure out what would make her happy if what made her happy was him.

Under her amused stare, he unfolded the paper and read:

Dear Hook,

I'm trying to be a good and supportive sister and help get Fiona and her ridiculously long veil down the aisle before I strangle her into submission with every hand-beaded, pearl-seeded foot of it. At the moment, sitting here knee-deep in crinolines and enough netting to outfit every member of *Downton Abbey*, I can't safely predict a win in that ongoing effort.

That said, I'd much rather be spending the time with you, sailing the high seas on our pirate ship. Especially that part where we stayed anchored in one spot for an afternoon and all the plundering was going on aboard our own boat. I've been thinking a lot about everything everyone has said and have come to the conclusion that the only thing I'm sure of is that I'm thinking too much.

I've decided it was better when I was just feeling things and not thinking endlessly about them. I especially liked the things I was feeling on our picnic for two. So this is all to say I'd like to go, um, sailing again. Even if there's no boat involved this time. I hope you won't think less of me for the request, but please take seeing a whole lot more of me as a consolation prize if you do. Also? Save me. Or send bail money. Sincerely, Starfish, Queen of the High Seas, Plunderer of Pirates, especially those with a really clever right Hook.

He was smiling and shaking his head as he folded the note closed and tucked it in his shirt pocket.

"Well?" she said at length.

"Apology accepted" was all he said.

"And?"

He slid a look her way. "And . . . what?" She'd made him wait three days, and punitive or not, he wasn't in any hurry to put her out of her misery. Plus, when he did, it was likely to be that much more fun.

"You're going to make me spell it out, aren't you? Don't you realize it was hard enough just putting it in writing?"

"I accept your lovely invitation," he said, then added, "I only have one caveat."

Her relief turned to wary suspicion as she eyed him. "Oh? And that would be?"

"Will you wear the crinolines?"

She bumped his shoulder with hers, hard enough to make him put his hand out to brace himself so he didn't topple off the pier.

"Is that a yes?" he asked, chuckling and putting his hands up as she turned toward him.

"You know, never mind," she said. "I don't know what possessed me to —"

"Proposition a pirate?" he finished for her, his smile spreading to a grin. "What did you expect, Starfish? Tea and roses?"

"And you wonder why I don't try to communicate more."

She went to boost herself up, but he reached out and took hold of her arms before she could so much as get her butt off the planks. Then he pushed her straight back down on the pier and, following her down, leaned over her so her side pressed against his chest. "You have one way of communicating that's exceedingly effective."

"I believe that's what I was trying to convey," she said, but any haughtiness she might have been trying to inject in her tone was utterly erased by the hunger that had her eyes dark and glittering for him.

"Maybe you should show," he said, lowering his head, "not tell."

"You really think putting your mouth near my teeth is a good idea right now?"

He kissed her nose, then the soft spot of her temple, then worked his way down the side of her cheek to her jaw. "If you still want to use those teeth by the time I get to your mouth, go right ahead," he murmured. "I'll deserve it."

Her response was a short gasp when he nipped her earlobe, then kissed the side of her neck, making it arch slightly off the pier. "Cooper —"

"I've missed you," he said as he worked his way to her mouth. "And not just this part." He claimed her mouth and she took him right in, kissed him right back. He drew away moments later before he was pulled under and smiled down at her. "Although I'm pretty fond of those parts, too."

"I know a guy who has a boat," she said, a little breathless, a smart smile on her lips now and hunger in her eyes.

"I know a guy who has a bed," he said. "A nice big one. About a hundred yards north of this very spot."

"A bed that requires a long walk through a crowded lobby," she reminded him.

"Do you think everyone thought we were playing tiddledywinks out there on that boat all day long?"

"Tiddledywinks? Really? You're adorable."

He winked at her. "I try. But okay, if my room is out, and I'm guessing yours as well, then —"

She let out a short laugh.

"What?"

"I can't believe I'm thirty-one-years-old, lying on my back on a pier in broad daylight — in my own hometown, I might add — trying to figure out a place to go make out."

"Is that what the kids are calling it these days?" When she stuck her tongue out at him, he took full advantage until both of them were a little breathless. He really needed to employ that method more often. It was surprisingly effective. Not to mention fun. "I also have a car, which can drive us in any direction you'd like to go. Another town, a private inlet, surely you've got the inside line on that."

"I don't know what kind of teenager you

thought I was, but you forget, I left here at eighteen, before I ever had reason to find anyone's inside line, much less where best to go play with it."

Now he made a face, and they both laughed. He rolled up to a seated position and pulled her up along with him. They both looked out at the water, then back to each other. "Boat it is," they said at the same time.

"But not Thomas's this time," she said as they scrambled to their feet. "It made me feel like — well, I don't know what, but not good — to have to sneak back aboard and stow all the sheets and towels in there before daybreak the next morning. Like some kind of reverse cat burglar or something. I had this whole story concocted about how I left my phone onboard and had come back to look for it, if by chance he came to move the boat while I was there. I have to tell you, I'd suck at being an actual pirate queen."

He pulled her against him, her back to his front, and looped his arms around her waist, leaning down to kiss the curve where neck met shoulder. "Don't sell yourself short, Starfish. And I think you'd make a lovely cat burglar. All decked out in tight black spandex. Mmm," he said, moving his hips a little. "Maybe we —"

"Don't even think about it," she said, then tipped her head back and looked up at him. "Unless you're willing to do the same."

He made a face. "You'd really want to see me in black spandex?"

"Mmm, maybe you're right. Not spandex. Oh, I know," she said, brightening. "You could be all classy, smooth cat burglar. You'd look amazing in a tuxedo," she said. "All black tie and Aussie accent." She wriggled a little.

"I'd rather wear the spandex," he said, frowning at the idea of getting trussed up in a monkey suit.

She laughed and said, "I figured as much." She turned in his arms and looped hers around his neck. "So how about we stop putting on a show for everyone out here and go find ourselves a floating playpen?"

He grinned. "Well, when you put it like that . . ." He leaned down, kissed her soundly, and tried not to let his thoughts stray to what came next. He'd exhausted himself with that the past three days and was thankful they were back to doing, not thinking.

"I'd tell you to get a room, but I happen to know you already have one."

The sudden intrusion of a deep voice with an entirely different accent made Kerry jump, and it was only because Cooper already had his arms around her that he was able to pull her back before they both went in the drink.

"Sorry," Brodie said with a grin as he covered the last ten yards at the end of the pier, a small mutt racing down the docks behind him. "Didn't mean to startle."

"So, an Irishman and an Aussie walk into a bar," Kerry said, recovering quickly and teasing Grace's husband as he stopped a few feet away. She bent down and clapped her hands as the scruffy mutt came skidding to a stop in front of her. "Hello, Mr. Whomper, and how are you today?" She gave him a good ear scratch, then laughed when he immediately wriggled over to his back in hopes of a belly rub to go with it. Laughing she obliged, then straightened, leaving the dog to sniff out Cooper's feet, hoping for more of the same from the newcomer.

"Heck of a watchdog you have there, Monaghan," Cooper said, squatting down to give the dog a good once-over.

"You realize," Brodie said, "you've just made a shameless love slave out of him for life."

"Well, he has good hands," Kerry said, then lifted her own in mock surrender when

342

both men looked at her. Cooper was certain his surprised expression mirrored Brodie's. "What?"

Brodie chuckled, and his grin had the same cheek Cooper had been told his did. The two men were about the same height and build as well, but the Irishman had shorter hair and green eyes almost the same color as Kerry's. "Well, not to put a damper on the, uh, festivities," Brodie said, "but Grace just gave me a shout, said she was trying to reach you. She'd have come out herself, but she's swamped with checking in a young family with four kids."

He was speaking to Kerry, who felt her pockets, then gave a rueful smile. "I must have left my phone in the truck. And four kids, did you say?" She looked to Cooper and wiggled her eyebrows. "Lots of distraction potential."

When Brodie cleared his throat she gave him an unapologetic smile. "Hey, you're the one doing all the festivity dampening. I can't be held responsible for what you might hear." She relented and patted his arm. "What did Grace want, did she say?"

"Something about a surprise bachelorette party for Fiona?"

"Oh, right! I told her I'd help her with that, and then —"

"Festivities happened," Brodie supplied. "I understand." And from the smile on his face, Cooper imagined he did indeed. "Do you want to use my phone to call her or did you want to —"

"I'll go on up and talk with her now, when she's done with her current check-in." She turned to Cooper. "Sorry, I promised."

"No worries," he told her and meant it. "I don't expect you to drop everything because I'm here. Besides, I like seeing the ebb and flow."

"Thanks," she said and bumped shoulders with him. She might have also snaked her arm around his waist and made a little detour to grab his backside.

"You know, what with all the weddings here and about, there's been a lot of talk about who'd be up to take on the challenge of the youngest McCrae," Brodie said, then stepped in and gave Cooper's shoulder a clap. "I'd say you look good for it, mate," he said with a grin. "I'll leave you two to it, then. And by *it* I mean —"

"Good-bye, Brodie," Kerry said, giving him a little shove, even as they both laughed. "I should have known not to encourage the incorrigible."

"You did start it," he said, then gave them a quick salute before jogging back down the pier, Whomper close at his heels.

Cooper took Kerry's hand in his and started down the pier after him, only to have Kerry tug him back. "I was thinking . . ." she said.

He grinned. "I thought you weren't doing that anymore."

"A different kind of thinking," she said, then batted her eyelashes at him.

"Ah," he said, taking her other hand and pulling her around to face him. "Tell me more."

"Well, I was thinking that if you go on up to the inn and sort of slip up to your room while the desk is in chaos with all the kids, I'll come in a few minutes later, when things have wound down, talk to Grace, then maybe, oh, I don't know, wander around a bit, wait for a lull, and find myself up at . . . what did you say your room number was?"

He pulled her close and kissed her up-turned mouth. "Six," he said, "and I think that's a lovely idea. I do wonder if those privacy screens are soundproof, though." He thought she'd swat at him again.

Instead she laughed and said, "You haven't met Langston. The man who designed the place? Trust me, they probably are. Bulletproof too. The man likes to mix his high-tech gadgets in with his historic replicas."

"So I noticed." He turned and they started down the pier, still hand in hand. "One other thing, then I promise I'll stop thinking, too."

"Okay."

"What about after? Getting back through the lobby, I mean. Assuming you'll need to leave at some point. For the bachelorette party, if nothing else."

"That's not until the weekend."

He grinned. "Your point being?"

"You know," she said, tipping up on her toes and kissing his cheek, "I like it when you do the thinking."

"Well, I was going to mention that, but —"

She pinched his butt, making him laugh.

"Careful or I'll swing you up and carry you up to my room over my shoulder."

Kerry spluttered a laugh, then said, "You know, it's almost worth doing, just to blow everyone's minds."

He pulled her closer. "Don't tempt me."

She batted her lashes again. "But I thought you liked it when I tempted you."

Now he slid his hand behind her and gave her a little pinch, making her skip a little step but laugh at the same time. "I guess I head that coming."

"There's a lot I'd like to do that has *com-*

ing in the description."

"Okay, okay, so assuming I will have to leave your pirate's lair at some point, then yes, how to do that without being the front-page story of the gossip gazette." She looked up at him, her expression serious. "I could always come down the ramp carrying a box of tiddledywinks. Then no one would suspect for sure."

"A real funny one, you are," he said dryly. "I was revisiting the whole black spandex cat burglar idea. Maybe you could sneak out under cover of darkness, shimmy down a rope from my window."

"Okay, you've given that particular scenario way too much thought." They were still laughing when they reached the end of the pier. "I'm going to pop over to the café to see if Delia can come help us brainstorm the bachelorette party. She's great at that sort of thing."

He bent his head for a quick kiss. "Grab your phone from the truck before you go in," he said.

"Why?"

"So I can send you suggestive and encouraging texts when you take too long with the party planning of course."

"Of course," she said. "I really might have to revamp my whole not-thinking plan and put you in charge."

He lifted his hands. "I'm willing and able," he said, then sketched a bow. When he stood, he slid his phone out and handed it to her. "To put in your number," he said when she looked confused.

"Oh, right." She did as he asked, then that mischievous light sparkled in her eyes as she took a moment and typed in a little more before turning it off and handing it back to him.

"What was that last bit?"

"Just helping to get that encouraging conversation going." She left him standing there, looking down at his phone then at her retreating back as she headed back around to the parking lot and her truck.

He pocketed the phone without reading the message, thinking he should probably be alone when that happened. And possibly naked.

"Yes, much better when we don't think." He planned to do his best to keep them both not thinking for at least the remainder of that day and, if he was lucky, all of the night, too.

CHAPTER SIXTEEN

Kerry stared up at the rope ladder that led to Cooper's room. Tempting. But she should probably be smart and mosey on up the ramps, all stealthy cat burglar–like. "On second thought . . ." She gave one last look around, but no one was paying any particular attention to her, tucked away in the back of the place as she was. Grace was still in the café talking to Delia and Alex about some event they were working on together with Owen Hartley, the town mayor, as part of the grand opening of the Cove's new recreation center. Calder's family's construction company had been a big part of getting the place built, which had been, in part, how he and Hannah had come to be together. It was located on the spot where Delia's original diner once sat, so there was a sentimental element to the whole thing for a lot of the townsfolk.

Planning Fiona's party had taken no time

at all, but from the size of the folder Owen had brought with him, chances were they'd be a lot longer dealing with that subject, so it was the perfect time to duck out.

She tucked her phone in the pocket of her knee-length jean shorts, then rubbed her palms on the denim to prepare for her climb. She smiled as she thought about the message she'd left on Cooper's phone. She knew exactly when he'd finally read it because less than a minute later she'd gotten a text that read: You don't play fair. And speaking of playing . . .

That had been thirty minutes ago and she'd been all but squirming in her seat in one of Delia's booths the entire time since. Fortunately, the other three women were so caught up in party planning, they hadn't noticed her distraction, but she hadn't chanced trying to text him back. She really didn't want to talk about Cooper, her relationship with Cooper, or what she was going to do about Cooper with anyone at the moment. She just wanted actually to be with Cooper. To that end, she grabbed the rope and started her ascent.

She was halfway up when she realized she should have at least let him know she was leaving the café because the trapdoor at the top of the ladder was likely latched on the top side.

She was two rope rungs from the top when someone hissed, "Psst," from the ground below her, making her wobble dangerously. Not because climbing the ladder was hard but she was in that whole please-nobody-see-me mode, and her heart was already beating halfway out of her chest.

Delia stood below her and mouthed "sorry" when Kerry finally steadied the swaying ladder enough to look down. Then she gave Kerry two thumbs-up and grinned as she did the universal zipped-lip-pocket-the-key hand signal.

So much for her career as a cat burglar.

Kerry smiled gamely and nodded but didn't say anything.

"I didn't get a chance to say it earlier," Delia said in a whisper loud enough to be heard . . . well, almost two stories up on a rope ladder anyway, making Kerry wince a little. "We really do like him. We're happy for you."

Kerry wanted to hiss *who's we?* but refrained. As far as she could tell, Cooper had spent the past three days befriending every man, woman, and lobster in Blueberry Cove. And every single one of them had managed to find a moment to tell her so. She was happy — truly — that everyone liked him but not surprised. He was a likable guy. And she was equally happy folks were happy for her.

Now she just wished they'd butt out and let her get on with being happy with Cooper. She managed to give Delia a little salute with half of one hand while still clutching the rope, and Delia gave her another enthusiastic wave, eyes sparkling. Kerry waited until Delia had scooted on back toward the café before turning her attention to the trapdoor. And almost had her second heart attack when she looked up, only to find Cooper staring down at her, his chin propped on folded arms, meaning he was lying flat on the balcony deck. He smiled and lifted his fingers in a little wave. "Nice of you to drop up," he said, a smile curving his lips but the glittering light in his blue eyes telling a different story.

His voice was deep and just a shade rough, which made her skin tingle in delicious anticipation. "I got waylaid by another of your throng of supporters and well-wishers so you only have yourself to blame."

"So I heard," he said. "I'll be sure to thank her later and tip double the usual when we order breakfast in tomorrow morning."

"Awfully sure of yourself, mister."

"Finish climbing that ladder and I'll be

happy to explain the source of my confidence." He wiggled his eyebrows. "Or, better yet, I'll show you."

"Well, if I'd known there was going to be show and tell, I'd have gotten up here sooner." She finished her climb and took hold of Cooper's hand as he levered himself off the balcony deck and pulled her all but bodily up through the trapdoor and into his arms. "My, my," she said, as he hauled her up against him, feet dangling off the floor, and held her there as he walked her into the room, using his elbow to hit the button to close the screens and turn them opaque. "The invitation didn't say clothing optional," she said, running her sandaled feet up the back of his bare legs. Which matched the rest of him. She let out a little laugh as he tossed her gently on the bed.

"That's because I wanted to peel your clothes off you," he said, following her down.

"Well," she said, stretching her arms up over her head, "if you must." She reveled in the way the two of them sank into the thick down mattress pad and even thicker down comforter that was layered on top. The word *sumptuous* came to mind. Even better, the bed didn't pitch and roll with each ocean swell, though that slow roll had provided a few key moments of its own, she recalled.

"Such a wicked smile you're wearing," he said approvingly, flipping her sandals off. "I think it should be the only thing you have on." He unsnapped her shorts, then slid everything off the lower half of her body in one smooth slide.

"You've been practicing," she said, though it was hard to keep the casual banter going now, seeing as he was slowly kissing his way past her ankle and on up along the curve of her calf. Her back arched off the bed as he made his way past her knee and began the slow, delicious trek up her inner thigh. "Now who's not playing fair?" she asked, breathless as he nudged her thighs apart; then she forgot about everything except the exquisite climb he was taking her on. He teased her with kisses, using his lips and tongue everywhere but where she most needed him to. He braced her hips with his big hands, keeping them pressed to the bed as he slowly took her up and up, until she was gasping, writhing beneath him. "Cooper," she begged, only it came out as a keening cry. "Please."

She cried out when he finally found that tiny knot of need and kissed her there, suckling her and sending her shooting over the edge, then keeping her there, sliding one finger, then two inside her. She was writhing in earnest now, wave after wave of pleasure vibrating through her. She had no idea how he understood her body so intimately, so perfectly, and didn't care. What she cared about was wanting him to replace those clever fingers with something a lot more fulfilling. To that end, she grabbed at his shoulders. "Now," she rasped, "now. I want you here." She pushed against his hand.

Then his hand was gone, and his mouth, too, but she was still rocketing, still buzzing, waiting, waiting . . . then she felt the bed dip as he kneeled on it, and her eyes flew open when she felt warm, bare flesh smoothing over hers as he slid his body up and into place. "Yes," she cried. "Please."

"Because you asked so nicely," he said, his voice a low growl, proving she wasn't the only one flying. He pushed her legs farther apart, moving slowly — too slowly — between them, his weight keeping her from arching into him and taking him fully. "Begged so sweetly," he whispered, his mouth on her throat.

He pulled her thighs up, urging to her wrap them around his waist. She did, arching almost violently against him, close to mindless now as he brushed the velvety soft tip against that damp, pulsing little bud. She needed him inside her like she needed air to breathe. "Cooper, I need —"

He swallowed her scream of release, kissing her, pushing his tongue into her mouth at the same time he pushed, slowly but fully, inside her. He slid an arm under her waist, pulling her up so he could sink even deeper on his second thrust, urging her to match him on the third. She was like a wild thing, completely uninhibited, completely with him. He pushed everything else away, emptied her mind of everything but their single-minded and unified need for each other.

If she felt unleashed, he took her like a man possessed of one goal and one goal only, and that was to drive them both to the limits of their control before shoving them together, flying over the edge. He was driving her up the bed, taking her almost ferociously, being met thrust for thrust by her pistoning hips. Her nails dug into the bunched muscles in his back, straining against him, glorying in the feel of his heavy weight on hers. She tangled her fingers in his hair as she pulled his mouth back to hers when he jerked it away long enough to suck in a lungful of air. "I love the way you fill me," she said, the words a hoarse rasp now.

His control snapped then, and he arched up, breaking their kiss as he sank even more deeply into her and shuddered his way through an almost violent climax, taking her with him, shaking, writhing, pumping, panting. He collapsed on top of her, then shifted his weight up on his elbows, his face pressed into her neck as he stayed buried deep inside her, still twitching as the last vestiges of his climax pulsed through him. She clung to him, her legs around his hips, arms around his neck, both of them breathing as hard as if they'd run a race.

Neither of them said a word, and Kerry closed her eyes and stayed in the moment, feeling, not thinking. Only what she was feeling wasn't any less dangerous or complicated than her thoughts. She chalked it up to raging pheromones or postorgasmic bliss. Who wouldn't feel half in love after being taken like that?

He finally eased out of her, still breathing a bit heavily. He rolled to his side and took care of the condom while she pulled off the shirt she was still wearing. He eased onto his back and reached for her, pulling her to his side, tangling his legs with hers and tucking her cheek to his chest. She slipped her arm around his waist and snuggled against the damp heat of his body. She loved how they moved together so easily, so perfectly. During, and after.

Neither of them spoke but simply lay there as their heart rates gradually slowed and their breathing returned to normal. He toyed with the ends of her curls and she pressed a small kiss over his heart, wishing, despite her attempts to keep her mind empty and simply revel in the bliss, that it could be this uncomplicated, this easy.

The intensity of their joining, in the moment, had felt driven by lust, fueled by their primal attraction to each other. Now, as they eased into the afterglow, it took on another feeling altogether. At least it did to her. Lying in his arms, feeling his hand soothing her back in languid strokes as his breath evened out, it was hard — impossible — to block out all the other emotions he stirred inside her. Emotions that had nothing to do with sex and everything to do with how much she cared about him, the man he was, the friend he'd been to her, a well-matched partner in work and now her lover. Her most exquisite, tender, ferocious, and beautiful lover.

Yeah, she really was in trouble here. Deep, deep trouble.

Could she reach for this? Would she want it always? Would this be enough to hold her, to satisfy whatever restlessness there was inside her that pushed her to move on, that prevented her from simply sitting still in one place forever and ever, amen? It seemed so simple, so easy, so obvious when she was with him. She was certain everyone watching the two of them together would tell her it was a no-brainer. And lying there right then, it felt like one to her, too.

But everyone else wasn't her. Hadn't lived her life. Hadn't felt the restlessness she'd apparently been born with. She didn't think there was some deep-seated psychological thing going on. She was happy, she was grounded, she was loved. She couldn't help it if she started feeling twitchy when she stayed in one place for too long. It was who she was, and she'd not only accepted that fact as truth, she'd reveled in it. She was grateful for the life she'd had thus far. She'd found a way to live the life of her dreams, a life that satisfied her mind, body, and soul. And that had not only been enough, it had been everything.

And then she'd landed in Cameroo Downs. And nothing had been the same since. Now she'd come home to Maine. She'd spent a lot of time the past three days thinking about what Cooper had said to her, and Hannah. Was she stalled here because she hadn't fully resolved her feelings about her time spent on his cattle station, with his family? Was that why she hadn't gotten the itch to go? Or was it that being with her family was enough for her now? There were so many changes with her family, so many new paths started, and she was honestly loving being part of it.

But what part would she play? She didn't want to run the pub forever. She was doing it for Fergus, not herself. And now that he had Maddy, her obligation was somewhat relieved. Maddy wouldn't be there forever — she had her own plans mapped out — but if he'd found Maddy, he could find another when she finally moved on. He'd made it clear he was clearing the decks for her. If she stayed in Maine, what would she do? What did she want to do?

So . . . now what?

"You don't have to sort out the whole of it now," he said quietly, still toying with her hair, lightly stroking her shoulder.

His voice was a rumble in his chest, beneath where her ear was pressed. She smiled against his skin and hugged him a little tighter. "Was there steam coming out of my ears?"

"Maybe a little." There was amusement and affection in his voice, and something a little sober, a little serious.

"I was trying not to," she said, then paused before adding, "I can't remember a time ever feeling this at peace." He deserved to know that much. He deserved so much more than that, but she could — should — give him what she did know, the parts she was certain about.

"Good," he said but didn't sound like he was reading any more into that than she'd intended.

Which was good, she knew, but didn't make her feel any better. "I meant what I said before," she said after a time, deciding that maybe she needed just to let all the words, all the feelings, tumble out, instead of keeping them spinning on an endless wheel inside her head. "About wanting it all." He truly did seem to understand the very real confusion she felt. He wouldn't take advantage of her confession, wouldn't use it to press his own preferred outcome.

"Define all," he said, his body fully relaxed, the air calm around them, still heated from their bodies, creating an intimate bubble of sorts, with the rest of the world on the outside.

"I want . . ." She paused, wanting to find the right words to explain. "I want a life with my family. One that includes seeing them more often than I did before. I like being part of our day-to-day, watching and being involved in the new lives they're all building. It's like a big new chapter has started, and I don't want to miss it."

He made a small hum of understanding, of agreement, then, after a moment, said, "But . . . ?"

She smiled again. He was so adept at reading her. If she thought about it, he always had been. It was why they'd worked so well together literally from her first day at the station. He was intuitive with her, with the animals, with his family. He paid attention. It was a trait so few people of her acquaintance had, and one she admired. She'd been drawn to that immediately. "But I don't know what my new path would be here. I'm enjoying being part of my family in the immediate sense, but I have no clear role here. I don't want to run the pub forever; it's not what I see myself doing. But nothing else here has popped up and grabbed my interest either."

"Maybe you need to make it happen, not wait for it to find you."

"I agree. I'd be willing, only . . . I really don't have a clue what that would be."

She could feel him nod, was happy that he let her ponder without trying to come up with ideas or solutions. He was good at doing that, too. Giving her space.

"What else?" he asked after a time.

She let out a long, slow breath and eased into the rest of it. "I want to know I can pick up and go if I feel the need. If I'm feeling all done with what I'm doing, I want to be able to go do something else, somewhere else, soak in new scents, new scenery, new people, new challenges." She smiled. She realized something else. "I miss the restlessness. The pull to head somewhere new, find something I've never seen, learn something I didn't know."

"It's comfortable, I would imagine," he said. "And comforting. It's what you know, what you understand. Makes you feel like you."

She nodded. "That's exactly it." It was a little overwhelming at times, how well he seemed to understand her, to get what she meant. But in the best possible way. "There's one more part," she said, finding the courage, knowing she needed to tell him the rest of it. "Of the all I want to have."

"Which is?"

She lifted her head then, propped her chin on his chest, and looked into his beautiful blue eyes. "You."

The light that leaped into those eyes was

almost startling in its fierceness. His hand stilled in her hair, his body seemed to vibrate a little, as if injected with a sudden shot of life. But he otherwise said nothing, didn't move, didn't roll her to her back and kiss her senseless. He just held her gaze and let her see everything her declaration made him feel.

That emboldened her to go on, to give voice to the rest of it. "I want to go back to Cameroo, see everyone again, see if it feels the same, if it still calls to me like it did before." She clung to his gaze. "Feel what it would be like to be there and be with you. Really with you."

She expected him to say something like he'd book her the next flight back, but instead he regarded her for a long moment, and she realized she was trembling by the time he spoke.

"That's a lot of all," he said.

She nodded, unable to say anything more.

Then he surprised a gasp out of her by reaching for her and pulling her up on top of him, slowing rolling to his other side and tucking her under the shelter of his body. He slid his leg between hers, leveraged his weight on one forearm, and cupped her cheek in his free hand. He stared down so intently, so deeply into her eyes, she thought she might drown in all that deep, dark, bottomless blue.

"Cooper," she whispered, for once not having any idea what he was thinking.

"Maybe there is a way to have it all," he said, lowering his head to hers. "If you want me, Starfish, we'll find that way."

"I do," she said, the sudden prickle of tears surprising her, but it was such a huge rush finally to admit it, to tell him. To tell herself. "But —"

"No buts," he said, kissing the damp from the corner of one eye, then the other. "We'll sort it out," he said. "It's what we do for the people we love."

If she hadn't already been certain her heart had tipped his way, it was definitely in free fall now. She reached up, stroked his face. "What have I done to deserve you?" she asked, quite serious. "Why me?"

"Because you're made for me," he replied. "I knew it from the moment I met you." He leaned in, kissed the side of her jaw. "It's not about earning or deserving. Everyone deserves to be loved." He lifted his head, and the intensity of his gaze was matched by the slow slide of his beautiful, cocky, sexy-as-hell grin. "We just have to be smart enough to recognize our perfect match when we find it."

Her smile matched his, her heart bumping hard inside her chest. "Are you calling me a dummy?"

"Not at all. I'm just saying that maybe some of us caught on a bit faster than others."

She tried to hook his ankle and roll him to his back but he was on to that move.

"Now, now, my little pirate wench, the only one with a hook is me." He rolled fully on top of her, then, bracing his weight even as he nudged her thighs apart.

"My, my," she teased, her heart full to bursting, "what a big . . . sword you have."

"All the better to pillage you with," he murmured, lowering his head again.

"I should tell you one more thing," she whispered, making him lift his head a bit, an eyebrow raised in question. "I'm protected. Makes traveling easier when you know what will be happening when," she explained. "So if you're okay with, uh, keeping your sword there unsheathed, I'm okay with —"

"Oh, aye, I'm very okay," he said, eyes gleaming that much more brightly.

"Good," she sighed, then tipped her head back and arched up into him. "Please feel free to pillage away."

He laughed, a deep, sexy, guttural laugh,

full of joy and promise. He moved slowly inside her this time, both of them groaning in appreciation of the increased pleasure with no barrier between them.

Their lovemaking was slow, yet all the more intense for the increased intimacy, as they kept their eyes open, looking at each other, kissing, playing, moving, enjoying.

And, for the first time, she let herself believe that maybe he was right, maybe there was a way to have it all.

CHAPTER SEVENTEEN

It was later, after they'd dozed and he'd pulled her into the shower upon waking, that Cooper started on a plan. She laughed at his timing.

"I do my best thinking in the shower," he told her, then poured bath soap in his hand and started rubbing her back. "I'm pretty sure I'll think even better if I have something more fun to be washing than my own self." He slipped his hands around to the front, making her squeal, then maybe moan a bit.

She smacked his hands away. "We can't. Or at least I can't. Not and talk at the same time. Back to the plan," she said, grabbing the soap from his hand when he just wiggled his eyebrows at her. "The hot water won't last forever," she warned.

He grinned but gave her soapy behind a pat and continued on where he'd left off. "I'm only saying that if you're living on Cameroo in a more permanent way, there's no reason you can't come back to Maine for an extended stay, to be with your family." He pinched her lightly, making her squeal. "Be the fun auntie with the cool presents and fascinating stories of life on a cattle station." He turned her to face him then. "Can you see yourself doing the work there, or is it like the pub, good for a time, but —"

"I loved working there," she said instantly. "That was at least half the reason I stayed as long as I did. It was the most fulfilling thing I'd done. Hard work, but such a good feeling when I finished up the day. And the horses . . ." She trailed off, then tipped up and kissed him. "I don't know about forever, but it's not like the pub. I do know that."

He kissed her back, until she almost forgot about the planning and encouraged him to get handsy with the soap again.

But he lifted his head just before they slipped over that slope again and stuck his head back under the spray. "That's good, then," he said. "Besides, I happen to know the boss, and when you wanted to come back home to Maine, he'd probably be able to work something out."

"Oh," she said, pretending to sound disappointed. "And here I had all these plans — really involved ones actually — on the many ways I would have encouraged him to see things my way." She ran a soapy hand down one of her arms. "There might have been spandex involved. Just sayin'."

He chuckled at that. "I'll be happy to be as obstinate about your plans as you'd like. And I don't know that I could come along on your trips back here, but we could trade holidays, perhaps, one on Cameroo, one here."

She brightened and felt her heart swell. He was trying. Really trying. "That's wonderful. Truly. And just knowing that there's time planned to see my family, to be home? I think that would be enough."

"If there's a special event, a niece or nephew decides to make an appearance . . . well, no worries. Auntie Starfish will be there."

She giggled at that. "And Unca Hook?"

He chuckled. "If I can." He finished rinsing the shampoo from his hair, then blinked the water from his eyes before pulling her under the spray with him. She squealed, but he quieted her with a watery, drowning kiss, then, mouth still on hers, eased her through the spray until her back was against the now-heated tiles, the water beating on his back. "And when you want to go on walkabout," he murmured, moving his mouth to her neck. "Maybe you could organize your-self a bit and I'll arrange to see if I could go with you."

She pushed at him, her eyes wide in delighted surprise. "You would?"

"If you're up for a traveling companion. I know you like the whole solo thing —"

He made an oofing noise when she wrapped him in a sudden, very tight hug. "I'm very up for that."

She could feel him grin against her hair. "Well, I've enjoyed my time here in Maine and was thinking I could stand to see a bit more of the world." He leaned her back against the wall again, smiled down into her upturned, beaming face. "And what better tour guide could a bloke hope for?"

"None," she said, kissing him with a loud, smacking sound on the lips.

He stroked the hair from her face, his expression turning more serious. "It's not that I would say no to you going on walk-about alone; it's your life to lead and I'll always have the station to deal with, but I do want to say . . . I'd worry about you if you did. And I might pout just a wee bit."

"You're probably ridiculously adorable when you pout."

He stuck out his lower lip and made the saddest face she'd ever seen.

She rolled her eyes, laughing, then leaned in and gently nipped his lip. "Seriously, how could I leave that face?"

He grinned, instantly transformed back to handsome devil. "Then my evil plan is working after all."

"You're such a pirate."

He pulled her to him. "And you're such a pirate's wench." He turned her around, wrapped her in his slippery arms, her back to his front, and began kissing the side of her neck, her nape, making her giggle.

They were well on their way to seeing just how long that hot water would hold out when Cooper's cell phone began to vibrate and ring. He ignored it the first time, but then it lit up again. And by the time they'd shut the shower off and grabbed towels, it was on its third round and both Cooper and Kerry were getting concerned.

He scooped the phone off the counter by the bathroom sink, looking at the screen. "It's Sadie," he said, looking clearly worried now as he swiped it on. "Hello, luv, what —" He listened, and Kerry could hear a very agitated and fast-talking Sadie coming through the line.

Her heart shot to her throat and her stomach squeezed into a sick knot as Cooper walked out into the bedroom and sat down on the edge of the bed. "Hold up, hold up now, Roo, what's this all about? I'm here, I'm here, no worries. Take a breath now, I can't understand you."

Kerry started chewing her nails as she watched the expressions shifting across Cooper's face as he listened. She couldn't hear Sadie now, but from the look on Cooper's face, whatever was going on back in Australia wasn't good. She took heart that he looked more concerned than devastated. *That had to be something, right? No one had died, then?* Her heart clutched hard, then fell even harder at his next words.

"I'm coming home, yes. I'll be on the next flight out. Is Cousin Mary there? Would you put her on? Yes, I love you, too. It's going to be okay, luv. Hang on to that and I'll be there in a jiff. You did the right thing, calling me. Yes, I know it is." He flashed a brief smile that didn't quite reach the bleak look in his eyes. "Yes, they can be hardheaded arseholes, and no, I won't hold the foul language against you. If they're going to behave like ones, that's just calling it like it is."

He paused while there was another torrent, and though he didn't relax, she could tell he was already starting to process what was going on, even as he continued to calm

Sadie down. "Yes, I'll call you again from the airport and give you my flight information. Yes, I'm off to book it right now. I'll talk to Cousin Mary when I'm back, okay? Just give her my thanks for coming and for staying with you. Have her text me all the information, room number and all that. I'll fly into Darwin, come directly there. Yes. All my love." He paused, then sighed, and his shoulders crumpled just a bit. "Don't cry now, luv, you've done the hard part. You say he'll be fine and he will. Tell him to quit scaring the nurses, and you, or he'll answer to me." He let out a watery chuckle, then, "Yes, true, and good on ya. I wouldn't want to answer to you just now either. You've done good, Roo. I'm proud of you. I'll be home before you know it."

He paused again, and his smile this time was sweeter, his eyes crinkling at the corners, his short laugh more heartfelt. "Aye. Yes. I'll tell her. I promise." He hung up a moment later, then dipped his chin, tapping his phone to his forehead for a moment before blowing out a long, uneven breath and turning it back on.

He didn't immediately explain and she didn't ask. Better to let him do what needed doing first. Kerry climbed on the bed until she was kneeling behind him and saw he'd opened an airline app and was punching in information. She knew he'd tell her what had happened once he put things into motion. She'd seen him in management mode before many times, calmly and efficiently handling any number of crises on the station, some quite critical, so she knew how he worked. Though, she had to admit, she'd never seen him rattled by it, as he was now, though he was doing his best to mask it.

She rubbed his shoulders, hating feeling so helpless, wishing she could do more. She also tried hard not to let her mind go spinning off on the part of this that would directly affect her. The part that meant he was leaving Blueberry Cove . . . and her. Today.

They'd just started figuring things out, but the key word there was *started.*

She shoved all that aside, along with the fear that whatever Sadie had just told him would somehow change everything, somehow render whatever plans they'd started to put into motion null and void. That he wasn't looking at her, or even registering her presence, wasn't all that reassuring either. Not that she was hurt by it; she wasn't, but as a measure of just how bad or life-altering the news he'd received actually was, it wasn't a big confidence booster either.

He finally turned his phone off again, and this time he tossed it on the bed next to him. Then, elbows still braced on his knees, he put his face in his hands, rubbing it with his palms, then raking his fingers through his hair.

She slid her hands away from his shoulders, but he reached up and covered them with his own. "So," he said, his voice sounding like gravel, thick with a tumble of emotions she couldn't quite decipher. "It seems that my family has decided to implode on me. Or, more accurately, on Sadie." He closed his mouth, shook his head, then muttered a string of swear words under his breath that made Kerry forget all about him leaving and put her focus right back where it belonged.

"What happened?" She tugged her hands free, then scooted around to sit on the edge of the bed next to him, shifting to look at him directly. "Is Sadie okay?"

"Other than being scared out of her mind and angry as hell at her other brother? Yeah, she's okay. But goddammit —" He broke off, reined it back in again.

"Cooper —" She was really worried now. Just hearing Sadie's voice over the phone had pulled her right back to Cameroo and the entire Jax family, as if the past year apart had never happened.

"So," he went on, agitation evident in his voice now, which scared her a little, because, from what she'd heard on his end, it seemed pretty clear that someone was in the hospital and, rather than simply being worried about that, he was pissed. As angry as she'd ever seen him in fact.

He continued. "Apparently my taking time off, coming to America to find you and see about giving the two of us a go, gave my brother, Ian, the gumption to do something of the same."

"What?" Kerry had absolutely no idea what she'd expected him to say, but it wasn't that. "This is about Ian? Is this —" She had to scramble now to keep up. "Is this about the woman you said he's been e-mailing?" Her eyes went wide. "Did he take off and leave your dad hanging in the middle of wet season —"

"Oh, he didn't just take off. He fucking eloped."

"What?" Now it was Kerry raking her hands through her hair, then simply leaving them there, clutching her head. She couldn't really wrap her mind around that.

"Sorry," Cooper said, heaving out a long,

heavy breath. "I shouldn't swear, but —"

"No, no need. Swearing understood. Approved even. What in the hell was he —" But then she remembered the hospital part and broke off. "Wait, so who's in the hospital?"

"That's the rest of it. So Ian decided because I was going after what I wanted and the world hadn't come to an end, seeing Dad had even sanctioned the trip and all but driven me to the airport himself . . . well, that gave him the head of steam he apparently needed to come clean about his own feelings on life and love."

"Okay," she said cautiously, not having any idea where this was going now. Clearly there was more. A whole lot more.

"According to Sadie, he went to Dad, told him that he really was in love with this girl — Prudence is her name — and wanted to marry her." He lifted a hand to stall Kerry's questions. "We don't know her, haven't met her, but we trusted in his judgment. He's never shown he was a bad judge of character before, and I'm sure this is no exception." He rubbed his hand over his face again, then said, "But it wasn't just that he was in love and wanted to get married. The real piece of news was that he apparently really liked being in the city while at university.

His new love — wife, now, I guess, *Jesus and jiminy . . .*"

He broke off again, shaking his head in disbelief, but Kerry just let him work his way through it, knowing quite well from the talk they'd had in this very bed earlier and had been continuing in the shower, that saying things out loud sometimes brought with them a whole new sense of clarity.

He heaved out a breath. "The bottom line is, he told Dad he'd be happy to stay on helping the station as a consultant — *a goddamn consultant* — but that he was going to go off, get married, and live in the city. Not in Darwin, mind you, but all the way the hell down in Perth. Might as well relocate to the moon for all the good that does us up in the north end."

Kerry could only imagine how Big Jack had taken that announcement, and feared she knew exactly who was in the hospital now, and likely why. "What happened then?"

"Sadie said Ian handled it all wrong, bungled it up, and Dad got his back good and up. The two got into a big blowout — World War Three, she called it — with the end result being instead of Ian planning a wedding and figuring out how best to start his new life in Perth, Dad kicked him off the station and told him not to come back.

So Ian ran off and eloped with the girl — Prudence — and Dad goes on and has a heart attack over the whole mess."

"Oh, no. But he's okay? Sorry," she said. "I overheard —"

"Yes," Cooper said. "It was a bad one and he's in surgery, getting a stent or something put in, but they say he should be fine. He'll be in a day or two at least."

"Poor Sadie; she must be scared out of her mind."

Cooper nodded. "I've never heard her like that; hope I never have to again. Though I can't tell you how proud I am of how she handled it. A true Jax, she is. Sadie was there with him when he had the attack, radioed our station master, and they radioed Royal Flying Doctors Service, who came by helo and got him, took him to hospital in Darwin. She —" He broke off again and pinched the bridge of his nose, and she could see him fighting his emotions. "She shouldn't have had to do that, dammit. She's a brave girl, as tough a nut as they come when need be. But goddammit, Ian, she shouldn't have had to be, not with her own dad, for Christ's sake. And me off on walkabout, not there to help."

Kerry shook her head, trying to absorb it all. "So . . . did she say what Ian said to make it go so far south? I mean, why Big Jack got so mad he booted his son out? I know he was counting on Ian and you jointly running the place, but he's run the place on his own and raised the two of you while doing it, so surely he knows it can be done, that you could take over by yourself. And he didn't get upset when you came here, so —"

"I don't know the particulars. You know my father and his temper, but . . ." He trailed off, then shook his head, still somewhat in disbelief. "I don't know what Ian said or what exactly set Dad off. I — I must admit, I'm stunned, too. I thought Ian loved the station, was proud of his role, both now and future." He looked at her, as bleak as she'd ever seen him, and she knew he wasn't really seeing her. "You heard him go on and on. What was that all about, then? All his big plans for the place?"

"He never talked to you about maybe wanting something different?"

Cooper shook his head. Then he seemed to snap out of his daze and immediately looked around for his clothes. "I'm flying back tonight," he said, grabbing his shorts and shirt. He finally looked at her — really seemed to see her for the first time since taking the call — as he pulled them on. "I'm sorry, Kerry —"

"No," she said, "don't apologize. Of course you need to go back." She couldn't help but notice he hadn't said anything about her going with him, but he was in crisis mode. "Is there anything I can do to help?"

"No, I've got the rental so that will get me to Bangor. I can turn it in at the airport. I'll settle with Grace —"

"I can take care of that part, have her put it on your card or whatever you reserved the room with, if you like. She'll understand about the cancelation; don't worry about that part."

"Yes, okay," he said, distracted now as he pulled his suitcase from the closet and began tossing things in. "Thank you."

"No problem." She watched him pack, feeling like she was sitting in the middle of a maelstrom; oddly calm, oddly still while life whirled in a tempest around her but not directly impacting her. Not yet anyway. That would happen after he was gone. She wanted to ask him, *what about me? About us?* But now was definitely not the time for that, and she felt awful for even thinking it. There would be time for that once things were settled and he knew what the fallout was going to be. They'd waited this long . . .

She rubbed her arms, unable to keep the inescapable chill from running through her. Things were happening in Cooper's family that would have big, life-altering implications. Implications she couldn't help but feel were somehow about to put an end to what they'd finally started here, before they'd even had the chance to begin.

When he was packed and ready, she stood, realizing she was still wrapped in a bath towel. "Will you let me know you made it back okay? And how Jack is doing? And . . ." She trailed off, feeling a burning sensation behind her eyes and willing herself to push it back. Now was not the time for that. She'd have plenty of time later. *Like the rest of your life, maybe.*

She'd hoped that when she finally spoke up, he'd snap out of the management mode he'd gone into, suddenly realizing he hadn't factored her, or them, into the immediate equation, and at least reassure her they'd talk once he'd gotten a handle on the situation. Or . . . or something.

But the look of remorse on his face, of unutterable sadness when he finally turned to her had creeping fingers of dread clutching at her heart so tightly, she thought she might not be able to take another breath.

"Kerry . . ."

She walked over to him, then, snapping out of her own little fugue state, determined to be part of . . . of whatever it was he thought he had to say on the matter.

"Don't look at me like that," she said, and briefly got a surprised glance, but the one that followed made her want to beat on his chest and scream *no!* "Don't come here and offer me — all but beg me to —"

He pulled her into his arms, then, over-coming her resistance, until she wrapped her arms around him, burying her still damp face and hair against his shirt, and shook. "I know you have to go back of course. I would fly you there myself if I could. But that doesn't mean —"

He tipped her chin up, and she looked into eyes that were as bereft as any she'd ever seen. She'd give anything, any amount, to make him smile, tease her, shoot her that cocky grin. See the hunger for her in his eyes again.

"Why are you doing this?" she asked, her voice breaking, seeing in his eyes what he was going to say. "It's not the end of any-thing."

"Ian's gone," he said. "Breaking free, liv-ing the life he wanted. I didn't even know he felt trapped. That was the word Sadie said he used. *Trapped.*" He pushed her damp curls from her forehead. "I won't trap you, Starfish. I couldn't bear it if —"

"But that's on me, not you. And we were working on that; we had solutions, ideas on how we —"

"Solutions I don't know I can honor now. Leaving the station —" He sighed and looked so bleak. "I don't know when or if that will be possible."

"But you said Jack was okay. They can do amazing things these days, surgically speaking. And he's big and strong as an ox. If anyone can come back from something like this —"

"He's had other health issues this past year," he said, surprising her into silence. "I didn't mention them, but . . . this isn't the first time he's been in hospital this year. It's his first heart attack, yes, but . . . this isn't going to be a small change. He'll need to make some big changes if he doesn't want to risk keeling over dead. We've all listened to the doctors, about his high blood pressure and whatnot, and while we didn't ignore them, we didn't push past Dad's willful stubbornness about them as hard as we should have. As you said, he looks big and strong as an ox, but I don't know what the future holds there." He trailed off, shook his head. "Sadie needs me. Needs the stability of me being there. And —" He broke off, looked into her eyes, and let her see all the love and feeling he had for her. "It's where I want to be most in the world, Starfish. I know my home; I've found my place in the world. I shouldn't — won't — keep you from finding yours."

"But —"

He kissed her, gently at first and then with all the hunger of a man who might never eat again.

Tears were trickling down her face now. "What if I want to come, if I know the risks, but —"

"You might be able to handle that," he said roughly. "But I'm not sure I could."

"Life doesn't offer any guarantees," she said, knowing she had to push, had to make him understand. She wouldn't get another chance. "I want to try. I want us to try. What happened to figuring things out because that's what you do for the people you love?"

He kissed her wet cheeks and pulled her close. "Can't you see?" he whispered hoarsely. "That's exactly what I'm doing."

And then he was gone.

She turned around, then sank down on the edge of the bed when her legs suddenly wouldn't support her any longer. "But what about the part where I'm hopelessly in love with you?" she whispered to the empty room. "Don't I get a say in how we figure things out for us?"

CHAPTER EIGHTEEN

Cooper guided his horse into the stables and out of the drenching downpour. He swung himself out of the saddle, then handed the reins to the stable hand once his feet were on dry ground. "Thanks for staying, Marco. Give her a good rubdown. She's put in a long one today. As soon as you're done here, you can head on out for the night."

The young man smiled, nodded. "No worries, Mr. Cooper." He rubbed the mare's damp mane. "How is Mr. Big Jack?"

"Doing well, thanks."

Marco nodded as he looped the reins over his hand and turned the horse around. "Please tell Mr. Big Jack that I've been keeping Marigold exercised for him. She'll be ready whenever he is."

A tired but kind smile curved Cooper's lips. Marco was Marta's nephew, and one of the most polite young men Cooper had ever met. No matter how many times he'd told Marco that there was no need for him to "mister" either Cooper or his father, Marco would simply nod and keep on doing it. When Cooper had pressed once, Marco had informed him that he was more afraid of his Auntie Marta than he was of either Cooper or Big Jack. "I'm sure Mr. Big Jack will be very grateful. Thank you, Marco."

The young man grinned. "No worries."

Marco led the mare down toward the other end of the stable and Cooper started to head back out into the rain, but at the last second opted instead to turn into the stable manager's office. It was empty this time of evening so he took advantage, slid off his wet canvas long coat and dumped the rain off his hat, then sat down behind the desk. It had been a long couple of days out checking the campsites, talking with his managers, checking on the cattle.

He both loved and hated the wet season. The northern section of the Northern Territory, where Cameroo was located, was in the tropical part of the country, and the wet season was like being wrapped up in 100 percent humidity at all times, rain or no. Fortunately, the herd looked great this year, with all things pointing to possibly one of the best culling numbers they'd had in years when it came time to take them to market. At the moment, however, he was tired right down to his very bones, and the wet felt like it went even deeper. There would be a very long, very hot shower in his immediate future, as soon as he walked up to the main house.

Which he should be doing now, but he just needed a moment of quiet first. Once inside, there would be Sadie, looking at him with either pleading or accusing eyes, and his father telling him all the reasons why he didn't need a full-time watchdog nurse. Cooper had had a long talk with Ian earlier in the week before heading out on horseback, but he still hadn't discussed it with his father and needed to, sooner rather than later. The longer their stubborn standoff went on, the worse it would be for all of them. And he had a bed to fall into that had never felt too big or too empty for one man to occupy . . . but did now.

That was partly why he'd volunteered to be the one out doing the circuit. Gossip traveled fast on the station, and he'd told Big Jack that he wanted personally to reassure his managers that things were okay with the family, that nothing was going to change in how things were run; their work and jobs remained secure. And all of that was true. But equally true was that he needed to get out of the house and away from anyplace that held direct memories of Kerry. The problem, he'd found out, was there was nowhere on Cameroo she hadn't made a mark, left an impression. Word had apparently gotten out about his reason for going to the States. He supposed he should have been prepared for that. He'd been prepared for the concerned questions about his father, and about Ian, but not the happy, hopeful questions about his impending marriage. Not prepared at all.

He leaned back in the chair, making the spring squeal a bit. He'd been back home for two weeks. He'd texted Kerry when he'd finally landed in Darwin, and again to let her know his father had come through surgery okay and was expected to make a good recovery, but otherwise, they'd had no communication. Although, he supposed, he hadn't been entirely forthcoming about his father's continuing condition; he hadn't seen any reason to worry her. He had been truthful when he'd told her back at the inn that Big Jack had some health issues, but while the stent had helped relieve some of his heart issues, that had been only a warning sign. His father wasn't out of the woods yet. Hence the hiring of the watchdog nurse. He'd opted for a male nurse who was bigger and scarier than his father; that was the only hope he had of getting Jack to follow doctor's orders and take it easy for a bit, focus on getting his blood pressure and other things back on track before taking on a full workload again, or any workload. The stress from Big Jack's fallout with Ian was still weighing heavily as well, on all of them, but none more than his father. And the old man was too stubborn to back down and admit he'd been a complete ass about how he'd handled it. Of course Ian hadn't done any better with his timing or his delivery.

Cooper raked his fingers through wet hair, swearing under his breath. He'd finally spoken with his younger brother three days ago, while on his way out on rounds, and it had given him a lot to think about. He supposed, if he'd been paying closer attention, Cooper would have realized how hamstrung Ian felt by his birthright ties to Cameroo, and that he'd basically been telling them he wasn't cut out to run the place all along.

Cooper prided himself on being pretty sharp, on reading people, on listening — really listening. And he felt he'd let his own brother down by not seeing what was really going on, not paying better attention.

Ian had been so over the top with his plans for the place, which Cooper had taken as enthusiasm. He'd also thought their father was listening to all those plans, open to implementing them. But, in talking to Ian, he'd found out that it wasn't that way at all. Big Jack still saw Ian as a kid, someone who'd been away at school but not getting the real education that only running and working the station could give him. He might have put a good face on it, but in truth, he hadn't seen Ian's ideas as credible and, when push had come to shove, he had dismissed every one of them out of hand, along with his youngest son's contribution. Cooper should have seen it coming, should have followed up with Ian, offered to help him get their father to step up, give him a chance.

The thing that had caught him more off guard when he'd finally talked to his brother was that, barring the unresolved issue with their father, Ian was happy. Happy with his new wife, happy in the city, happy with his new job, working for a company designing ways to improve irrigation and other large systems for the cattle stations in Australia. He was taking his education seriously, and his love for his heritage, just applying it in a different way than by running the place directly. He'd found a solution — a good one — that honored his birthright but didn't consign him to a life he didn't want.

Cooper knew his father would eventually come around to seeing that. He just had to find the right way to bring the two to the table to talk it out. A way that brought Ian and his wife, Pru, back into the family fold and didn't send Big Jack back to the hospital.

Then there was Sadie, who still hadn't quite forgiven him for not bringing Kerry home with him. And, if truth be told, that was the real reason he was sitting in his stable manager's office right then and not standing under a stinging hot shower spray. In the turmoil of his rushed departure from Maine, he hadn't passed along Sadie's request that he tell Kerry that Sadie wasn't mad and hoped the two could communicate going forward. It had been an honest oversight. He hadn't been together or in control of anything when he'd left Blueberry Cove.

He'd taken care of that oversight after he'd gotten to hospital and Sadie had asked after Kerry. He hadn't gone into any particulars with his sister on what had happened while he'd been in Maine but had gently let her know that it wasn't going to work out with him and Kerry, that her life wasn't meant for sitting in one place forever. He had given his blessing for Sadie to communicate with Kerry if she still wanted to, and had let her know that Kerry had felt bad about not staying in touch before, and had included Sadie's request when he'd texted Kerry about his dad's surgery.

Other than her reply, thanking him and asking him to pass along her well wishes to his father, they hadn't communicated since. During that time, he'd been forced to admit his reasons for giving Sadie the green light to connect with Kerry hadn't been so altruistic as all that. He knew he'd closed the door on that part of his life, but he'd also realized over the past week that in his rush to make everything right, in his shock over his brother's sudden defection, he'd overreacted, overstepped, and, stupidly, idiotically, ended the best thing that had ever happened to him.

He'd told himself he'd done it for all the right reasons and still thought that maybe it had been the right thing to do. What stuck with him, though, was that he hadn't even given her a say. He'd asked a great deal of her when he'd just barged back into her life, and instead of tossing him out on his ass, she had eventually done as he'd asked and given him — them — a chance. And just when she was finally finding her way to him, he'd abruptly pulled the rug out from under them, slammed the door shut, and taken off. He knew Kerry well enough to know that had he turned right back around, apologized, asked her to forgive the knee-jerk reaction, she very likely would have, chalking it up to the stress of the moment. But he hadn't done that. And now the deed had been done, and Kerry had made it clear she respected his choice with her silence. So, hard as it was, maybe it was for the best, and he should respect her choice, too.

But she hadn't been silent with Sadie. He knew the two were talking, though Sadie wasn't more forthcoming than that about the nature or content of their e-mail and messaging conversations, other than to make it clear she thought all three men in her family were idiots.

And she likely had a point.

He wondered when and how his life had gotten so complicated. And how he was going to get it all back on track. He'd lost count of the number of times he'd instinctively found himself wanting to turn to Kerry, to talk over this issue or that problem with her, ask for her thoughts, work his way through all of this with her clear-minded, pragmatic view helping to guide him toward the best solutions. He missed her at the end of the day, turning to her to soothe the savage beast and help take his mind off his troubles. In a very short time they'd fallen right back in the rhythm they'd always had, even when dancing around the hunger and the bigger life questions they were tackling. And now, back on Cameroo, his memories of her there were that much brighter, so many forgotten little details, all the many reasons he'd fallen in love with her now in full-blown Technicolor, there in the forefront of his mind.

The fact was, even if he had made a mistake in leaving her behind, he was now solely in charge of Cameroo. His role at the station had forever changed. Ian wasn't coming back — not to live and work the station anyway — and nor should he. He'd found his path. And if and when his father was able to take on a more active role again, it would be in a different capacity going forward. Cooper was okay with that. Unlike his brother, he couldn't imagine life anywhere but on the station, had been grooming himself toward this eventuality his entire life. He hadn't expected the shift to happen as it had, as suddenly or as soon, but given the fact that he had taken over the reins, he couldn't up and leave, head off to Maine, or take off on walkabout or anything else. Even if he organized the work structure so he could be away from the station, he had Sadie to take care of for at least several more years, and his father to watch over for who knew how long. Possibly longer than he could foresee. He was well and truly tethered. Happily so, but what could he offer Kerry now?

And what would he say to her, if he could? I'm a jackass who let go of the best thing I ever found? The thing I came halfway around the world to get back? Kerry had gone far outside her comfort zone to even consider a life with him, and she'd finally gotten to the place where she could see it happening, or at least see herself giving it an honest try.

He'd asked that of her. *Just give it an honest try.* But, when push had come to shove, he hadn't given her the same consideration. He'd decided for her.

"Oh, for the love of Mary, just get over yourself, mate. It's done. You've coshed the matter over the head and killed it dead, haven't you? Maybe it's for the best after all, then. She won't want to be tied down to this place and the likes of you and all this drama. You don't have time to sit around feeling sorry for yourself either. You've got a station to run, a herd to get to market." He pushed away from the desk, stood, and grabbed his hat. *And a father to talk sense into, a brother to bring back into the fold. And a sister to apologize to for not giving her the sister of the heart she needed. The woman of his heart, whom he needed right now, too.*

He shut down the lights in the office and the stable, which was quiet now, except for the snuffling noises of the residents occupying the long row of stalls. He headed back out into the deluge and on up to the house. A hot shower, maybe an evening snack in the kitchen, and a good long night's sleep in his own bed, would help get his head on straight. Help him focus on what was and not what might have been.

He saw the lights on in the back of the sprawling homestead and opted to go around and in through the mudroom off the kitchen. Sadie was probably in there doing homework. He'd risk the attitude just for the chance to give her a kiss on the head. He always missed his family when he was out riding the rounds. He purposely ignored the little voice asking him what he'd do when Sadie finished growing up and headed off, when his father eventually passed on to his great reward. What would he come home to then?

"Like life isn't hard enough, mate. Don't borrow more sorrow." He pulled open the back door to the mudroom and slid out of his heavy canvas slicker and hat, then pried his muddy boots off. He heard chatter coming from the kitchen and smiled. Good; Sadie was done with homework and watching the telly. Maybe he'd fix a sandwich and join her, spend some time in the same room in companionable silence, and see where that got them. He'd put off shower and bed for that. End what had become a maudlin day on a more promising note.

He pushed through the door, smiled at Sadie, and mustered up a hearty hello, thinking she was so grown up now, she didn't launch herself at him with those tight bear hugs she used to give him when she was little, when he'd come back after being out in the beyond for days. He missed those hugs. He was halfway to the fridge when he went completely still, then slowly turned to look to the kitchen table. Where Sadie sat, her schoolbooks open in a sprawl in front of her. Remains of dinner still on a plate off to her left. The telly on the counter, however, was dark.

The chatter hadn't come from there. It had come from the woman seated at the table, next to his sister.

He almost turned and walked back out the door, then back in again, to see if perhaps now he was the one with the health issue. Because either he was dreaming or he was hallucinating.

"Hello," Kerry said from her regular perch at the family table, seated next to an all but radiantly beaming Sadie.

"I needed some help with this," his sister said, motioning casually to the books and notebooks, though there was nothing casual about the beacon of fierce hope that shone from her pretty blue eyes. "I hope you don't mind that I got my old tutor to come back." She turned to look at Kerry, her happiness so evident in every inch of her face, it made Cooper's heart squeeze.

And he couldn't afford for his heart to squeeze because it wasn't even pumping at the moment. He'd be up in bed next to Big Jack any moment now.

"Yeah," Kerry said, her smile trembling a bit. "I hope you don't mind."

"I — no," he said, surprised he could get even that much out. "I don't mind at all."

Just then the door that led off to the living room opened and in sailed —

"Fiona?"

She beamed at Cooper. "Hello, handsome. About time you showed up. Wow,

401

you're really soaked. Sorry," she went on, looking at Sadie. "I didn't hear him come in. I didn't mean to spoil anything. I was just getting refills for everyone." She scooted over to the fridge, grabbed a few bottles of root beer, then sailed back through the door to the living room. "Pretend you never saw me!"

Kerry rolled her eyes at Sadie, who just shrugged and giggled. "Family. What are you gonna do?" she said.

"Right?" Kerry responded.

Cooper did turn around then and walked straight back through the door to the mud-room, where he stood staring, sightlessly, through the window, toward the stables he'd just come from, which were completely obscured from view by the rain. Had he fallen and hit his head? Was he, right now, lying out there in the mud and muck some-where, going off to his own great reward and hallucinating the happy ending he'd dreamed about, then ruined because he — the door opened and closed behind him and he turned to find Kerry standing in front of him.

"Maybe we shouldn't have sprung this on you," she said. Then she smiled, that dry, devil-may-care curve to her lips he'd missed almost more than breathing. "But then, fair's fair," she said. "I didn't get a heads-up when you came barging into my life, unannounced and uninvited."

"No," he said, still mentally scrambling, still not entirely certain he wasn't dreaming. Or dead. "I suppose I didn't." He looked past her to the door and nodded. "Was that —"

"Fiona? Yes. Ben is here, too. They made a last-minute change in honeymoon plans. I hope you don't mind."

"Uh, no. No. That's good. That's —" He broke off, pinched the bridge of his nose, then looked at her again. "You're really here."

"I really am." It was the nervousness, the hint of vulnerability that had entered her eyes that finally snapped him out of his temporary daze.

"Why?" he asked. "I mean, beyond the algebra homework of course."

"It's pretty hard algebra. I might need a refresher course."

"Kerry —"

"I'm here for you," she said, then let out a long, shaky breath, making him realize just what her apparent insouciance was costing her. "You know Sadie and I have been talking. She's kept me up-to-date with everything going on, including that you don't seem too happy these days."

"That's not her place —"

"I'm not so happy either, Cooper. I miss you. Like I miss breathing. More than I thought I was capable of missing anyone. I even think — I know you did what you did because you thought it was the right thing to do. And maybe it was. At the time. And maybe it gave me the chance to realize that, while I might not have figured out what I want to do with the rest of my life, I do know what I don't want to do for the rest of my life. And that's live one that doesn't have you in it."

"I —"

"I know things have changed here. I know the things we talked about, about you going with me if I need to race off to see this temple or that high mountain stream, can't happen. At least not anytime soon. I'm willing to risk that if you are." She took a step closer. "I'm willing to risk some time apart if and when I need it so we have all the rest of our time together." She took another step and he could see the fine trembling in her shoulders. "I'm willing to risk loving Cameroo Downs, loving your family" — she looked him straight in the eyes — "and loving you, even if that means I'm risking the danger of losing everything I care about in

404

the world, were something bad to happen." She took another step. "Which is a really good thing." She looked up into his still stunned face and said, "Because I already love Cameroo Downs. And your family." Her voice shook now. "And I very much, with all my heart, love you. I think I have since we started all this, two years ago." She smiled then and let out a watery laugh. "Sorry; I'm a little slow on the uptake sometimes."

It wasn't until he started to speak that he realized he was shaking, too. He reached up, touched her check. "You are real," he said, then grinned when she rolled her eyes. "I — just checking." Then he framed her face with his hands, struggling to keep the touch gentle when what he wanted to do was pull her all the way inside him and keep her there forever and ever. "Because I don't think I could stand losing you a third time, Starfish. I'm barely functional as it is."

"So I've heard," she said, then half laughed, half caught her breath on an emotion-filled gasp of air.

"Have you, now?" he said, his own voice choking up. "I'll have a talk with that one after."

"After?"

"After this." Then he pulled her tightly

into his arms and lowered his mouth to hers, the joy filling him so swiftly and so fully, he truly feared he might burst with the intensity of it. "I've missed you," he said hoarsely when they broke apart, gasping for breath. "More than I thought possible."

"Me too." She held on to him just as tightly. "I really do love you, Cooper. And I want to be here. In fact, I can honestly say, standing here right now, I can't imagine wanting to be anywhere else."

He brushed the damp from her cheeks. "That's good. Because I don't know that I could let you go." He pulled her back into his arms. "But yes to the rest."

"What rest?"

He looked down at her. "If — when — you need to go off, fill your soul, feel different earth under your feet, I'll do my best to handle missing you. As long as you promise to always come back."

She nodded, sniffling. "Like a boomerang; you won't be able to get rid of me."

He chuckled, still getting past being stunned, then kissed her again, and this time the relief, the joy, started to shift to that all-consuming hunger that was always there for them and, he suspected, always would be.

With that in mind, he went to scoop her up, thinking his family and hers would have to understand if they needed a little time alone, when she pressed her palms against his chest.

"Wait. I have one more thing I have to ask."

"Anything."

She smiled. "Is that marriage proposal still on the table?"

He grinned. Just when he thought his heart couldn't get any fuller. "Why, Starfish, I thought you'd never ask."

"Is that a yes?"

"That is the most resounding yes there will ever be."

Her face split wide in a smile, but there was still something else, some nervousness, along with the happiness, filling her eyes. "Good. Because, well, there's something else I didn't tell you —"

The air was suddenly filled with the sound of applause, whistling, and a few catcalls. Cooper looked behind her to see not only Fiona, Ben, and Sadie crammed in the doorway to the kitchen but Hannah and Calder, along with Logan and Alex, too.

"I sort of brought witnesses," she said. "And the rest of the wedding party with me."

"Like we were going to trust her to handle it on her own," Fiona said with an affectionate snort, wiping tears from her own cheeks as well.

"I — that's —" He looked at Kerry, then back at the throng in the doorway, and his face split in a wide grin. "That's bloody brilliant." He scooped her up and spun her around, much to her squealing dismay and the utter delight of her sisters. "What of Fergus?" he asked when he'd finally set her down, her family rushing in to hug them both, the men slapping his back and everyone more or less talking over each other.

"His doctor said no to the long flight, but —"

"I've got it worked out for him to be at the ceremony via computer," Sadie chimed in.

"The ceremony, is it?" he said. "You've really been up to all kinds of good on that computer, then, haven't you?" At her smiling, watery nod, he pulled his sister in for a hug and got the bear hug squeeze he'd been missing in return.

She looked up at him, eyes shining. "You're not mad at me? For not telling?"

He leaned down and kissed her on the head. "I love you, Roo," he said, and her eyes filled at his use of the nickname he'd given her as a toddler, saying she bounced around, more kangaroo than human. He

408

tipped up her chin. "You've become a lovely and strong young woman, Sadie Eloise Jax. I'm so proud of you. Thank you for holding us all together."

Now it was her turn to surprise him by letting out a huge, shuddering sigh. "I'm really, really glad to hear you say that." She turned, and he could feel her shaking. "It's okay," she called out, over the chattering hubbub in the mudroom, now packed to the gills with warm bodies. Cooper looked over their heads as another shadow filled the doorway.

"Ian," he said, his breath well and truly knocked out of him now. A moment later, a petite brunette joined him, her own smile tentative but bright with hope.

Cooper made his way through the rapidly parting throng and wrapped his brother up in the tightest of hugs, his own eyes burning. "So good," was all he could get out. "Thank God."

"I didn't give you a chance to be at my wedding," Ian said, hugging him back, his laughter filled with rough emotion, too. "So I sure as hell wasn't going to miss yours."

Cooper laughed, then managed to ease back enough to meet Prudence, who seemed every bit as lovely as her smile. She was quieter than the rest, but he saw her quiet, steady strength and the love she felt in the way she looked at his brother and, as importantly, the way Ian looked at her.

"And Dad?" Ian asked, when he was done getting his own bear hug from his sister. He looked at Sadie. "Did you tell him —"

"What's all this now?" came a booming voice from the doorway. "Somebody having a party and didn't invite old Jack? Haven't you heard? I'm dying and can't be disturbed. But I'll be damned if you're going to leave me in my room to —" He broke off his commentary when he spied Kerry in the midst of the crowd. "Well, well," he said, a smile crossing his grizzled face. "It's about time." He held his arms out and Kerry didn't hesitate. She walked right into them and hugged him back fiercely, if the look on her face was anything to go by.

"It's so good to see you, Big Jack," she said. Then she leaned back and thumped him on the shoulder.

He frowned and rubbed the spot, but the affection and love he had for her was there in his happy and relieved eyes the whole time. "What was that for?"

"Scaring us half to death. Don't do that. And listen to Nurse Bertram. Or you'll be answering to me along with your daughter there. Who I'm here to tell you is no one to

410

be trifled with."

"Don't I know it." He chuckled at that and pulled Kerry under his beefy arm. "Well, don't push a man to have a heart attack just to get his family back in line and maybe I won't have to make things so hard." It was just then, as everyone was jostling to introduce themselves, that Jack spied Ian on the other side of the throng.

Silence fell. It was as if the room held its collective breath.

"Dad?" Ian said, walking through the quickly parting crowd. Prudence followed behind him, their hands joined. "I'd like you to meet my wife. Prudence Weller Jax, this is my father, Jackson Jax."

She had seemed quite shy to Cooper, so he was happy to see her lift her chin to meet his father's gaze head on. She extended a dainty hand, and in a calm and sincere tone filled with honest happiness, she smiled and said, "Mr. Jax, it's a real pleasure to finally meet you. Ian has told me so much about you, and I've been so excited about this moment. You've raised a wonderful man, whom I love very much. I just know we're going to have a wonderful future together, and I'm really looking forward to spending time with you and Cooper and Sadie, and becoming a real part of your family. Thank you for welcoming me. I hope you can all make it down to Perth at some point and meet my family. I know you'll love them, too."

Everyone's gaze shifted on whole to Jack, who seemed a little taken aback by the sincerely delivered speech. He took a moment and cleared the gruffness from his throat before taking her hand in between his two much bigger ones and saying, "Welcome, Prudence. I'm glad to see that whatever mistakes I might have made raising him, he apparently knows a lot more than his old man did about choosing the right woman. Welcome to Cameroo Downs. I'm glad you're here." He looked from her to his younger son. "I'm glad you're both here."

And then Marta was there, ringing the dinner bell, telling everyone she'd gotten the kitchen set up with food and coffee, and to come in out of the mudroom already.

Cooper took Kerry's hand and held her back while everyone did as Marta commanded and filed back into the house.

"You have a pretty sharp, amazing little sister," she said, then laughed. "She's going to be a real handful for someone someday. And I think your new sister-in-law is going to give everyone a pretty good run for their money, too. I like her already."

Cooper nodded yes to all of it before pulling Kerry back around and into his arms. He saw Sadie's face peek through the window of the mudroom door as she discreetly closed it, then waved and gave him two thumbs-up before pulling the curtains shut.

He would have to find some way to thank his sister later. He wondered how hard it would be to wrap up the entire world and put it under the tree for her come Christmas. He looked back at Kerry. Because that was exactly what Sadie had wrapped up and given to him.

"Are you sure you want to sign on for this cattle drive, jillaroo?" he asked her.

"Oh, indeed I do." She slipped her arms around his waist. "You just try to stop me."

He grinned. "Well, I tried that once and we see how well that worked out."

She tipped up on her toes and kissed him. "And aren't you glad I didn't listen to you?"

"More than I can say, Starfish." He pulled her up off her feet and kissed her, and it didn't take any time for it to shift to something needier and far hungrier than a simple kiss on a side porch would fulfill.

"Do you think they'd miss us in there?" Kerry murmured against his mouth. "If we, uh, went out and inspected the grounds?

Or . . . something?"

"You know, there's a separate entrance to my quarters around the back. But it's thumping rain out there, luv."

She nodded toward the window. "It's stopped. Look. You can see the moon."

He looked out to discover she was right indeed. He pulled her over to the window, then looked down to find her eyes sparkling a particularly mischievous shade of emerald in the wash of the golden glow. "A starfish moon," he said, thinking from now on the two would always go hand in hand.

She smiled at that, the girlish smile that only he got from her. And he felt the world tilt back into place and settle there, comfortably, right where it was supposed to be.

"I love you," he said, pulling her up on her toes again to kiss her. He was going to need a lot more of those.

She smiled up into his face, the truth of her words shining from her eyes. "I love you back."

He took her hand and pulled her to the back door. "Come on," he said and shoved his feet back into his boots.

And they went outside; then, to keep her feet dry, he hitched Kerry up on his back, much to her squealing delight, and took off across the back of the property, letting the light in the sky guide their way.

He thought that whatever happened along their journey, wherever their paths led them, they'd always have the comfort, the strength, and the power of knowing their hearts were united as they looked up at the same starry sky.

Under a starfish moon indeed.

Epilogue

Sadie slid her father's plate of half-eaten wedding cake over and helped herself to a nice frosting-filled bite. He didn't need to be eating any more of it anyway, she reasoned.

Smiling, her heart so full of love and happiness she thought she might burst, she looked out across the makeshift dance floor they'd put together under the large white tent, out behind the main homestead. They'd put it up because it was wet season, but the skies had remained surprisingly clear for the afternoon's events. Still, she was glad they'd put the tent up. With the white, twinkling lights Fiona had strung around the edges and into looping swirls inside, under the pointed peak, it was so pretty and romantic, it made her sigh.

Kerry was a beautiful bride, as Sadie had known she would be, though Kerry certainly hadn't. It had been Sadie's idea to dig her brothers' mother's wedding dress out of the attic, see if they could make it work. She didn't remember her own mom, and her father didn't talk about her, but she'd heard many, many stories about his first wife, mother to Cooper and Ian, who'd passed away from an aggressive form of brain cancer and whom she was privately convinced was her father's one and only soul mate.

She didn't know what she thought about her own mother and tried not to, for the most part. She had come to understand that her father had married her out of grief and loneliness, and that while he hadn't been able to fix whatever was wrong between her mother and him, he did love his daughter more than the sun and the moon combined. She'd never doubted that, and when she did think about her mom, she thanked her for at least getting that part right. She might be unresolved about her mom taking off before she was even old enough to form memories of her, but Sadie knew she was better off having been left behind.

She wished Cooper and Ian's mother had been her mother, too. And privately pretended that was true, rationalizing that if she'd lived longer, and had another child, it could have been a daughter. A daughter like

Sadie. One of the strongest images she had of Cooper and Ian's mom was in her wedding dress, in the framed photo that still sat on her dad's nightstand.

It wasn't a traditional dress by any means, as the woman who'd worn it apparently hadn't been all that traditional a sort, which was partly why Sadie loved it and all of why she'd thought it would be so perfect for Kerry. It wasn't white; quite the opposite. It was bold and bright, made out of traditional aboriginal cloth, with a neckline studded with hand-carved and hand-painted beads, a sheathlike bodice, smooth and elegant despite the bright colors, then gathered in at the waist, which was wrapped in row after row of tightly rolled cloth, each band a different color, tied in the front in a huge, wild, intricately knotted bow, from which hung beads and feathers and other natural found objects their mother had collected in her wanderings. Another reason Sadie knew she was her heart mother, if not her real mother. She had the wandering in her, too. Then there was the skirt below all the bands, which was full and soft and flowing, with all the colors in the bands at the waist woven together to form a beautiful, free-flowing pattern.

Sadie had thought maybe she'd made a

mistake, asking her father about it, when his eyes had gotten all watery, but he'd nodded, said it shouldn't just lie up there going to the moths. So, among her, Fiona, and Alex, they'd worked on it and adjusted things until they got it just right. Kerry had been bowled over by the dress, and Sadie knew, from the moment she'd laid eyes on it, that Kerry understood it was the right dress, the right thing. If she hadn't, then seeing her brother's face when Kerry had stepped to the end of the grass aisle that led from house to tent, which had also served as their wedding chapel, had answered the question for her.

That look had been matched only by the huge, beaming smile on Kerry's face when she saw that Cooper had donned a tuxedo for her, something that apparently had inside meaning for the two. Sadie didn't care why he'd worn it but thought she'd never seen a more handsome man than her big brother. The contrast between him looking all slick and sharp and her looking like she'd stepped out of a tribal union had made the wedding even more perfect than Sadie could have dreamed.

It was the perfect day. She watched her brothers dance with her new sisters. She'd known Kerry was her heart sister from the moment they'd met. Sometimes she knew things, though she kept that to herself. And she'd known about Kerry. Her gaze shifted to Prudence, who had just been stolen away by her new father-in-law for a Bertram-approved waltz and felt her heart settle. She didn't know this sister-in-law well yet, but just watching her with Daddy Jack told Sadie everything she needed to know. She was so petite, so quiet, and yet she wielded such calm confidence, Sadie knew she'd be the perfect divining rod between Ian and their father. Things were better — much, much, better — but she knew it would probably always be a bumpy road, with Ian's new ways butting heads with their dad's old ones.

Her gaze drifted back to Kerry, who was twirling now with Sadie's computer tablet, having a dance with her Uncle Fergus, who'd been part of the festivities all day via the Internet and Skype. Sadie didn't even want to know how much data that was burning through but figured she'd be excused, given how much it obviously meant to Kerry to have him there.

Paths. Kerry had told her so many stories about her adventures. She'd confided to Sadie during their talks after Cooper had come back to Cameroo that she was worried, or had been, about the prospect of staying in one place, whether she had it in her to put down real roots, and that was one of the reasons she hadn't written to her as she'd said she would.

Sadie might only be fourteen but she could tell just from watching Kerry with her brother that she'd have a hard time wanting to be anywhere else. Plus, Sadie knew things. And she had a feeling about them. Her feelings were never wrong.

So now her brothers were settled, Cooper with Kerry and Ian with Pru. And her father had Bertram, and Marta and Kerry and Prudence to keep him in line . . . which meant Sadie could start thinking about her own future. Her own path, and where it might lead.

She finished off the last of the mango-filled butter cake and smiled as she scooped up the last of the creamy frosting with her finger and popped it in her mouth. She was going to be an adventurer, like Kerry. A wanderer, like her heart mother, who'd given her her brothers. Sadie had always known it, but meeting Kerry had cemented the knowledge.

She would travel far and wide, see many wondrous and glorious things.

And she knew just where she was going to

start. She was going to start in the same place Kerry had: Blueberry Cove, Maine. With the ocean right there any time she wanted to look at it, fresh seafood on every menu, seabirds in the sky, and snow. Lots and lots of amazing, wonderful snow. She couldn't wait.

There was one place in particular that called to her. Kerry had told her about this amazing little shop, Mossy Cup Antiques, run by the same family of women for as long as had been recorded. Eula March was the current proprietor, and Sadie was excited to meet her. But, more than that, she was excited to see the big, live mossy cup oak tree that grew, straight up through the middle of the shop and out through carefully constructed holes in the roof. There were all sorts of stories about her famous workroom, which only Eula and Logan's wife, Alex, were allowed into. Sadie had already pulled Alex aside a half-dozen times, begging her for every last detail. Were there really elves in that tree? Was the workroom really a magical place?

Yes, she'd start with Mossy Cup. And the oak tree. She had plans. The shop had been there as long as the town, longer maybe, because there was no record on file of it being built. It had always just been there. As had the oak tree.

Eula didn't know it yet, or maybe she did, but Sadie Eloise Jax from Cameroo Downs, Australia, was going to be the first person ever to climb that tree, the first one to get all the way up into its highest branches. To find out all of its secrets. She knew it.

She had a feeling.

FIONA & BEN'S BLUEBERRY-LEMON CAKE

WITH LEMON–CREAM CHEESE FROSTING

In *Starfish Moon,* there were two wedding cakes: Fiona's blueberry-lemon cake and Kerry's mango-filled butter cake. I mean, you can't have too much wedding cake, right? Because, you know . . . *cake*! So I thought I'd share one of the recipes with you, and given the Maine setting of *Starfish Moon,* along with the other books I've set in Blueberry Cove, Fiona's wedding cake recipe seemed like the perfect thing!

The recipe below is for a three-layer cake, perfect for a smaller gathering. It can be increased in size, but in order to keep the blueberries suspended throughout the finished cake (and not all sunk to the bottom) this is a dense crumb cake. Keep the cake pans shallow and make sure to support anything taller than three layers.

BLUEBERRY-LEMON CAKE

1 cup (2 sticks) unsalted butter, softened

1 1/4 cups sugar (granulated)

1/2 cup light brown sugar, packed

4 large eggs, room temperature

1 tablespoon pure vanilla extract

3 cups all-purpose flour, sifted

1 tablespoon baking powder

1/2 teaspoon kosher salt

1 cup buttermilk

2 tablespoons lemon juice (fresh squeezed)

1 tablespoon lemon zest (fresh)

1 1/2 cups fresh blueberries (frozen is okay; keep frozen until use)

Directions

1. Preheat oven to 350° F.

2. Grease and lightly flour three 9″ × 2″ round cake pans.

3. Use a mixer (standing type with paddle attachment is great) to beat the butter on high for approximately 1 minute.

4. Add granulated and brown sugars and beat on medium-high for another 2 to 3 minutes. Scrape the bowl as needed.

5. Add in the eggs and the vanilla. Beat on medium until everything is fully combined, up to 2 minutes. Scrape the bowl for complete blending.

6. In a separate bowl, whisk together the

flour, baking powder, and salt, then slowly add to the mixing bowl and mix on low. Batter will be very thick. Scrape bowl and paddles as needed.

7. Add the milk, lemon juice, and lemon zest and beat until just combined. Scrape and stir with spoon to make sure all is blended.

8. Carefully fold in fresh or still frozen blueberries. The batter is very thick, so stir gently to distribute as evenly as possible, but don't overmix.

9. Spoon the batter into the prepared cake pans in even measure. Note: You can use parchment rounds on the bottoms of the pans to help with removing the cake later.

10. Bake for 20–25 minutes until toothpick test comes out clean.

11. Let cool in pans on racks for 15 minutes, then remove from pans and cool completely.

LEMON–CREAM CHEESE FROSTING

2 8-ounce packages of brick-style cream cheese

3/4 cup (1 1/2 sticks) unsalted butter, softened

4 cups powdered (confectioner's) sugar

1 teaspoon lemon zest

1 teaspoon pure vanilla extract

Directions

1. Using your mixer, beat cream cheese and butter until light and fluffy.
2. Gradually add in the powdered sugar.
3. Mix in the lemon zest and vanilla extract, then beat on medium until smooth.
4. Cover and refrigerate to firm, approximately 30 minutes.

Frosting the Cake

1. If cake tops are uneven or not level, use a bread knife to carefully slice off the top to make flat.
2. Put the first layer of completely cooled cake on the plate or cake stand.
3. Spread an even layer of frosting on the top of that layer only. Don't frost too thickly so the layers added on top won't slide.
4. Add the next layer and repeat, frosting an even layer to the top only.
5. Add the final layer and frost the top.
6. Brush any loose crumbs from the sides of the layered stack of cakes.
7. Frost the sides of the cake, then the top. Add additional frosting to sides and top as needed or desired.
8. Garnish the top as desired. A small gathering of blueberries with a twirl of lemon tucked in looks beautiful.

9. Keep cool in refrigerator until serving. (Garnish just before serving.)

The employees of Thorndike Press hope you have enjoyed this Large Print book. All our Thorndike, Wheeler, and Kennebec Large Print titles are designed for easy reading, and all our books are made to last. Other Thorndike Press Large Print books are available at your library, through selected bookstores, or directly from us.

For information about titles, please call:
(800) 223-1244

or visit our Web site at:
http://gale.cengage.com/thorndike

To share your comments, please write:
Publisher
Thorndike Press
10 Water St., Suite 310
Waterville, ME 04901